FOR

THE **SISTERS CHASE**

"Part mystery, part road novel, part family saga, *The Sisters Chase* had me riveted from the first secret to the last revelation. Mary Chase is a force of nature and a truly unforgettable heroine."

— LISA LUTZ,
author of *The Passenger* and *How to Start a Fire*

"A beautifully written family drama with a mystery at its core, *The Sisters Chase* is a layered and lovely book about the bonds of love crashing up against the rocky shore of the world. Mary Chase is thorny and fractured and fascinating, and I will not forget her or her struggle to bring her sister to a place of peace and safety that she only half believes in. Sarah Healy's novel, wise and fierce and bittersweet, broke my heart in all the best ways. This is one you'll want to pass along."

— JOSHILYN JACKSON,
author of *The Opposite of Everyone* and *gods in Alabama*

"*The Sisters Chase* hits all the right marks. Wonderful characters, so believable that it still surprises me they aren't real people, a heart-wrenching story about love, loyalty, the bonds that can't be broken, and the true nature of survival. This is the kind of book that you read late into the night, eyes heavy, and wake up thinking about until you've finally finished the last page."

— CHEVY STEVENS,
author of *Never Let You Go* and *Still Missing*

"Sarah Healy's *The Sisters Chase* is the deeply moving and thrilling portrayal of three women driven by love, loss, and the deep desire to make things right. This is a story that stayed with me long after I turned the last page."

— CARLA BUCKLEY,
author of *The Things That Keep Us Here* and
The Deepest Secret

"*The Sisters Chase* is a deliciously compulsive read, a miniature mystery of love, survival, and sisterhood written on the scale of the human heart. Deceptively simple, gracefully realized, and occasionally wicked, it lingers like a summer dream after the last page is turned."

— AMY GENTRY,
author of *Good as Gone*

"The Chase girls, aptly named, are always, it seems, on the run, chasing a better life, a place where they'll be at home, be safe, and where the secrets of their past won't come crashing down on them. Sarah Healy has created, in Mare and Bunny, characters so real and flawed my heart ached for them, and I so, so wanted them to find that safe place called home. *The Sisters Chase* is exquisitely written and full of surprises, love, and loss; it is clearly the work of a writer at the top of her game."

— JENNIFER MCMAHON,
author of *The Night Sister*

"Sarah Healy's *The Sisters Chase* will stay with me for a long time. It's a heart-rending tale of survival filled with deftly revealed surprises and twists. In less skillful hands, Healy's deeply flawed young protagonist, Mary, might have been unlikable, but here she's redeemed by her love and compassion for her younger sister, Hannah. In fact, I ached for Mary as her plans to save herself and Hannah fall apart and tension builds. Each chapter ends on a note of suspense and surprise that demands you turn the page. An exciting read!"

— DIANE CHAMBERLAIN,
author of *Pretending to Dance* and *The Silent Sister*

THE
SISTERS
CHASE

ALSO BY SARAH HEALY

Can I Get an Amen?

House of Wonder

THE
SISTERS
CHASE

Sarah Healy

BLACKFRIARS

BLACKFRIARS

First published in the US in 2017 by Houghton Mifflin Harcourt

First published in Great Britain in 2017 by Blackfriars
This edition published in Great Britain in 2018 by Blackfriars

1 3 5 7 9 10 8 6 4 2

Book design by Rachel Newborn

A CIP catalogue record for this book
is available from the British Library.

ISBN 978-0-349-13453-6

Printed and bound in Great Britain by
Clays Ltd, St Ives plc

Papers used by Blackfriars are from well-managed forests
and other responsible sources.

MIX
Paper from
responsible sources
FSC® C104740

This imprint has no connection with The Order of Preachers (Dominicans)

Blackfriars
An imprint of
Little, Brown Book Group
Carmelite House
50 Victoria Embankment
London EC4Y 0DZ

An Hachette UK Company
www.hachette.co.uk

www.littlebrown.co.uk

For my sons,
Noah, Max, and Ollie

THE
SISTERS
CHASE

One

BUNNY

I WAS IN THE GROCERY STORE *the other night waiting to be checked out, and in the line next to me were these two girls. They were nineteen, maybe twenty years old. And as they stood there leaning on their cart, they let their heels slide out of the backs of their clogs and picked at their chipping nail polish. One flipped through a gossip magazine while the other looked on. When they straightened up, you could see the indentation of their belly buttons through their T-shirts. They were just girls, Mare. And I wondered if you ever got to be a girl like that.*

Then a song came on. It's big right now; you would know it. And as soon as they heard it, these two girls look at each other, and without a word, they let their heads drop back and they opened their mouths and you should have heard the voices that came out. You should have heard how beautifully these girls sang. Now everyone was looking at them, not just me. And for a second, I could have sworn you were there. That you had come up quietly behind me. Listen to them, Bunny, *you'd say. I'd turn and you'd be smiling, your lips apple red, the hood of your sweatshirt pulled up like a cloak.*

It happens like that. I'll be in the grocery store or waiting for the train or out on a run. *And suddenly you come into my mind and it's like I'm underwater. Like the rest of the world is above me and I'm watching it through the ripples and shimmers of the surface. And I'll remember how on those days when the ocean was calm, you'd take me into the water and we'd sink down to the bottom and stay there for as long as we could. My need for breath always sent me bursting to the surface, but it seemed like you could stay down there forever, your black hair swirling around like smoke.*

I don't tell many people about you, Mare. Or at least I don't tell them much. But I framed some of your drawings and put them up around the house. And sometimes Daniel and I will have friends over, and I'll see someone staring at one. Who did this? *they'll ask, not looking away, their nose near the glass.*

My sister, Mary, *I'll say.*

Two
1977

I T HAD BEEN A DAY AND A HALF since the baby was born, and still she did not have a name. Diane stared down at her, a dim yellow light illuminating the hospital room. A tiny fist escaped the swaddling blankets, and Diane gently spread it open with her thumb as if she were unfurling the frond of a fern. Looking at the wrinkled palm, at the translucent crescents of fingernails, she brought the little hand to her face and inhaled the child in, inhaled her newness, her purity. She was worth it, of course; she was worth everything that had been and would be sacrificed. "Sweet girl," Diane whispered.

The maternity ward was without sound that night, and Diane felt as though they were sheltered in the belly of a boat as it drifted across a still black sea. Mary stood at the hospital room's single window, her forehead resting against the cool glass, her eyebrows tensed as she peered into the night. Even at fourteen, Mary's beauty had a ferocity to it, an elegant savagery. Diane let her head loll against the blue vinyl chair as she stared at her daughter's back, at her reflection in the window.

"How ya doin', Mary, honey?" she asked.

But Mary was silent.

Diane looked back down at the baby, feeling the warmth of her in her arms. She hadn't wanted her, had mourned her coming birth. When she learned with certainty that there was, in fact, a baby, she cried for two days, pacing around the motel and muttering about how stupid she was. How she, of all people, should have known better. How this was going to ruin their lives. But that was all incomprehensible now. Their family was now three: she, Mary, and the baby.

She and Mary had left Sandy Bank, New Jersey, and their home at the Water's Edge Motel in September. It was usually only the summer people who left then. Even though the motel closed soon after Labor Day, Mary and her mother always stayed through those months of churning gray seas and empty streets with the rest of the locals. Mary hadn't wanted to go. There was a boy, of course. Someone Mary would have to leave, though she wouldn't say who. And so she subjected Diane to terrifying acts of rebellion intermixed with frigid weeks of silence before their departure, but Diane insisted that this baby had to be born elsewhere. That she had to be born in a place without winters. So Diane pulled Mary out of school and they drove south, migrating slowly through small towns where people spoke with languid words until they reached their destination.

Bardavista, Florida, was a small city on the Gulf of Mexico whose business was shrimp and the United States Navy. And during that winter, Diane and Mary stayed on the barrier island of Bardavista Beach, which then had only a smattering of motels and beach cottages. Together they walked in silence over sugar-white sand from their cottage up to Ft. Rillieux. The fort was an enormous structure occupying one end of the narrow semibarren island. When they first visited, Diane found Mary reading a placard about Geronimo, who had been held there for a year of his life.

Diane read over her daughter's shoulder. "Geronimo," she said. "Isn't that something?"

Mary was quiet for a moment. "One of his wives died here."

"In Bardavista?"

"She's buried in the big cemetery. Over the bridge."

Diane and Mary kept to themselves in Bardavista and people let them. At thirty-four, Diane was still young. She liked to think that people assumed she and Mary were sisters. Maybe even two young naval wives walking together on the sand while their husbands donned uniforms and defended the nation.

Diane worried about Mary during those months. Worried that she was supplanting the needs of one child for another. Worried that something essential was being drained from her wild, lovely daughter. Mary used to sit alone on that beach that winter, a sheet of paper resting atop the phone book in her lap. She'd draw creatures rising up out of the sea, pelagic dragons, their massive bellies turned skyward as they breached the white crests of waves. Mary had always been an exceptional artist.

Diane had been twenty when Mary was born. It was she and her father at the Water's Edge then. Vietnam was about to become the event horizon for a generation of young men, and so, perhaps sensing the inevitability of that conflict, boys began crisscrossing the country like creatures at once pursued and in pursuit. They would show up every so often at the Water's Edge with an undirected hunger in their eyes, searching for something for which to long. And one day a boy with thick dark hair and a tall broad body parked his motorcycle in the lot of the motel and came in, addressing Mr. Chase as "sir" and asking for a room.

Mr. Chase looked down through his glasses as he took the boy's name and where he was from.

"Vincent Drake," he said. "From Bardavista, Florida."

Mr. Chase gave a murmur of recognition. "I hear it's beautiful down there."

And as Mr. Chase filled out the paperwork in his slow, careful script, Vincent Drake looked out the window behind the front desk at the pretty girl who was shooing away seagulls from the Dumpster as she heaved in another overstuffed trash bag.

After shutting the lid, Diane came back into the office, eyes and mind elsewhere as she started to say, "Daddy, the . . ." Then she noticed Vincent Drake and her words slowed a bit. "Dumpster is full." And the boy found something for which to long.

Diane didn't have the opportunity to tell Vincent Drake that she was pregnant. Her father spent months calling town clerks' offices, but they never did find a young man with that name near Bardavista. And though mother and daughter walked those beaches together for weeks, Diane never told Mary why she had chosen there, of all places, to wait out the arrival of another child. Diane wasn't even sure if she herself knew.

Sometimes during that winter, Diane would look at her daughter as if remembering the man who said his name was Vincent. Mary resembled him physically, but where his presence was most apparent was in Mary's boldness. In her opportunistic charm. In the way she could tell wild, outrageous lies with a steady-eyed calm.

Mary had a similar expression on her face now as she stared out of the window of the hospital room. Diane shifted, feeling the fatigue in her body reach down to her bones.

"Mary, honey," Diane said. "Can you hold the baby for a minute?"

Mary didn't move. Diane shifted slightly in her seat, suddenly feeling the enormity of raising another child on her own. She was going to need Mary, she knew. She was going to need her girl.

"Mary," she said, her tone sapped of patience, her words lingering and long. "I need you to hold your sister."

Mary's eyes found her mother's in the window's black glass, all that was unspoken passing in a look.

"Why?" asked Mary.

Diane held her daughter's gaze. "Because I have to go to the bathroom, Mary."

Mary turned slowly and looked at the baby, her arms at her sides. Diane struggled up, cradling the infant in one arm while pushing herself up with the other. "Mare . . . ," she said, keeping her awkward hold. "Can you?" She felt herself slip slightly, fall back against the chair, and the baby let out a mewling cry.

And to Diane it looked like reflex, like some primal need to protect the being with whom she shared blood — a tribal sense of duty. But Mary darted forward, sliding her arms beneath the baby and pulling her into her chest. Diane watched them for a moment, watched as Mary started to sway, calming the child.

"I'll be right back," she said, but Mary was still looking at the baby, some internal battle silently being waged.

In the bathroom, Diane turned on the water and sat on the toilet, letting it run and run, letting it drown out everything else. She wasn't sure how long she stayed in there. It could have been five minutes. It could have been twenty. And when she opened the door, Mary was sitting in the blue vinyl chair, the baby still in her arms. Diane watched them for a moment.

"So," Diane said. And Mary started slightly, as if she hadn't heard her leave the bathroom. "What are we going to name her?"

"Name her whatever you want," Mary replied, though she couldn't quite look away from the baby's small face.

"She's going to need you, Mary," said Diane. It was something Diane knew without understanding how. "Do you know that?"

Diane walked over and sat on the edge of the hospital bed facing her daughter. Diane waited, knowing that Mary was a girl whose loyalty was fierce and rare and absolute. Knowing that Mary was deciding, right at this moment, whether or not to love this child, whether or not to give herself to her entirely. The baby squirmed in Mary's arms and the expression on Mary's face slackened and at that moment Diane knew it was done. Raising her chin, Mary looked at her mother, and said simply, "Let's call her Hannah." And with those words, it was as if Mary had slashed the palm of her hand and offered her blood as oath.

Soon the three of them would return to Sandy Bank, and the whispers and gossip would rise like a tide and then eventually recede. The father of Diane's second baby, it was said, had swept in and out of her life in much the same way as the father of her first. Another Vincent Drake had come to the Water's Edge, laid Diane down on a sand dune, and given her a child but nothing more.

Three

1981

I N THE DARK, MARY FELT THE PRESENCE of the small
light-limbed body next to her. She and her little sister
lay with their heads on the same pillow, Mary's dark hair
mingling with Hannah's light. Hannah had inched in as close
as she could and wrapped both of her arms around one of
Mary's as the story Mary was telling grew almost unbearably
climactic for a four-year-old.

"Princess Hannah and Princess Mary raced as fast as they
could through the forest, the briars *ripping* the skirts of their
gowns and *scratching* their hands and faces," said Mary, skill-
fully riding the wave of her tale. "Because behind them . . .
they heard the *wolves.*"

Hannah gasped. "The evil *queen's* wolves?" she asked, as she
hugged Mary's arm tighter.

"The evil queen's wolves," confirmed Mary.

Mary could spin masterful stories and often transformed
the room she and Hannah shared at the Water's Edge into a
land of beauty and magic and danger. A land where they were
princesses, always running, always pursued. A land where no
one was to be trusted except each other.

"And just as they reached the edge of the Black Woods"
—Mary's voice built as if she were giving a speech from a
grandstand— "a wolf came *leaping* out of the dark, its mouth
open, its fangs bared. But Princess Mary drew her sword and
plunged it into the beast."

"Does that mean she killed it?" asked Hannah, the words
coming out as an urgent breath.

Mary smiled at her sister and nodded, relishing Hannah's
utter absorption, her lack of disbelief. "Then Princess Mary
pulled Princess Hannah onto her back, and together they ran
out of the Black Woods, falling out of the forest just as the rest
of the pack reached its edge."

"So they were safe?" asked Hannah, desperate for confirma-
tion. "The wolves didn't get them?"

"They were safe." Mary leaned over to kiss her sister on
the line where her hair met the skin of her forehead. "Don't
worry, Bunny. The wolves can't leave the Black Woods."

DIANE DIDN'T LIKE THE STORIES that Mary told Hannah.
"They're too much for her," she'd said one morning, piling a
plate high with the powdered sugar donuts that they set out
for the motel's guests. "She doesn't understand that they're not
real."

Mary looked at her mother, her gaze sharp. Mary bristled
when her judgment regarding Hannah was called into question. "She likes them," she answered, taking a donut from the
stack. It was past Labor Day, so only a handful of the rooms at
the motel were occupied, but Diane was a believer in customs.

"Yeah, well," started Diane. She let her head drop back as
she rubbed her eyes. "I like a lot of things that aren't good for
me, too." Diane had grown heavier since Hannah was born,
her stomach and thighs thickening until her figure, once so
girlish, was now matronly. Everyone assumed it was baby

weight, but Diane blamed her schedule and never having time to eat a proper meal or get a full night's sleep. Since her father had died, she ran the Water's Edge alone, taking a second job as a cocktail waitress at one of the casinos down in Atlantic City to make ends meet during the off-season. "So listen," she said, letting her hand drop to the counter. "Mrs. Pool is going to make you girls some dinner tonight. I had to pick up Tina's shift so I won't be home." Diane looked at her daughter. "Can you watch the front desk when you get home from school?"

"Yeah," said Mary, brushing her dark hair over her shoulder. "Sure."

Diane's eyes remained wide as she looked at her daughter, as if to communicate both her distrust and concern. "Because someone needs to be here from three o'clock on. Mrs. Pool can cover until then." Mrs. Pool lived next door to the Water's Edge, which was, incidentally, not on the water's edge but several blocks away. Having sympathy for the woman who was raising two children alone, Mrs. Pool often helped Diane with both the girls and the motel. "And when I say *here*," Diane said, slapping her open palm on the laminate wood countertop for emphasis, "I mean *right here*."

"I got it, Mom."

Diane continued to stare for a moment, then looked away, grabbing the now empty donut bag and crumpling it against her chest. "Alright," she said. "Okay." Mary looked coolly at her mother until Diane changed the subject. "So school is starting off good this year?" she asked.

"Yeah," said Mary, leaning in and draping her slender arms over the counter. "I talked to Mr. Alvetto about options. For college." At eighteen years old, Mary should have graduated from high school this past June, but her and her mother's winter in Florida had put her behind, and she would now be graduating with a younger class. Intelligent without effort but often disrespectful in the classroom, Mary maddened teachers who didn't know exactly what to do with the bright, beautiful girl who was so free with her disdain. Rumors flew around about Mary and certain administrators, perhaps as a way to explain the girl who was generally considered to be a problem but tolerated nonetheless.

"Good girl," said Diane.

That afternoon, Mary got a ride home from school with one of the handsome younger boys. Barely acknowledging him as she lifted her bag from the floor, she pushed open the door to his Dodge Omni and shut it with her hip, heading toward the yellow single-story structure that was the Water's Edge. Walking over the crushed-oyster-shell parking lot, Mary pushed open the glass door to the wood-paneled office, where a soap opera flickered on an old television set and Mrs. Pool sat reading *Woman's World.*

At the jingle of the door, Mrs. Pool glanced up from her magazine. "She's sleeping, honey," she said, knowing that all Mary wanted was Hannah. That was all she ever wanted.

"What time did she go down?" asked Mary, setting her backpack down.

Mrs. Pool glanced up to the clock. "About one."

"I'm going to go wake her up," said Mary. Then softening her face beseechingly, she asked, "Can you stay a little longer, Mrs. Pool? I want to take her to the beach."

Mrs. Pool's husband ran fishing charters out of Sandy Bank, often leaving before sunrise and not returning until well after sunset. She was rarely in a rush to get home. "Take your time," she said, then she turned back to her article on satisfying and inexpensive meal solutions. Everything about Mrs. Pool was yielding.

Mary hurried back outside over the concrete walkway to the room next to the office, the room she shared with Hannah. She pulled a bright orange coiled cord off of her wrist, then sunk the key it held into the lock. As she pushed the door open gently, the dim room flooded with light. "Hey, Bunny," she said.

Hannah took a sharp breath, sitting up in bed, her eyes still closed, her hair wild.

"It's time to wake up," said Mary, who slipped off her shoes and walked over the permanently sandy carpet to Hannah, sliding into bed beside her. Their room had two double beds, but many nights they slept together in Mary's, sinking down under the comforter that always felt slightly damp.

"Are you home?" asked Hannah, repositioning herself to rest her head on Mary's chest, her face still puffy with sleep.

"I am," answered Mary, as she stroked her sister's hair. "I was thinking that we could go down to the beach."

With her eyes still closed, Hannah answered. "*Mmm*kay."

Mary let Hannah wake up, then helped her go to the bathroom and put on her sandals. She hoisted Hannah onto her back and, with Hannah's arms wrapped around her neck, began to walk over the sandswept road to the beach.

They left their shoes at the beginning of the narrow path that cut between the dunes and led to the ocean. Mary took Hannah's hand, and they walked together down to the stretch of shore where the waves made their rapid advances then their defeated withdrawals. Mary dug her hands into the sand and came up with tiny translucent sand crabs tunneling furiously to return themselves to the safety of depth. She'd put them into Hannah's palm, and Hannah would shriek as she felt their tiny legs against her skin. And all the while Mary kept a watchful eye on the man who was casting his fishing line into the surf, his legs covered with sand to the knees. He was one of the guests at the Water's Edge, staying in room 108.

When he appeared finished and ready to return to the motel, rod and tackle box in hand, Mary turned to Hannah.

"Okay, Bunny," she said. "We should head back. Mrs. Pool's waiting for us."

With Hannah again on her back, Mary kept a respectful distance from their guest as she followed him back to the motel. And when they arrived at the Water's Edge, Mary watched him set his rod and tackle box down outside his door, then head inside his room. Pushing open the glass door to the office, she set Hannah down and scooted her inside. "Mrs. Pool," she said, her body still outside the office, her head leaning in, "can you watch Hannah for one more sec? I've just got to go to the bathroom."

Mary walked around the back of the building to the rear of room 108, not hiding the sound of her footsteps, her hands sunk easily into her pockets. Passing the window, she listened to make sure the water was running. She knew it would be; the man would want to get the sand off of his legs. Mary then slipped back around to the front of the building, pulled another key chain off of her wrist, and carefully opened the door. Only her eyes moved as she scanned the room. The man's shorts had been dropped on the floor in front of the television. From the bathroom came his mumblings and the spatter of the shower. Mary moved no faster than she needed to. She picked up the shorts and coaxed a wallet from their pocket. Quickly counting four twenty-dollar bills, she took two of them. Then she returned the wallet to its place and was out of room 108 just as quickly as she had come, the water in the bathroom turning off just as the door clicked shut.

Sliding the forty dollars into the pocket of her cutoffs, she walked back to the office and stepped inside as Mrs. Pool picked up the ringing phone.

"Water's Edge Motel," said Mrs. Pool, her voice gentle and agreeable as always.

There was a stretch of silence while Mrs. Pool listened. Hannah sat on the floor, playing with a naked Barbie doll.

"No, this is Alice Pool," she said, the concern already spreading on her face. "I'm a friend of the family."

Then Mrs. Pool's trembling hand shot up to cover her mouth. "Oh, my Lord," she said, her eyes finding Mary's, the soft skin underneath her chin quivering. "Where is she?" And at that moment, as Mrs. Pool looked at her, Mary knew what had happened, if not how. Mary knew right down to her bones.

Four

1981

THE TELEVISION BABBLED AWAY in the background, but Mary still heard the click when Mrs. Pool put the handset back into its cradle. Her hand hovered there while the other covered her mouth, her fingertips jailing her words. Mrs. Pool then took a breath, her shoulder slumping with her exhalation, as if something vital had been drawn from her lungs.

"Alice," said Mary. It was the first time Mary had ever called her by her first name.

Mrs. Pool turned to Mary, her eyes like chasms. "Mary," she said. "Your mother."

Hannah was now looking up from her Barbie, her hands still holding it upright, keeping it standing.

Mary felt her body leaden. "What happened?"

Mrs. Pool's face rounded. "There was an accident," she said.

IT WAS MRS. POOL WHO DROVE to the hospital. She shook and prayed in the front seat, honking the horn at a car that was slow to react at a green light, then jumping at the sound of it. *Hail Mary, full of grace, the Lord is with you.* Over and over, she made the sign of the cross. Mary sat in the back with Hannah, stroking her hair as Hannah laid her head in her lap. Mary just stared straight ahead and breathed in and out, forcing herself to remain still.

Hannah looked up at her. "What was the accident?"

Mary's hand stilled on Hannah's head. "It was a car accident," she said, her words not sliding easily from her throat.

Hannah's eyes went to the near distance, then she looked at Mary once again. "Did Mom get hurt?"

Mary stared at her sister's face, at the eyes that looked up at her as if she were a deity, then she nodded. "Yeah, Bunny. She did."

Diane was dead by the time they arrived, having sustained massive internal injuries when her car slammed into a telephone pole on Route 73. The doctor addressed Mrs. Pool when communicating Diane's passing, speaking in hushed, quiet words. Mary stood with her back to them, looking out of the window at the parking lot with Hannah gripping her leg. The sky was flat blue and faded, making everything outside look as though it were already of the past. And Mary remembered sitting with her mother and Mrs. Pool as they watched the royal wedding in the office of the Water's Edge not so long ago. Diane had gasped when she first saw Diana, her dress filling that horse-flanked carriage. *You kind of look like her, Mom,* Mary had said.

Hannah cried and rubbed her face against Mary's thigh, not fully understanding what had happened, what any of this meant. Not understanding the way Mary did. "It's gonna be okay, Bunny," Mary whispered. "You've got me. You've got Mary."

The police investigation would determine that Diane Chase had fallen asleep at the wheel. Witnesses would describe the

Ford Fiesta drifting off the road in a smooth arc until it hit the pole head-on. The casino had been slow so she had left work early that day. She had told a coworker that she was going to go home to take a nap.

When Mary, Hannah, and Mrs. Pool returned to the Water's Edge that night, Mary lay down with Hannah in their room and told her a story in which the two princesses encountered a magical pool in the forest, the water from which could turn a person to stone with one sip. Princess Mary had just filled a vial with the water when there was a knock on the door.

"It's Alice," said Mrs. Pool. "And Stan."

It was with great effort that Mary hoisted her sister onto her hip and opened the door for their neighbors. Mr. Pool held his baseball cap to his chest. Mrs. Pool carried a bucket of fried chicken.

"I'm so sorry, Mary," said Mr. Pool. His eyes were water-blue and earnest, and his skin was brick brown. His bowlegs made him an inch or so shorter than he might otherwise have been.

Mary nodded.

"We thought maybe you girls should eat something," said Mrs. Pool, nodding toward Hannah.

Mary looked at her sister. *Am I hungry?* Hannah seemed to ask. *Do I need to eat?*

"Yeah, Bunny," Mary answered, her words coming out slowly, as if there were just a few drops of them left. "You should eat something." And Mary followed the Pools to the office, where they sat on the couch with a bucket of fried chicken and a bag of biscuits on the coffee table. The Pools looked nervously at the girls. Mary picked up a drumstick so that Hannah would, but Hannah just watched until Mary took a bite. Mary swallowed without chewing, feeling the meat slide slowly down her throat. Hannah followed suit, her eyes not leaving Mary.

They sat there in silence until the drumsticks were done. Until Mary finally looked at the Pools. "I should get Hannah to bed," she said.

Mr. Pool rose quickly, extending a hand to Mrs. Pool as she strained to rise. "Course," he said, his hat again at his chest.

Mrs. Pool looked at Mary, her eyes warm and wet. "I'll be back first thing."

Mary watched the Pools walk across the parking lot to their home, Mr. Pool's hand on Mrs. Pool's back, their heads hung low. *I just don't know what they're going to do, Stan,* Alice would be saying. She would be crying freely now, her sobs soft and feeble things. *I just don't know what those poor girls are going to do.*

From beside her, Mary heard Hannah's small voice. "Are you sad?"

Mary's hand found the curve at the back of Hannah's head. "I am, Bunny."

"Because of Mom?"

Mary nodded, her brain above her left eye pounding, feeling as if it were knocking on her skull.

"What happened?"

Mary closed her eyes, feeling the pain in her head and color and pulses and light. "She had to go away."

"Is she going to come home?" asked Hannah.

But Mary said nothing. And Hannah let her face drop against Mary's thigh, where she rubbed her tears away, back and forth.

When Hannah's eyes started to slip shut, Mary finally carried her from the office. She lifted her up, her head rolling back against Mary's forearms. Mary felt weak, as if her knees might buckle, as if her arms might give.

She set Hannah in bed and pulled up the covers, not bothering to change her clothes. Then she went to the bathroom, closed the door, and stuck her pointer finger down her throat, feeling her fingernail cut the soft tissue at the back. When she leaned over the toilet and wretched the Pool's chicken into the bowl, she tasted blood.

IT WASN'T LONG AFTER HER MOTHER'S DEATH that Mary learned there was no money. That Diane Chase's estate — if it could even be called that — was in the red.

"The motel owes a significant amount in back taxes," an attorney in a brown suit told her, his elbows resting on his laminate wood desk.

"What does that mean?" Mary asked sharply. But Mary knew what it meant. It meant that the only inheritance Diane Chase had for Mary and Hannah was the Water's Edge. And it would be like a stone tied to their necks, pulling them slowly down through the depths.

"It means that the debts owed by the Water's Edge are likely to exceed the value of the business, including the property itself."

He took his glasses off and looked at Mary. "It's quite an unusual situation," he said. "To have so much responsibility at your age. You're only eighteen." And Mary hated him. She hated that his plump fingers had run over their mother's private documents and papers. She hated the way he looked at her now, with leering curiosity. Because it wasn't just the Water's Edge that belonged to her: it was Hannah. In the eyes of the law and everyone else, Mary was Hannah's guardian.

"Well, this has been incredibly useful," said Mary, standing abruptly. "Just incredibly fucking useful."

That night, while Hannah lay sleeping, Mary stood in front of the utility sink and stared at the steady stream of water coming from the faucet, slowly grinding her jaw from side to side. The laundry room at the Water's Edge was tiny and down to one working fluorescent bulb, but Mary had taken to going there since Diane died, sitting on the concrete floor and leaning against the washing machine as it worked, feeling somehow steadied by its rhythmic motions.

When the water was near scalding and its steam thickened the air, Mary pulled an old plastic bucket from one of the makeshift wooden shelves and stuck it into the sink, letting it fill. She grabbed a scrub brush and a container of Comet, and marched out into the cold night, the hot water sloshing onto the ground as she walked. Then she pushed open the door to a vacant guest room, went to the bathroom, and dropped to her knees. She plunged the scrub brush into the water and let her hands linger there, thinking of nothing quite as satisfying at that moment than the shocking temperature, than the heat against her skin.

She went to a new room each night and scrubbed it clean. She cleaned until her heart would pound and strands of her hair would stick to her neck and her forehead. She cleaned until the skin of her fingers would pucker, then crack. And when she ran out of rooms, she started over again. So it was on the floors and the tubs and the sinks that some of Mary's ferocity and fear was unleashed.

It was after another such evening that she returned to her and Hannah's room to find Hannah awake, lying limp on the bed with a terrible cough. "Bunny," Mary said, rushing to her sister. And that night, Mary sat in the bathroom with Hannah on her lap, steam filling the air and calming Hannah's breath. When she fell asleep again, Mary held her still, watching her chest rise and fall, tensing as her body quaked with its periodic coughs. Mary was late to homeroom the next morning; Hannah hadn't wanted to go to Mrs. Pool's.

"Nooooooo," she whined, her arms wrapped around Mary's neck as Mrs. Pool tried to pull her away. "I want to stay with yooouuuuu."

"You can't, Bunny," whispered Mary into her hair. She kissed the top of her head. "I have to get to school."

And when Mary had walked into Mrs. Violette's classroom and the squat, dowdy teacher asked for a note, Mary went right past her and sat at her desk, acknowledging neither the teacher nor her request.

"I asked for a *note*, Miss Chase," repeated Mrs. Violette. Mrs. Violette hated Mary. Hated her beauty and her insolence. Hated her mind. Mrs. Violette, unlike many of the teachers at Bergen Shores, was entirely unmoved by Mary's recent loss.

Mary rested her feet against the chair in front of her. "I don't have a *note*," she spat.

"Then get back *up*," began Mrs. Violette, relishing her words, overenunciating each of them. "Go to the main office and *get* one."

Mary stared at her for a moment, then made a noise of disgust. "Stupid bitch," she muttered, shaking her head.

Without another word, Mrs. Violette marched out of the room, and Mary took down her pony tail, shaking her long brown hair loose over her shoulders and looking out of the window as the class began to buzz and pulse with her defiance. *Did you hear that shit?*

Mrs. Violette returned with Mr. Alvetto who said—all stern and somber—"Miss Chase, please come with me."

With her arms crossed, Mary walked behind Mr. Alvetto through the school's silent hallways into the main office. He nodded once at Bonnie, who sat at the front desk, and Bonnie smiled. All the women who worked at the school thought Mr. Alvetto was handsome. Mary followed him into his office, and he turned and closed the door behind her, and it clicked shut.

When he looked back at Mary, her face was in her hands. "I know I shouldn't have said it," she said, her voice muffled and wet with emotion. "I've just had such a short fuse lately."

"Mary, please, sit down," he said, but instead of sitting,

Mary rushed him, burying her head into his chest and letting out a quiet sob that could break your heart. "I know what you're going through has been very difficult," started Mr. Alvetto, gently laying a paternal hand on her back, as if thinking this were a moment he would soon be proud of: one when he would deftly handle the behavioral difficulties of a grief-stricken girl. "And all of us here at Bergen Shores are here for you."

Mary took a deep breath, the sort a mournful girl might take to steady herself, but as her chest filled, it pressed against Mr. Alvetto's. "I know," she said.

"But the language you used toward Mrs. Violette cannot be tolerated."

Mary lifted her chin and looked at Mr. Alvetto with big wet eyes, then made the slightest adjustment of her hips. "I'm sorry," she said, letting her gaze drop as she took another breast-expanding breath. She felt his hand drop down just a fraction of an inch lower on her back. "I feel terrible."

She shifted her weight just a bit more, pushing her hips ever so slightly forward. So subtle were her motions that no one except Mary herself would be able to recognize their artful deliberateness. Mr. Alvetto backed up suddenly, red faced and flustered.

"You shouldn't blame yourself, Mary," he sputtered, while trying to hide the bottom half of his body behind his desk. "I think you need to take a little more time to cope with what's happened. Why don't you take the rest of the day, and we'll start fresh tomorrow?"

And Mary almost laughed. Sometimes she just couldn't believe how easy it was. But instead she made her face look tortured and let her gaze drop down to her feet, thinking only of her pleasure at the thought of Mrs. Violette learning that she had been given the afternoon off. "Okay, Mr. Alvetto."

"I'll handle everything with Mrs. Violette."

Mary nodded, still trying to look ashamed and remorseful. "Thank you."

So Mary went home, picked Hannah up from Mrs. Pool's, and took her to McDonald's for lunch.

"When's my birthday?" asked Hannah, as she took a bite of her cheeseburger.

"On February fourteenth," answered Mary. "Valentine's Day."

"I'm going to be five."

Mary made herself smile. "You are."

They got back to the Water's Edge just as the mail truck was pulling away, leaving a fresh crop of sympathy cards. There was a thick one on the top from her mother's cousin, Gail. Their Christmas card always included a photograph, and Mary recalled the way her mother had always studied it when it came. In the last, she was posed with her husband and son on a cream-colored couch, a large abstract painting hanging in the background. Mary had heard her mother make enough comments to know that Gail and her husband had money—he was an entrepreneur and had recently been elected to the state senate. *They think they're God's gift.*

After Mary put Hannah to bed that night, she filled another bucket with water and carried it—sloshing and steaming—into another guest room. And that night as she cleaned, she pictured Gail's husband, with his tanned skin and dirty blond hair. She pictured Mr. Alvetto blushing and hiding behind his desk. She pictured the lawyer with his shabby suit and fat fingers.

Her hands were red and raw, her skin thin from the water and the cleansers, but Mary scrubbed and scrubbed and scrubbed. She knew that she wouldn't raise Hannah in Sandy Bank. Sandy Bank was where people died. Her grandmother had died during childbirth, bleeding to death on the delivery table. Her grandfather had lingered for only three months after his diagnosis. And her mother had driven her car into a telephone pole, her organs pulverized. Even the town itself died every winter.

No, she and Hannah wouldn't stay in Sandy Bank. They would leave. They would disappear, two princesses escaping in the night, running through the Black Woods with wolves at their heels. It was the two of them now, the last of their house. They would be deceitful when they had to, they would use the powers they were granted, and they would make their way back to the one person Mary always knew she would once again find. And that evening, as the knees of Mary's jeans grew stiff and wet, as her hands went back and forth, she devised her plan.

M ARY NOTICED THE WAY HANNAH sat up in the backseat, angling herself to get a better view of the palm-shaded gatehouse at the entrance to Co-coplum Estates. An elderly black man stood from his stool and waved the Mercedes through, tipping his hat to Gail, but Gail was too busy sizing up the two girls in her backseat to notice.

"We're so glad you're able to spend Christmas with us," said Gail, her red lips forming a false smile, her voice carrying an anxious lilt. "It was just such a surprise."

Mary softened her face. "We just wanted to be around family," she said, wrapping one of her arms around Hannah. "And the card you sent was so nice."

Mary watched as Gail's smile faltered as she recalled the rote sentiment and empty offer she had included in the sympathy card she'd mailed after Diane's death. *If you need anything at all, we're here for you. You are not alone.* Gail had surely thought it classy, elegant — that morsel of sympathy tossed from her jewel-bedecked hand. Mary had to look out of the window to keep from laughing. She remembered the silence on the other end of the phone when she first called her mother's cousin. *Hannah and I are hoping to come for Christmas. We bought our tickets!*

Cocoplum Estates was a cluster of massive homes with white stucco exteriors and orange clay roofs set against a cloudless blue sky. Their backyards all had kidney-shaped aquamarine pools and enormous central air-conditioning units that whirred in unison to create a constant pervasive white noise. There were tennis courts and sidewalks and a marina, but Mary didn't see a soul outside aside from the hunched gardeners with sweat-slick faces who tended to the sprinkler-fed lawns.

"Here we are," said Gail, as the Mercedes turned onto the smooth black driveway of one of the nearly identical homes in the community. Sailing into the garage, Gail brought the car to a stop, then turned to look back at her cousin's daughters once again. Hannah was leaning in close to Mary, shrinking against the enormity that surrounded her.

"Alright, girls," said Gail, opening the door. Thick humid air rushed into the cool, clean car as she swung her tanned, tennis-toned legs onto the concrete. She then took a deep strength-gathering breath before rising. "Let's get your bags."

Mary took Hannah's hand. "Come on, Bunny," she whispered.

The girls followed Gail to the back of the car, where she popped the trunk and stared down at the three large suitcases the girls had brought with them. It did not look like the luggage of two girls who had come for a weeklong visit. It looked like the luggage of guests who planned on staying for a while. "Oh, my goodness," Gail had said, when she saw Mary haul the suitcases off the baggage carousel at the airport, a manic laugh sputtering out. She looked at Mary, clearly hoping for reassurance that the planned duration of their visit had not changed or that the enormity of their bags could be otherwise explained. But Mary had just smiled sweetly. "I hope these will fit your car."

Gail reached in and pulled out the smallest of the three bags while Mary picked up the remaining two. With Hannah at her heels, Mary followed Gail's padding steps as she pulled open the door that led to the kitchen.

"So here we are," she said, unable to resist the rush of pleasure she felt when displaying her home. Like a docent revealing the prize work in a museum's collection, Gail Dackard extended her hand toward her kitchen and the mauve and gray living room beyond. "Chez Dackard."

"Wow," said Mary, as she took in the room, with its arches and columns and gaudy abstract art. "This is beautiful."

"Well," Gail demurred, as she set her purse on the countertop next to a vase containing spiky sprays of birds-of-paradise. "It's home."

After a quick tour of the house, Gail showed the girls to their room. Leading them up a wide staircase to the second floor, she glanced behind them to ensure no footprints had been left on her cream carpet. Hannah stuck tightly to Mary's side and averted her eyes each time the path of Gail's gaze neared her. The room in which they would be staying was large and comfortable, and had its own private bath; and Gail felt the need to walk them through the suite, pointing out the bed and the sink and the closet.

Finally, Gail said, "Alright, I'll let you girls get settled. Ron will be home soon with Tim, so feel free to wash up or have a rest." She forced another smile. "Make yourselves at home." And then she ducked out of the room.

The moment the door clicked shut, Mary and Hannah fell into each other, giddy and grateful to be alone again. *"Oomph,"* joked Mary, as Hannah's head hit her hip with a thump. "Take it easy, Bunny."

Mary sat down on the bed and pulled Hannah onto her lap. Hannah looked at Mary with wide, earnest eyes. "This is a really pretty house," she said, as if the fact were somewhat worrisome.

Mary rested her hand on Hannah's head, pushing her hair away from her face. "It's pretty enough."

"They have a light made out of *diamonds*," said Hannah, referring, Mary assumed, to the baguette-prism chandelier that hung over the dining-room table.

"The light was nice."

"And everything is pink."

"Well . . . if Princess Hannah and Princess Mary lived here, they'd make it even *prettier*. There would be a big golden bed and a ballroom with velvet curtains and windows that went from the floor all the way up to the *sky*."

"*Yeah*," said Hannah, her eyes full of worlds Mary created. Mary smiled as she watched Hannah's gaze lifting up through the ceiling into the heavens.

For the next hour, Mary opened bags, put a few things in drawers, and lounged with Hannah. Hannah lay on the bed and asked questions about the plane they had flown on and about when they were going to go back home.

"Well, we can go back in about a week if we want to," replied Mary, as she pulled out her enormous cosmetic case and set it on the dresser. The green floral bag was dingy with makeup and carried with it Mary's exotic powdery scent. She pulled out a tube of lip gloss and leaned into the mirror. "But we're going to see how it goes," she said, as she slicked it on.

Mary had used the insurance payout for Diane's car to purchase their tickets to Miami. The Pools had arranged for Diane's funeral, and Mary gave them most of the money that she had gathered and saved to help with the costs. But she now had only a few hundred dollars left. Diane hadn't purchased life insurance, perhaps because she was so young. Or perhaps because she was already financially burdened without the additional monthly payment. It was a gamble coming to Florida; Mary knew that. She took a small aerosol can of fragrance from her bag, leaned her head back, and sprayed a cloud of the scent onto her neck, her hand circling as she did so like a bird in dizzy flight. Then she took an appraising look at herself. She really was beautiful. She thought this without joy or emotion. She thought this with the focus of someone who had just put down her last dollar on what had always been her lucky number.

MARY AND HANNAH SAT BESIDE EACH OTHER at the dinner table. Gail passed around a bowl of pasta salad; she had made chicken nuggets for Hannah. "So, Tim," said Gail, in a hostess voice. "Mary and Hannah are your second cousins." Gail smiled at her shy, sullen son. "And Mary's only a couple of years older than you."

"Second cousins," mused Ron, who sat at the head of the table, occupying it fully with both his ego and physical presence. "That means you two could get married."

Tim blushed and scowled and mumbled something toward his plate, but Mary let out a gracious and appreciative laugh, leaning forward and smiling back at Tim's father. "Well, maybe we'll start with being friends," she said.

Though his father watched him, waiting for him to engage in repartee with the lovely young woman seated across the table, Tim — seemingly so ill-suited to being Ron Dackard's son — continued to stare at his plate. Diane had nurtured a deep jealousy of her cousin and had spoken enough about Gail's husband for Mary to know that Ron hadn't come from an illustrious background. He was the son of a postal worker. But having made a series of very shrewd business moves early in his career, he now owned a large chain of automobile-maintenance shops called LubeTime, which specialized in the thirty-minute oil change, and he had leveraged his success into a budding political career. Mary sensed that Ron could be merciless and single-minded when it came to getting what he wanted. She could tell because she was, too.

"So, Tim," said Ron, stabbing a bite of his pasta salad. "Are you going to show the girls around the neighborhood after dinner? Take them down to the marina?"

Tim's head jerked up, his expression half-terrified, half-furious.

"That would be fun," Mary offered, smiling at Tim and then his father.

"Ron," whined Gail, with a soft, annoyed chuckle. "It's a school night. And I'm sure the girls are tired."

There was a collective glance toward Hannah, who had just surreptitiously put a whole chicken nugget in her mouth. Hannah's eyes widened at the attention. She had been quietly consuming her dinner hoping that no one would notice her. Mary gently took her chin.

"Are you tired, Bunny?"

Mary nodded once, almost imperceptibly, and so Hannah did, too.

"Well, maybe once Hannah goes to bed, Tim can take Mary down there," decreed Ron Dackard.

Mary and Ron and Gail spent the rest of the dinner mentioning the goings-on of family members that none of them knew very well at all and agreeing that Florida was pleasant in the winter but that the North, with its change of seasons, had its own charms. Hannah and Tim sat silently eating. Ron asked Mary how she was managing without Diane. And Mary sighed, looked at Hannah, then stroked her sister's head. "We're hanging in there," she replied, in a voice that wasn't quite her own.

Mary helped Gail clear the table and load the plates into the dishwasher while Tim escaped to his room and Ron pretended to enjoy playing hide-and-seek with Hannah.

"So your mother's finances . . . ," Gail began, as she and Mary stood together in front of the sink rinsing and loading. "Are you girls provided for?"

Mary's chin dropped as she handed Gail a plate. "She did what she could."

"Well, that motel," said Gail, the anxiety making her voice tinny and shrill. "I'm sure you could get something for the motel."

"I don't know if it's going to be enough."

And Gail turned the water hotter, higher.

When Mary put Hannah to bed that evening, she filled their big pink bathtub to the brim, adding way too much bubble bath so that Hannah was surrounded by peaks of white fluff. "When we last saw our beautiful princesses," Mary began, starting to spin one of her tales, "Princess Hannah was trapped in the cloud kingdom." But Hannah wasn't in the mood for a story tonight.

"Mary?" started Hannah, her light blond hair messy and wild, her eyes almost disproportionately large. "When can we go home?"

"Oh, Bunny," said Mary, lifting her hand out of the water to place it on her sister's head. "It'll be soon."

Hannah looked down into the soapy bubbles, and Mary could tell by the set of her chin that she was trying not to cry. "I miss Mom."

Mary watched Hannah for a moment, and she felt a tugging inside her, painful but precious and pure. "I know," she said.

"When can we go save her?"

Mary's hand whirled slowly through the bubbles. "I'm not sure."

Hannah hadn't understood the funeral, hadn't understood what it meant to be dead. As she stood staring at the enormous flower-ringed box with its lid shut tightly, Hannah kept asking where their mother was. And so Mary told her a tale, whispering in her ear that Diane had been on a journey and was pricked by a poisonous thorn, and now she would sleep unless Princess Hannah and Princess Mary could find the enchanted scroll, the words of which held a magic powerful enough to bring back a dead mother.

HANNAH FELL ASLEEP EARLY, Mary tickling her back until her eyes slipped shut. Then in the dark of their room, Mary applied another coat of lip gloss, ran her fingers through her hair, and moved silently back down the wide cream-colored stairs.

Gail and Ron were facing each other, their arms crossed over their chest, their whispers turning into too-eager smiles as soon as Mary entered the room.

"Hey," said Ron, clapping his hands together on seeing Mary. "There she is!"

Gail took a sip of her white wine and looked away while Ron summoned Tim on the intercom system. "Tim!" he said curtly. And that was all it took. Tim came slinking down the stairs, hands in his pockets, his chin elevated regally. He brushed silently past both Mary and his parents, and went right out the door that led to the garage, leaving only stares in his wake. It was a fledgling defiance that Mary recognized at once. "Well," she said, with a good-natured shrug. "I'll see you in a bit."

Ron made a noise of disgust toward his son, as Mary followed Tim out the open door into the humid night.

"Hey, Tim!" called Mary, as she jogged to catch up with him. He was walking quickly without looking back. "Wait up."

But Tim didn't slow nor did he look at her even after she had reached him. For a minute or two, they walked in silence as Mary worked to keep his pace, sprinklers spitting and whirring in the dark between spotlight-illuminated palms.

Finally, Tim spoke, his eyes gazing straight ahead, his steps not slowing. "My mom doesn't want you here. She thinks you're looking for a handout."

He had meant it to sting. Mary took a moment to think tactically. Tim didn't like girls, she could tell. So her usual arsenal was of little use. But Tim went on. "She put some of her jewelry and the silverware in a safe-deposit box," he said. "She thinks you're going to steal it."

Mary stopped suddenly, and the surprise of it made Tim stop, too. He turned around to look at her. She stared at him for a moment, and she saw the effort it took for him to hold her gaze. Looking Mary in the eyes could be like staring into the sun. "You could," she said, nodding her chin in his direction. "You could take something and say it was us after we're gone."

Tim let out a vicious laugh. Mary had been right to play off his hatred for his parents. He was imagining it now, a pair of diamond earrings sitting in his sock drawer as his mother went wild, pulling her room apart looking for them. "They're such assholes," he spat. "My mom pretending to be all perfect, but she's so scared that her dead cousin's kids are going to ask her for some money that she told me that we have to keep Christmas 'humble' this year. In case you guys saw how much shit she usually buys. We're going to have a second Christmas on New Year's when I'll get the rest of my presents."

Tim turned and started walking again, head down, hands in his pockets.

"What about your dad?" asked Mary. It was a deliberately ambiguous question, one open to interpretation.

"He and my mom don't even talk. She goes upstairs every night after dinner with a glass of wine and takes a sleeping pill. He sits in his office and counts his money." Mary found his angst charming — a quaint offering from a native son.

Tim stopped abruptly and gestured in front of him — a grandiose sweep of the hand. Mary looked up. In front of her were rows of beautiful boats gleaming white in the night and bobbing on the black water. "The *marina*," said Tim, with false pomp.

Mary had seen plenty of boats, often walking down to the harbor in Sandy Bank with Hannah to watch as the summer people launched their vessels. But unlike the Dackard's tacky bourgeois home, these yachts reminded Mary of something rarer than money. These yachts were white stallions pawing at the dark liquid earth, ready to take her to faraway lands.

"It's beautiful," she said, the sentiment plain and uncalculating.

"It's supposed to be," said Tim. Then he looked sharply at Mary. "My mom said that she heard things about you." Mary felt herself rise ever so slightly — a reflexive response to a challenge. "She said she heard that you're wild."

Mary smiled, her teeth ultraviolet white in the dark. A gentle gust of warm air licked her skin, but she didn't respond. She just pulled an errant strand of hair off of her face and looked past him.

"I can get cocaine," dared Tim.

"Oh, yeah," said Mary, with a laugh, as she turned to walk back toward the house. Now it was Tim who was struggling to keep up with her. "That's cool."

She and Tim walked more companionably home, Mary asking him what he liked about school. *Nothing. Maybe History.* And what music he was into. *Duran Duran. Talking Heads.*

"I saw Duran Duran in New York," said Mary.

"Where?"

"The Palladium."

And Tim nodded with respect.

When they arrived home, Tim went to walk upstairs without a farewell, intent on keeping his anger intact at least within the four walls of his room. "Good night," Mary stage-whispered, as he took the steps two at a time.

He might have mumbled something in return, but Mary couldn't tell. The house was silent now. Tim in his room, Hannah in theirs. According to Tim, Gail would be sleeping the heavy dreamless sleep of a pill. And Ron would be in his office. Mary waited a few more minutes, listening to the water run in Tim's bathroom, then shut off. Listening to the low murmur of the television coming from Ron's office.

Then she walked quietly through the dim room, running her fingers over Gail's things, letting them slide over the back of the leather couch and across the thick brushstrokes of the paintings. Beyond the glass doors at the far end of the living room was the brilliant pool, glowing and sunk into the earth. Mary opened the door and stepped out, kicking her shoes off and feeling the cool stone on her feet as she walked to the pool's edge and stared down into it. Filled with light, it looked like a liquid gem, its facets rippling.

With unhurried motions, Mary pulled off her shirt, letting her body work its way out like a snake shedding its skin. Mary then unhooked her bra, letting it drop beside her feet. She felt the warm night air on her bare breasts. Her shorts came off, then her underwear. She waded quietly into the pool, and despite its warmth, the water brought rise to goose bumps on her skin. Having grown up by the ocean, Mary felt good in the water, as though it were her natural habitat. Quickly, she submerged, swimming confidently out to the center of the pool. Once she arrived, she turned back to face the house and let her limbs circle around, her body glowing in the light. She looked up at the house and found the window to Ron's office. And then she treaded water and watched until she was sure there was movement. Until she was sure she saw the curtain being pulled ever so slightly farther back.

MARY STAYED IN THE WATER until the skin on her fingers began to wrinkle and crease. When she emerged, she did so as a Venus, liquid spilling from her skin and running down her limbs in thin channels under an enormous white moon.

Gathering up her clothes, she padded toward the house, feeling the uneven stone beneath her feet. She began to hum the Temptations' "Just My Imagination," which had been Diane's favorite song. She passed the door to Ron's office and saw the television's quick flickering light under the door. She imagined him in there, his back to the bookshelf, his heart pounding in his chest as his hand pressed against the front of his trousers. With her arm sliding up the rail, she took languid steps up the staircase, leaving damp footprints behind her.

She opened the door to her room, and the light from the hallway rushed in. Hannah was lying on her back in bed, her hands palms up, as if she had surrendered something. Mary pulled a T-shirt from her bag and slipped it on, then got into bed beside Hannah. Her wet hair stuck to her neck and soaked her shirt, but her limbs felt loose and light, and the white cotton sheets were cool against her skin. The air conditioner hummed, and Hannah emitted her tiny snores, and as Mary let her fingertips glide up and down Hannah's forearm, she felt for the first time in a long time that everything might be okay.

Hannah woke before Mary the next morning, wriggling in close to her and waiting until Mary raised her long lean arms above her head and stretched. Mary slung one leg up over the covers, then looked down at Hannah.

"What are we supposed to do here?" asked Hannah, her voice small, her brow two tight lines. In Sandy Bank, days passed without needing to be filled. Here, even Hannah sensed that would take more effort.

"I don't know," said Mary, smiling. "I guess we're just going to see what Gail and Ron have planned."

Mary helped Hannah get dressed, then did the same, pulling on cutoffs, and then rubbing her legs with baby oil so they shone shimmery slick. They held hands as they took the stairs, listening to the voices already in the kitchen, which came in brief bursts between ponds of silence. *The Allens invited us for dinner Thursday. Tim needs a check for the Orlando trip. The sprinkler at the end of the driveway is broken.*

When Mary and Hannah entered the room, Ron, who had his newspaper open on the glass-top table in front of him, gave his hands a clap. "There they are!" he said, beaming. He looked at Tim, who was standing in the corner leaning against the wall, eating a bowl of cereal.

"Good morning," said Mary, smiling as she paused just inside the large room.

"Morning, girls," answered a tight-lipped Gail, who was at the counter slicing a cantaloupe.

"What do you all have planned for today?" asked Ron, looking from Mary to Gail and back again, his arms crossed over his chest. "Gonna do a little sightseeing? The Seaquarium is always fun."

"Well," chuckled Gail, giving her husband a searing glance. "I'd love to take the girls around, but unfortunately I have a lot to do to get ready for the holiday. I was thinking that Mary and Hannah might like to just relax by the pool." Gail placed her perfect wedges of melon into a glass bowl.

Mary made her expression one of stoic disappointment. "Oh," she said, with a brave smile. "That'll be nice."

Ron regarded her silently for a moment. "Oh, come on now," he said. "We can't let you sit around the house all day." He turned to his wife. "Honey, you do your shopping. I'll take the girls around."

Gail smiled, her hand at her neck. "Ron," she said. "Don't you have to get to work?"

"Nah . . . ," he said, with a magnanimous swat. "I just get in the way there anyway."

Gail looked at Tim. "Well, you can all do something," she said. "Tim doesn't have school today."

Ron forced himself to acknowledge his son. "What do you say, Timmo?" he asked, his sarcasm bleeding into the edges of his words. "You want to get out of the house?"

Tim abruptly deposited his cereal bowl on the table. It sloshed milk onto the glass. "I'm going to Zack's," he said, as he rushed out of the kitchen.

And on that day, as Gail drove from the tennis court to lunch with friends, then to the Galleria, she'd check her lipstick in the rearview mirror, only mildly annoyed that Ron had shown such alacrity as a tour guide for the orphaned Chase girls. It was, after all, better than having them alone in the house all day. So while Gail purchased gifts for her husband and son, and even herself, Mary was coyly biting her lip as she snapped pictures of Ron with her Polaroid camera. *So Hannah and I can remember our trip.*

So it went for the next few days—the accidental meetings of feet and ankles under the table, the playful stretches that exposed a swath of smooth belly. Gail couldn't really be blamed for not noticing. Mary was so careful, so subtle. As it was the holiday season, Gail had plenty of excuses to get out of the house away from her burdensome houseguests, so Mary's most overt advances were timed with Gail's frequent absences. But Mary made no such accommodations for Tim, whom she often caught looking at her as if she were something mesmerizing but terrible.

Ron played his part well, too, lingering after breakfast when he would have typically departed for work, coming home early and offering to take the girls for a ride on the golf cart—all under the guise of being a good host.

"They're going to want to stay," Mary heard Gail whine on Christmas Eve; she listened outside Gail and Ron's bedroom door while they finished wrapping gifts. "You mark my words; they're living high on the hog here, and this visit is going to end up being longer than a week."

"Oh, please, Gail," snapped Ron.

"I just think giving them that kind of gift is going to make things worse!" Gail's voice whistled like a kettle. "It's inappropriate!"

"You can tell me what is and what is not appropriate when you earn a fucking *dime*, Gail!" bellowed Ron. "Because until then, every cent that is spent in this house is *mine*, and I'm the only one fit to deem what is and isn't *appropriate.*"

And on Christmas morning, when Mary and Hannah opened their matching gold lockets, Mary beamed and let her eyes go wet. "Thank you," she said, her voice a sob-suppressing whisper. "I can't tell you how much this means to me."

Gail gave Mary a tight smile and took a sip of her mimosa, her crossed leg bouncing while Ron beamed. "You're welcome," he said.

"Isn't it pretty, Bunny?" she asked Hannah, who was staring at her own golden oval. "It's a necklace."

Mary pulled Hannah's from the box and draped it over her neck, watching as Hannah brought the locket close to her face for inspection.

"Can someone help me put mine on?" asked Mary, her eyes moving between Gail and Ron.

After a moment, Ron spoke up. "Sure," he said, in a manner that was intended to mask his eagerness, but Mary saw his pleasure as he started to stand. She walked over and handed him the box with a Bambi smile, then turned and lifted her silky black hair to reveal the curve of her bare neck.

And as Ron fastened the gold clasp, his fingertips brushing her skin, Mary stared across the room at Tim, who appeared to be the one person who might have fully understood just what Mary Chase was playing at. But no one could have been more helpless to stop her.

Ron was in good spirits the rest of the day, his mood having an inverse relationship to his wife's. They both downed drink after drink, moving from mimosas to Bloody Marys to vodka tonics, but as Ron grew jovial, Gail became dark. She remained perched on a stool in the kitchen for much of the day, watching as her foolish husband openly flirted with her very young cousin. Maybe Gail thought she'd have a serious talk with him about it later. Maybe she thought she'd nip this transgression in the bud and put an end to his nonsense. *You're making a fool of yourself!* she'd say. *You realize that you're old enough to be her father?* She had no idea how close Ron was to the precipice.

Tim had disappeared to his room as soon as the gifts were opened and only resurfaced briefly for dinner, where he took a few bites of the beef Wellington and scalloped potatoes that his mother had purchased from a local caterer and heated in her professional-quality range. Gail went to bed soon after dinner as well, disgusted and annoyed by her husband's display but thinking it nothing more than a middle-aged man's pathetic diversion and taking *two* sleeping pills that night to tamp it from her mind. Mary put Hannah to bed, and then it was just she and Ron.

He was sitting on the sectional when she came back downstairs, his arm resting on the seatback. Mary's lip gloss was freshly applied, her hair was brushed, and in her hands was her Polaroid.

"I want to take some more pictures," she said. "This place is so pretty."

Ron patted the seat next to him. "Come sit."

Mary obliged and took the seat next to him. She stretched her long tanned legs out over Gail's cream leather as she looked about the room. "Gail has such good taste."

Ron looked down and exhaled at the mention of his wife's name. "Gail has *expensive* taste," he said, and then he looked at Mary, this sugar-sweet young beauty who had never run up his American Express bill, had never insisted on private school for his pussy son, or made him go to couple's therapy.

Mary sunk down lower into the couch and rolled onto her hip to face him. Then she snapped another photo. "Merry Christmas," she said, with a giggle, as he leaned forward, rubbing his eyes and blinking against the surprise of the flash.

"Give me that," he teased, as he groped for the camera, his eyes still closed. Mary tried to hold the camera above her head as he blindly reached for it. Mary let out small playful shrieks and laughed as she maneuvered away from his grabs. But then came the inevitable moment of their tussle when his body found its way on top of hers, their faces inches apart, and she smelled the liquor on his breath. And from the quick flash of doubt that crossed his face, Mary saw that she might lose him, so she adjusted her hips and bit her lips and let out a barely audible little moan. Then she loosely aimed the camera that she still held extended out in her arm to point the lens at Ron and herself. "Say cheese," she said, with a coy smile, as she hit the button. His mouth fell on hers to the mechanical sound of the print being pushed from the camera.

And though Mary felt reflexive arousal at Ron's gyrations, she was able to judge his state of mind with near scientific clarity. At that moment, he was thinking of nothing besides being with her. He would have fucked her right there on his wife's nine-thousand-dollar sofa.

"Come on," she whispered, her voice baby soft. "Let's go to your office." And she twisted out from under him, camera still in hand, and ran giggling to his office as he staggered after her, drunk with want.

Mary put the camera to good use that night, using the nine remaining photos wisely, pretending it was all a playful little game. And when Ron flipped this beautiful girl onto her knees and had her from behind, she was sure that he had never before in his whole life been quite so happy.

Ron fell asleep that night on the leather couch in his office, naked. When he was lightly snoring, Mary extricated herself from his embrace and set to work, gathering up the photos that had been strewn around, then heading up to her and Hannah's room to pack. She worked silently and quickly, refolding clothing and zipping the bags in the dim room, her hair tangled, her lips feeling raw.

At just before six in the morning, Mary loaded herself up with their luggage and brought it down to the garage, setting it just behind the automatic door. Then she went back up to the bedroom for Hannah. She slid her arms underneath her sister's sleeping body. Hannah gave a startled intake of breath as she was lifted, then she settled against Mary, her eyes never opening. As Mary hurried down the stairs, Hannah made small noises, as if her consciousness were floating up to the surface.

The cab glided up just as Mary peered through the glass of the garage door. She pressed a button and the door rumbled to life, rising obediently.

Seeing Mary carrying Hannah, the driver had gotten out. "Can you get the bags?" Mary asked him, tilting her head behind her to the luggage that sat on the concrete floor.

The driver just nodded, looking at the beautiful Mary and the sleeping Hannah and the hideous grandeur of the house behind them. And as Mary settled Hannah into her seat, he hauled the three bags into the trunk, got back into the driver's seat, and with unuttered urgency, sped away from chez Dackard.

"Where are we going?" asked Hannah, whose eyes were now open.

Mary adjusted in her seat, feeling the vinyl stick to her skin. She twisted a finger though a loop of her sister's hair. "Away."

Though Mary couldn't have known it, Gail had already roused, the rumbling of the garage door having woken her. She had seen the bed empty next to her and shuffled down to Ron's office. Ron, still naked, raised his head when his wife entered the room. It was with a politician's practicality that he immediately wondered what exactly Gail knew, where exactly Mary was, and how exactly he could explain it all away.

Mary, as it turned out, was at that moment pulling out of Cocoplum Estates, staring at the bright red sunrise that had made its advance in the morning sky.

"Red sky at morning, sailors take warning," said Mary, as she angled her head to better see the road, her arm around Hannah.

"What does that mean?"

"It means that there'll probably be bad weather later."

From the front seat, the cab driver met Mary's eye in the

rearview mirror. He was a black man who wore a short-sleeve button-down shirt and a baseball cap. If Mary had asked, he would have told her that his name was Terrance.

"You going to the airport?" he asked, his words long and languid.

"No," said Mary. "The B & M Diner."

"The B & M?" he asked, questioning.

"Yeah," replied Mary. "The one by the *Herald* building."

The streets were quiet as the cab glided through them; talk radio playing low enough for the words to be indiscernible. As the sisters made their way out of affluence, the buildings tightened and rose, and the sun burned through the early-morning haze. "This is right here," said Terrance, finally, pulling up to a silver diner on the corner. He watched Mary look at the sign. "They got good steak and eggs."

Mary paid the fare, and Terrance lifted the Chase girls' bags out of the trunk, resting them on the sidewalk. "You want some help with those?" he asked, as Mary slung one over each shoulder, lifting the third to her chest.

"I got it. Thanks."

The Chase girls went inside, taking a booth near the window. Two bags were stuck next to Hannah, the third next to Mary. When the waitress came, Mary ordered Hannah a stack of silver-dollar pancakes and a glass of orange juice.

"Anything else?" asked with waitress, without looking up from her order pad.

"Yeah, I'll take a coffee," replied Mary, closing the menu and extending it toward the waitress. "And the steak and eggs."

"They're famous here."

"That's what I heard."

"That'll be right out."

"It's okay," Mary said. "We're not in a rush."

After the waitress left, Mary went to the pay phone outside and stared across the street at the large sand-yellow building with enormous words affixed to its exterior. THE MIAMI HER-ALD. Then she dialed the number that she had committed to memory.

The phone rang several times until the machine picked up. Gail's smooth, practiced voice came over the tape. *You've reached the Dackards, please leave a message and we'll return your call just as soon as possible.*

"Hello. This is——"

Mary heard the line being picked up.

"Mary," he said, his voice steel smooth. And she couldn't help but smile.

"Good morning, Ron."

She heard him exhale loudly. "Where are you?"

At that, Gail's voice burst into the background, her words running together in an indiscernible shriek. Ron put his hand over the receiver. "Shut the fuck up, Gail!"

Only when Gail was quiet did Mary speak again. "Did you have fun last night, Ron?"

She heard Ron try to steady his voice. He was opportunistic enough himself to recognize the trait in others. "I had a lot to drink, Mary."

"That you did, Ron." A couple passed, the man was following the woman, shouting at her in Spanish. *"Crees que puedes hacerlo mejor que yo?"*

"Why don't you tell me where you are?" he said, with the forced calm of a hostage negotiator. "I can come pick you up and we can work this out."

Mary's smile grew broader. "I'm at the B & M Diner," she said, relishing the pause. "Right by the *Miami Herald.*" And she would have given anything to see Ron's face as he finally and fully put the pieces together. "You're going to meet me here in three hours with ten thousand dollars in cash."

"You're out of your fucking mind." His words were said through locked teeth.

"And if you don't," continued Mary, as if he hadn't spoken, "I'm going to walk across the street and tell the reporters an interesting story about a freshman state senator and his wife's cousin." She paused, knowing that Ron was recalling the pictures and the look on his face as he smiled for the camera, cupping the breasts of a very pretty, very young girl.

Seven

1981

MARY STOOD AT THE DESK of the dealership watching the damp man with strings of hair running across his bare scalp count the stack of money she had handed him. Stopping suddenly, he looked up at her, his face inquisitive and hopeful. "Are you that famous fashion model?" he asked, his accent more rural than she had heard elsewhere in Miami.

Mary looked at him for a moment as he waited for her reply. "No," she said plainly, before slipping her sunglasses back down on her face and looking away. The man returned to the stack of bills, but his question had made him lose count, and she heard him swear under his breath as he started over again. Perhaps he was wondering how else a girl would be able to pay cash for a car — albeit a used one — if she wasn't a famous fashion model.

Mary stayed silent as the man finished, feeling the remainder of Ron Dackard's money against her leg, to which it was strapped with an ACE bandage. Once he had totaled the $3,200, he slid the title toward her. "Alright. You've got yourself a car." Mary picked up the paper, her eyes running over its seals and signatures. "Lemme go get the boys to bring it around," he said, straining slightly with the effort of standing. Then he carried himself to the backroom with his wide chugging gate.

Once he was out of the room, Mary bent down toward Hannah, who was staring into a dismal-looking little fish tank that contained only three common goldfish circling their scum-walled environs. "We're going to have such a fun trip, Bunny," she said. Hannah looked up at her. The past few months had been hard on Hannah, Mary knew that.

"Are we going home now?"

Mary squatted down so that their eyes were level, and she shook her head. "We're going to do something so much better."

"What?"

Mary turned to see the black Chevy Blazer round the front of the building and idle, like a loyal steed. Then her eyes returned to Hannah. "We're going to have an adventure," she said, the words feeling round and perfect on her tongue.

The Chase girls drove north, hugging the coast before drifting toward the center and taking the great artery that cut through the peninsula of Florida to the heart of the south. The elevation seemed to slope downward until Mary felt their destination grow nearer. It was something she was drawn to without knowing why, like her own magnetic north. And when the swamp finally did come into view, its still waters reflected the steadily falling sun like an inverse earth.

Years earlier, Mary had read about Tammahuskee Swamp in a magazine, and the images from the article had settled in her mind, found shelter there. The heavy-footed cypress trees, their branches swathed with veils of gray moss; the carnivorous pitcher plants, hooded and red veined; the black cottonmouths, slipping between land and water—they all seemed to be the inhabitants of the fairy-tale world Mary so often created for

Hannah. Mary recalled that the swamp used to be home to panthers, but they had been eradicated. And as she glanced out her window at the orange sky, she wished that they were still there, lurking in the bush, their bodies pressed low.

Up ahead, a sign came into view and Mary read the white letters, then made a smooth turn onto the dry pine-flanked dirt road at the entrance to the park. "This is it, Bunny," she said, finally letting herself feel the weariness from the past days and weeks and months. It was a relief to be with just Hannah, in a place both water and land, where the past and the future seemed to meet, where Mary could prepare for what came next. "We're here."

Mary pulled up to the campground offices and put the car in park. They had stopped only twice, exiting the highway and finding themselves on wide roads lined with unfamiliar fast-food chains. When Mary saw a Kmart, she pulled in, and with the Dackards' money, Mary bought a tent and two sleeping bags.

"Do you want to stay in the car while I run inside?" Mary asked. The sun had sunk out of sight, and under the pines, the air outside was cool and getting colder.

Hannah opened her car door. "No," she said. "I wanna come."

She followed Mary up the wood ramp to the drab gray building. Mary pulled open the clattering screen door, then propped it open with her hip as she pushed in the larger wooden one and scooted Hannah in ahead of her. A small gray-haired woman looked up. She wore a handknit-looking sweater over an ill-fitting uniform.

"Evening," she said, with a nod. "May I help you?"

"We're here for a campsite," she said.

The woman glanced up again at Mary, then back down at her ledger. "Do you have a driver's license?"

Mary took her wallet from her bag and pulled out her license, handing it to the woman, who slid her glasses up her nose before tilting her head back to examine the small card. Then she set it down beside the ledger and began to transcribe Mary's name. "You girls have come a long way," she said.

"We were visiting family," Mary replied. "Down in Florida."

The woman then pulled a photocopied map from a stack. "You'll be in campsite 21. You'll want to park just in front of it." Then she looked at Mary as if Mary were a young scout under her command. "You have equipment, I assume. It's going to get down into the forties tonight and you'll need proper sleeping bags. Most people don't come this time of year."

"We have bags," answered Mary, as she took the map and stuck it in her back pocket. She rested her hand on Hannah's back as they turned to leave.

"The closest grocery store is Harvey's," the woman called after them. Mary stopped and looked back. "Just a couple of miles down the road. They'll be closed by now, but they open at eight in the morning."

Mary nodded. "Okay," she said, with a single nod. "Thanks."

Then the girls walked back out, hearing the screen door bang shut behind them. "How hungry are you, Bunny?" Mary asked, as she opened her car door, stepping aside to make room for Hannah.

Hannah looked up, then shrugged. "Only a little," she said.

"Do you think another PB&J would be enough for tonight?" she asked. "We could get something warm in the morning."

"I guess," replied Hannah, before scrambling up into the car and across to the passenger's seat.

Mary got in beside her and navigated by headlight the short distance to campsite 21, which was a small alcove with a picnic table sitting on patchy balding grass. Mary noticed a shiver run through Hannah as they got back out of the car. She popped the tailgate and pulled out one of the three big suitcases they had brought with them to Miami, then she opened it and took out Hannah's purple down jacket and tossed it to her sister. "Here, Bunny," she said. "Put that on."

Hannah caught its sleeve as the rest of the jacket landed by her feet. She wasn't old enough to wonder why Mary had brought her winter coat with them to Miami. "Do the alligators stay in the water?" she asked, slowly sliding the jacket on.

"Oh, yeah," said Mary, as she pulled a hat down over Hannah's head. "Don't worry about them. They can hardly move on land."

Hannah gave her a solemn look, and Mary cupped the back of her head.

"You'll like it here, Bunny," she said. "It'll be a good place to stay for a couple of days."

Hannah nodded, the way an adult does when processing information that doesn't seem to make a whole lot of sense. "Why did we leave Gail's house?"

"It was just time to go," said Mary.

"Ron was mad when he came to the restaurant."

Mary recalled how he had walked silently in, his jaw like a jutting crag of rock, and sat down. Without a word, his eyes boring into Mary's, he had slid her a gloriously fat envelope. She held his gaze while she fingered each bill under the table, counting them out. Then she slid him her own envelope, the one with the Polaroids.

"The Dackards were nice, but we couldn't stay there forever," Mary said, as she pulled the tent, still in its package, from the back of the Blazer. "Now come on. Help me get this thing set up."

Mary spread the components of the tent on the ground in front of her and set to work. Her long lean arms secured stakes and threaded poles through fabric channels as Hannah held the flashlight. The night was a dense black, hung with the moon and its companion stars.

As Mary worked, she drew the attention of two men in the nearest occupied campsite, who had positioned themselves to watch her. With gray beards and black leather jackets, they reclined against their picnic table, their hands curled around cans of beer and their faces illuminated by the undulating flames of their fire. Beside their tent were two large luggage-strapped motorcycles parked on a blanket of dead pine needles. "Let us know if you need any help," they called, their gravelly voices playful.

Mary heard the pop of wood as their fire consumed it. Her head jerked up. She looked at the men, her hazel eyes more yellow than brown.

But she said nothing.

Once the tent was up, Mary unrolled the sleeping bags and set them inside, then hung her flashlight from a small hook at its peak. Scooting back out, she stood at the entrance and looked at Hannah. "Check it out," she said, tilting her head toward the tent.

Hannah stuck her head in and was taken with it at once, scrambling in and lying on her back atop one of the sleeping bags. Her hands were beneath her head and her teeth were visible through her smile.

"You like it?" asked Mary, bending down toward the entrance. The tent with Bunny in it reminded Mary of the Easter eggs Diane used to buy her, the ones made of sugar with a window into an intricate scene inside.

Hannah nodded. "It's like where rabbits live," she said.

Mary chuckled. "Yeah," she said. "Perfect for a bunny."

On her back, Hannah gazed up at the tent's ceiling, and Mary knew that it was turning to vines and roots and moist brown earth in her sister's mind.

Mary gathered sandwich makings and then followed Hannah into the tent. "We can pretend that we're Princess Mary and Princess Hannah, and that this is an enchanted forest," she said, assembling a sandwich, using her knees like a countertop.

"And that we just got out of the Black Woods," said Hannah, curling her arms around her small body.

"And that there's a magical creature here that looks like a huge cat, and if we can find him, we can ride on his back and defeat the evil queen."

Hannah's head fell back onto the tent floor. "How many nights do we get to sleep in here?" asked Hannah, giddy.

"A bunch," answered Mary, as she handed Hannah a PB&J. "We can stay until we don't want to stay anymore."

Hannah took a bite of the sandwich and smiled contentedly, her gaze softening as her mind drifted to lands faraway. "Do you think that scroll might be in here? The one that could help Mom?"

Mary stroked Hannah's head. "I don't know, Bunny" was all she said.

The girls each ate three sandwiches, and then Mary helped Hannah zip up in her sleeping bag.

"Night, Bunny," she said, kissing her nose.

"Can we look for the magical cat tomorrow?"

"First thing," replied Mary, then she picked up the sandwich makings. "I'm going to go stick these in the truck."

She had just shut the car door when the men called to her from their campsite across the way. "Want to come sit with us?" the younger one said, his voice just starting to slur. "We got some beers."

Mary looked from side to side, then walked briskly to the men, somehow seeing everything around her, sensing it as coolness and heat, light and dark. The men elbowed each other excitedly at the approach of the girl with the black hair. When she stopped, she stared at them for a moment before speaking. "Did you hear?" she asked. The men looked at each other, trying to determine if they were equally confused. "About the attack?"

Finally, the young one, the braver one, spoke. "What attack?" he asked, his free hand finding its way under his arm. Beside them, the fire snapped and danced.

"The panther. One dragged a man into the swamp by his throat. He was kicking the whole time, but his throat was filled with blood so he couldn't scream."

The men looked at each other nervously. "We didn't hear anything about that," the older one said, trying to sound dismissive.

"You won't. The state's trying to keep it hush-hush. They don't want people to know that the panthers are back," she said. And as quickly as she came, she turned and left, stalking back through the dark with quick, quiet steps, leaving only silence in her wake as the men watched her behind the flames.

Back at site 21, Mary unzipped the tent and, finding Hannah still awake, climbed in. Without a word, she lay next to her. And when Hannah's eyes finally slipped shut, Mary reached for a novel that she had taken from Gail. Its unread pages were cool and virgin, and Mary slid her fingers inside to flex the spine. She balanced a flashlight against her shoulder and held the book above her face. They wouldn't be going back to the Water's Edge, Mary knew that. And as she read, with a strand of her dark hair tucked into the corner of her mouth, she felt a pulling in her chest. She remembered the day several years ago when her heart opened up, then closed back around the object it so desired.

Eight
1982

I T WAS THEIR MOTORCYCLES THAT WOKE HER, the burn of them as they roared out of the park. Mary lifted her head, her gaze turned toward the sound. Next to her, she heard Hannah breathe sharply, then saw her eyes struggle to open. Mary rested her head back down and let it roll toward her sister. "Morning, Bunny," she said, as Hannah propped herself up and glanced around the tent, looking disoriented. "How'd you sleep?"

With her eyes still swollen from sleep, Hannah thought for a moment. "Good," she said.

"We need to go into town," said Mary. "We need to buy some food."

Hannah made a grunting noise, and she squirmed her way onto her belly, burying her face into the bag's plaid flannel lining.

"Come on, Bunny," said Mary, nudging her sister with her foot. "We'll find a diner or something."

Once in the Blazer, Mary turned the heat up to high. Next to her, Hannah had her coat pulled tightly and her chin sunk into her chest. Mary laid her fingers over the vent until she felt the air turn warm.

"Here," Mary said, taking Hannah's hand and placing it where hers had been. "Put your hands here."

The town nearest the campsite was a small grid of streets that housed churches and shops and offices in small two- and three-story buildings. Mary found a small restaurant, and she and Hannah parked down the street, then silently took a seat at the counter while the locals gave them inquisitive glances over their menus and newspapers. They were accustomed to tourists visiting the swamp, but not two girls alone, not at this time of year.

"Do they have waffles?" whispered Hannah.

Mary looked over the menu. "Yeah," she answered back.

And when the waitress approached and asked the girls what they would like, Mary gave her the most charming of smiles, and with the languid drawl she had first heard on that trip with her mother so many years ago, she said, "I'd like two eggs over hard with bacon and hash browns, please. My sister here will have the waffles with a side of ham." Then she set her menu down, and as the waitress began writing the order, Mary gave Hannah a wink.

After breakfast, the girls went to the grocery store, filling their cart with cereal and donuts and oranges, with bread and milk and ice for their cooler. And as they drove back to camp, Mary felt content and warmed, knowing that Hannah was fed. Knowing that they had enough money to ensure she would be so again. Back at the campground, in front of site 21, Mary put the truck in park and turned to her sister. "Whaddaya say we go see this swamp?"

It would begin that way each day. They'd start their mornings in winter coats and hats, their bodies still stiff from the ground and the temperature. But as they walked, the sun making its way up in the sky, their muscles would become warm and loose, and the hair under their hats would grow damp. They'd stay gone all day, eating lunch on the trail and not starting back until the afternoon light began to turn golden. It was during those days that Mary began to feel restored, that the past few months began to fall away like a husk. And so it was that the wounds left by Diane's death started to heal over.

Their first excursions were limited by dry land and what could be seen on foot as they traveled over boardwalks and paths. And each day, they ventured farther, dared to go deeper, until, after nearly a week, the girls found their way into the swamp's damp heart.

The man who rented them the canoe operated out of a small shack inside the park's borders. He chewed gum and wore windshieldlike sunglasses that hid his eyes.

"You know there's gators in them waters," he said, watching Mary help Hannah into their vessel, his hands on his hips.

Hannah, who you might not have thought was paying much attention, suddenly looked up. "Do they ever bite people?" she asked.

The man's tongue darted from his lips, and the corner of his mouth lifted in a smile. "Not if you don't fall in."

Hannah's eyes widened, and Mary tilted her head to find her sister's eyes. "Bunny, if you fell in, I'd dive in right after you."

The man looked to the side and laughed, not knowing the truth of it. As he gave the canoe a push from the dock, he called, "Watch out for water moccasins, too! Those sons a bitches will chase ya!" Hannah looked back at him while Mary took strong, solid strokes, guiding their little canoe away.

The girls made their way through lily-blanketed channels and waterways lined with cypress, the trunks of which looked like the slender legs of some towering ancient beasts. Mary consulted the compass but she didn't need to. The swamp had seeped inside her. She knew its direction, its nearly indiscernible flow. She paid attention to the way the vegetation gathered or spread, to where the waters were choked or clear. And as the canoe rounded a cluster of trees, there, staring at them from behind a tangled clump of greenbrier, was a cat.

IT WAS THE COLOR OF COAL and stood with its massive head hung low. Its enormous paw splayed out over the soft earth, and its yellow eyes didn't leave Mary's even as its long tail flicked like a blade of switchgrass.

Mary pulled in a rush of breath, a stomach-punch gasp that made Hannah stiffen.

"What?" whispered Hannah, but Mary couldn't say a word.

The cat took a soundless step forward, and its mouth opened so that Mary could see the pink of its tongue, the white of its teeth. She felt her breath become shallow. Suddenly, Hannah shouted, "Look!"

Hannah's was the only voice that could have pulled Mary away. Hannah was pointing toward a fallen log. "An alligator!" she said.

And it was only a second that Mary took her eyes off the cat, but when she looked back, it was gone. "Do you see him, Mary?" asked Hannah.

Mary searched the swamp, lifting her chin to see past trunks and through tangled branches and ferns, searching for his black snakelike tail.

"He's right there!" said Hannah, turning back to tug on the leg of her sister's jeans.

Mary's eyes lingered on the spot where her cat had stood before looking in the direction of Hannah's pointing. Her gaze arrived just as a large alligator pushed off a log into the water, his body entering with a dull splash, like a stone statue come to life.

"Did you see that?" asked Hannah, looking back at Mary, beaming.

Mary nodded, her words stuck in her throat. "That was cool," she finally said.

"Yeah," agreed Hannah. "We saw an *alligator*."

"Good eyes, Bunny," said Mary, feeling a loss enormous and unexplained.

MARY AND HANNAH SPENT TWO WEEKS in the swamp before they packed their Blazer and left. "Good-bye, Tammahuskee!" called Mary, as she made a quick right onto the main road. "We'll miss you!"

"Yeah, bye, swamp!" echoed Hannah, having seemingly aged years during those two weeks. "We'll come back some-day!"

After several miles, Mary looked over at Hannah. "Do you know where we're going now?"

"Where?" asked Hannah, home no longer on her mind. Home no longer a place that was even real.

"To the beach."

Instead of heading north, Mary cut back and traveled west. They drove through farmland and smalls towns that held only churches and jails until turning south again and crossing the state line. Once again in Florida, Mary drove Hannah to the white sand beach on the Gulf of Mexico where she was born.

They arrived that same day, pulling up to the weather-battered stone of Ft. Rillieux well before sunset. They got out of the truck, and Mary grabbed the bouquet of red carnations she had purchased at the market just over the bridge and walked to the fishing pier that jutted out into the Gulf. After the tea-colored swamp, the Gulf — with its aqua waters and rhythmic waves — was like a counterstretch. Mary closed her eyes, feeling the sun on her face. "Mom and I came here," Mary said. "A few months before you were born." Then she looked down at the flowers in her hands. "Here," she said, pulling the bouquet apart. She extended half of the blooms to Hannah. "Let's toss these in."

Hannah took the flowers and looked down at their red petals. "Why are we going to throw them in?" she asked, not looking at her sister.

Mary felt the bottomlessness in her stomach that she had felt during those first weeks after Diane had died, when she would scrub the floors until her hands bled. "For Mom," she said, looking out at the pastel sky and sea. Then she took a flower from her bunch and tossed it in. Mary looked at Hannah, and Hannah, understanding somehow what this meant, did the same. With her brow tightened and her eyes filling, Hannah tossed her flowers in one by one with her sister.

"Is Mom going to find them?" asked Hannah.

"Yeah," replied Mary. "She'll find them." And the girls stood there in silence watching as the red flowers scattered and parted ways in the vast blue sea.

MARY AND HANNAH SPENT THE NEXT several weeks on the road drifting gradually but purposefully northward. They lived out of the Blazer or the tent or, when needed, small forgettable motels like the Water's Edge. They saw the Smokey Mountains and Graceland and the feral horses of the Outer Banks. And after Bardavista, Hannah didn't ask for Diane again. Anyhow, it had always been Mary to whom Hannah was fixed. It was as if Mary were the sun that Hannah orbited while Diane was a mourned but nonessential moon.

Since they left Sandy Bank, Hannah had turned five and Mary nineteen. They lived like the girls from one of Mary's stories, bonded and inextricable, the line where one ended and the other began a malleable, gossamer thing. And it was in front of another silver-sided diner that Mary put the Blazer in park. Then she shifted to look at the passenger seat, where Hannah was sleeping. Hannah wouldn't understand what had brought them to this place, of all places. She wouldn't understand that in an inevitable way it was always where they were headed. No matter their direction.

Mary reached over to give her sister a gentle rousing. "Bunny. We're here."

Nine

1982

MARY AND HANNAH SAT ACROSS FROM each other in the booth of the sunny Rhode Island diner.

"Where are we?" asked Hannah.

"We're in a nice town. It's called Northton. We're going to be here for a while." Mary glanced out the window at the parking lot and the wide busy road beyond. "Stay here for a sec," she said. "I'm going to go get a newspaper."

Mary slipped her sunglasses on and walked out the front door of the diner over to a red metal box. She pulled a few coins from her back pocket, dropped them in, and opened the door, pulling out a thick newspaper.

Mary opened the door to the diner, and the cool air from outside collided with the humid grease-scented air from inside. She slid in the booth, opened the paper, and flipped to the thick classified section.

Without looking up, Mary responded to her sister's unasked question. "We need to find a place to live," she said.

"What do you mean?" asked Hannah. After their time as nomads, the idea of living somewhere had become foreign.

"You need to start school," said Mary, not looking up as she read the description of an available apartment.

"School?" Hannah said the word as if she'd never heard it before.

Mary glanced up, then looked back down at the classifieds. "Yeah, school."

"Are you gonna come?"

Mary was silent for a moment, not exactly pleased with what came next for either of them. "No," she answered. "I have to get a job."

The girls' lunches were set down and they consumed them in silence, Hannah slowly eating her grilled cheese and fries, Mary's eyes scanning the ads, not looking up even as she ate her cheeseburger. When they were finished, Mary walked up to the cashier to pay. "Do you have a phone book?" she asked the woman perched on a stool in front of the register.

The cashier reached under the counter and pulled up a thick yellow book, setting it with a thud on the counter. Mary opened it, leafing quickly through the white pages, toggling back and forth until she found the page she was looking for. Then she tucked her black hair behind her ear and ran her finger down the row of black letters until she stopped. Her finger then traveled horizontally across the page and she looked up suddenly. "Can you tell me where Northton Avenue is?" she asked the cashier.

The cashier pushed her large gold-templed glasses up on her nose to get a better look at the girl in front of her. Mary, with her sun-darkened skin and yellow brown eyes, must have seemed like some strange half-domesticated species. "You just take the highway down one exit and take a right on Burke Street," she said. "Northton crosses Burke after a half mile. You can't miss it. Beautiful homes there."

"Thanks," said Mary, putting her change in her back pocket and ushering Hannah out of the front door.

"Where are we going to sleep tonight?" asked Hannah. It was a familiar question and one asked without anxiety.

"I don't know yet," said Mary. "We're probably going to find a motel." She opened the driver's-side door, letting Hannah climb in ahead of her. "But we need to go see something first."

Mary followed the route the cashier at the diner had given her, taking the highway, following Burke Street, where they passed stately old homes with large oak-lined lawns. The diner had been a humble touch in what was a very nice town, with its wide sidewalks and shiny black lampposts; it was as well regarded as Newport, just a few miles up the coast.

Turning onto Northton, Mary looked at the house numbers, counting them down in her head until she came to 1264 Northton Avenue. It was a lovely old stone Tudor, sweeping and graceful, with neatly trimmed hedges and a long flat driveway. Mary pulled in, keeping the Blazer at the edge of the driveway but facing the house. The tiny panes of the windows shone and shimmered in the sun, and Mary could see an expansive patio at the side of the house. With its peaked roofline and rambling scale, it looked like a house from a fairy tale. It looked exactly as Mary had thought it would.

"What is this place?" asked Hannah.

"It's a house," replied Mary. "It's pretty, right?"

Hannah nodded. "Yeah," she said. "Really pretty. It looks like a castle."

Mary put the truck into reverse. "Maybe we'll live here someday, Bunny," she said, as she backed out of the driveway.

Mary followed her route in reverse as she drove, heading south on the highway until they were in a town that she hoped had a motel they could afford. Mary had been thrifty with their money, even making a little more of it with her fearlessness, her opportunism. They had slightly more than five thousand dollars left, enough to get an apartment and hold them over until they got settled. When she thought of the Dackards, which was not often, she felt no remorse for what she had done. It wasn't pleasant, but it was necessary. Sometimes Tim's face would come to her unbidden. She'd see the rash of pimples on his neck, his expression as he watched her brush against his father. But if she had a regret, it was in demanding only ten thousand dollars. In retrospect, she should have asked for more.

The girls found a motor lodge fifteen miles away from the house on Northton Avenue and the town where Mary planned to make a home. It was off of a traffic circle, and as Mary checked in, Hannah stood at the wide front windows watching the cars enter and exit. The office was in a brown A-frame structure, with a single-story row of guest rooms extending to either side.

"May I see some identification?" asked the man at the front desk. On the wall behind him, Mary saw a sign that read, in a looping hand-done script, YOU MUST BE TWENTY-ONE YEARS OR OLDER TO RENT A ROOM AT THE ARBOR MOTOR LODGE. In the types of places she and Hannah stayed, they rarely encountered age requirements.

"Actually," said Mary, adopting the earnest eyes of a fawn. "I just can't believe what a ninny I am sometimes." She was familiar enough with this type of man to know that the bumbling, softheaded young beauty routine was particularly effective. "My sister and I are driving up to Maine to visit our grandmother, and I left my driver's license at home. My mom is mailing it to her house." Then Mary bit her lip in a gesture both apologetic and hopeful. "But I won't have it until we get there."

The desk clerk looked from Mary to Hannah then back to Mary, both bothered and thrilled to be dispensing a scolding. "You really shouldn't be driving without your license," he said. "You should have turned back the minute you realized it was gone."

"I would have," said Mary. "But we were already five hours away."

"How old are you?"

"Twenty-two," said Mary, without pause.

He looked at Mary and she knew she had him. "I'm going to need payment in advance," he said, the slick strings of his hair sliding forward on his bald head as he bent down to pull a key from under the counter.

"That's no problem," said Mary. "Thank you so much."

"Uh-huh," he said.

MARY SLID THE BRASS KEY into the knob and opened the door to their room. Hannah walked in ahead of her, holding her backpack and the stuffed tiger Mary had won for her at a fair. The room was paneled in wood and had two twin beds covered with brown and blue plaid polyester bedspreads. White drapes were hung around the single window that looked out onto the parking lot, and the carpet was a dusty blue. On the chest of drawers sat a television with a sign written in that same loopy hand above that read, NO PORNOGRAPHY. But the room was clean and smelled like Pine-Sol, and it reminded Mary of the place that used to be home.

Whenever she was in a cheap motel room, Mary thought of the Water's Edge. Of sharing a room with Hannah. Of Diane being alive and Mrs. Pool living next door and of waking up at dawn and walking down to the beach, where the line of the horizon was infinity, where the world didn't have an end. "This place isn't so bad," she said, as she dropped her bag on the floor. Then she walked into the bathroom and flipped on the light, giving her surroundings the quick appraising glance of someone who had cleaned many rooms. "You wanna take a bath, Bunny?" she asked. Whenever the Chase girls rented a motel room, they took the opportunity to bathe. Mary turned on the water, and it rushed from the faucet with an aerated hiss, the sound of it hitting the tub making a comfortable clamor. Mary pulled off her tank top and unhooked her bra, letting it fall to her feet. She was undoing the button to her cutoffs as Hannah shuffled in.

"Are there bubbles?" asked Hannah.

Mary stepped out of her shorts, leaving them in a pile on the linoleum floor. She reached for the paltry selection of toiletries beside the sink and picked up a bottle of shampoo. "Yeah," she said, reading the label. "We can make bubbles."

Hannah lifted off her T-shirt, and Mary reached to help her get it over her head.

"Owww!" she said, as Mary pulled it off.

"Sorry, Bunny," said Mary. "It's those ears. You've got bunny ears."

Mary helped Hannah out of her shorts, which were at least a size too small. Then Mary slipped out of her underwear, which bagged and drooped after too much washing, too much wearing. Mary turned and looked at herself in the mirror. It hadn't been often during the last several weeks that she had occasion to stand in front of a mirror naked. She had grown thinner since Diane died, with her ribs visible through her skin. Her breasts were still full, and she brought her hand to one, feeling its weight. Her hip bones jutted out, and between them was a dark thatch of hair. Hannah was standing next to her, watching her sister look at herself.

"Why does yours have hair?" asked Hannah, who was naked as well, looking like a skinned rabbit — tiny and bare, her pale belly and chest a bathing suit in reverse.

Mary chuckled. "Yours will, too, someday."

"When?" asked Hannah.

"When you get a little older."

"How old?" asked Hannah.

Mary thought about Hannah's age, about when she herself first started puberty. "I guess in five or six more years," Mary said, stunned by the brevity of childhood.

"Good," said Hannah, as she squirmed her naked bottom onto the edge of the tub and dropped herself into the water. "I want a hairy one."

Mary gave herself one more glance, then picked up the shampoo bottle and stepped into the tub after Hannah. Ever since Hannah was a baby, she and Mary had taken baths together. Hannah used to sit up between Mary's legs, but she had gotten too big for that. Now they faced each other, Hannah at the faucet end and Mary leaning against the back of the tub. Mary dumped some of the shampoo into the water. "Stir it up, Bunny," she said. And Hannah began swishing her hand back and forth through the water until the bubbles rose and frothed.

Leaning over, Mary brought the water to her face with her hands, rubbing off the dirt, rubbing off the ten or so days it had been since she last had a bath. She tasted the salt of her skin in the water, felt her sweat-starched hairline.

After the girls were out, they put on the cleanest clothes they could find in their bags. Then Hannah lay on the bed watching cartoons, the water from her damp hair seeping into the white pillowcase. Mary pulled out the newspaper with the ads that she had circled and began making phone calls. *Hello, I'm interested in the apartment I saw listed in the* Observer. Sometimes they would ask where she was employed. One landlord asked her if she was married. Mary always had an answer. *I'm a student at the university. My fiancé is in the service.*

Finally, she put the phone down. "We've got some good places to look at tomorrow," she said, as she pulled her own damp hair into a ponytail. Then she slid in bed next to Hannah, and Hannah tossed her skinny legs over one of Mary's thighs.

Mary smoothed back her sister's hair, which was curling as it dried. "Do you want me to tell you a story?" asked Mary.

"Yeah," said Hannah, turning away from the TV.

Mary stood and pressed the button to turn it off, then got back into bed with Hannah, their cheeks resting on the same pillow as they faced each other. And Mary told Hannah a story about the princesses who boarded a white ship and set sail over a silver sparkling sea to the green isles. But when they had almost reached their destination, a great tentacle burst out of the water.

"At first, the princesses didn't know what it was. They heard only the rush of water. Then they saw it, rising up, its slick skin shining in the moonlight. But then it turned to the princesses, and it looked to them like a *thousand* eyes."

"Oh, my gosh," said Hannah, the covers drawn up to her chin, her words a gasp.

"And then as fast as the strike of a snake, it lunged for Princess Hannah," said Mary, her words building momentum. "But Princess Mary grabbed Hannah and pulled her out of the way, and the girls raced below deck, the tentacle following them. Princess Mary beat it back with her fists, and Princess Hannah used an old candlestick as they fought to get the hatch closed. And when at last they turned the lock, they fell to the ship's damp floor, their hearts pounding."

"Did it come back?" asked Hannah.

"I don't know," said Mary, as her eyebrows darted up. "We're going to have to find out." Then she kissed Hannah's forehead. "But it didn't come back that night."

The girls slept beside each other while the second bed lay empty. They were unaccustomed to space, unaccustomed to distance from each other's breath. Hannah fell asleep first, as usual. As Hannah lay with her jaw slack and her mouth open, Mary thought. She thought about a white boat on silver water and a night long ago. She thought about the stone house on Northton Avenue and its wide green lawn. She thought about the people who lived there and who they were. And she thought about how she would cross a vast sea to get inside.

THE WINDOWS OF THE DAY CARE that Hannah attended after school were obscured by snowflake chains and construction-paper Santas. But as Mary walked quickly up the concrete path in the cold early-evening dark, she could see her sister at a table drawing by herself as the single worker who was left busied herself with straightening and cleaning and preparing to close. It had been several months since the Chase girls had arrived in Northton, and they had settled into what many would call a life.

Mary paused outside the day care and watched her sister in the illuminated room, which was supposed to be bright and cheery but always struck Mary as the type of place that no one would be if they really had a choice, like a nursing home. Like an institution. Mary saw Hannah's gaze turn her way as if sensing her presence, so Mary waved, then took a few brisk steps before reaching the glass front door. She pushed it open, and with a screech of chair on tile, Hannah rushed to her, wrapping her arms around Mary's legs and pressing her face into her thighs. They stood there for a moment, their breath rising and falling in unison. "Hey, Bunny," Mary said, rubbing the back of Hannah's head. "How was school?"

Hannah leaned her head back and looked up at her sister, her expression full of mischief and news. "Guess who came to our class?"

"Who?"

"*Santa.*"

"*Santa?*" asked Mary. Hannah's teacher had sent a note home saying that the class would be receiving a special visitor the day before Christmas vacation; Mary had assumed that one of the parents had volunteered to dress up.

Hannah nodded. "Uh-huh," she said. "He came and we all got to tell him what we wanted for Christmas."

"What did you ask for?"

"A horse," she said. "But don't worry. Mrs. Murphy already told me that Santa doesn't bring horses." Hannah's voice was light and unperturbed, but Mary felt herself tense. Mary didn't like Mrs. Murphy. She didn't like her imperious air. She didn't like that she had called her in soon after Hannah had begun kindergarten to talk about what she referred to as "Hannah's lack of social skills."

"She hardly knows how to play with the other children," Mrs. Murphy had said, her shoulders back, her torso resting atop her round bottom. "And her lisp just makes matters worse."

Mary looked at her with cold steady eyes. She had known that Hannah was having trouble with some of the other little girls in the class. "Her *lisp?*" she said.

"Yes," said Mrs. Murphy. "She has a defect in the pronunciation of the *s* and *z*—"

"I know what a *lisp* is," interrupted Mary. Mrs. Murphy bristled, but Mary continued to stare, her black hair falling past her shoulders, her eyes flashing yellow.

After that meeting, while the Chase girls were taking their

evening bath, Mary leaned back against the tub in their apartment's tiny bathroom and tilted her head, watching her sister as she dunked an old Barbie under the water. Hannah looked up at Mary with her wide earnest eyes. "She's a really good swimmer," Hannah said.

"Bunny," Mary had said. "You're going to start getting some extra help at school. With saying certain sounds."

Hannah's face became still and suspicious. "What sounds?"

And so twice a week, instead of going to recess, Hannah was taken to the speech therapist's office where she practiced her sibilant s's. And though the instruction was helping, Mary hated Mrs. Murphy for hearing Hannah's lisp. For hearing it when she didn't.

Mary pulled Hannah's project from her cubby. "Don't listen to Mrs. Murphy," said Mary. "Santa may not be able to bring you a horse this year, but I bet you'll get one someday."

"Either a horse or a cat," said Hannah.

Mary smiled. "A horse or a cat," she repeated.

Mary gathered up the rest of Hannah's things and put them in her backpack. Then, resting her hand on Hannah's back, she guided her toward the door. Mary pushed it open and a burst of cold rushed in. Hannah paused and turned to look behind her. "Bye, Tammy!" she called to the woman, who was now zipping her coat.

The woman smiled and offered her own farewell. "Bye, Hannah!" Then she looked at Mary. Neither Hannah's teacher nor the women who cared for her after school knew quite what to make of Mary. "Merry Christmas," she said, with a polite nod.

Mary found a smile. "Merry Christmas."

Walking back down the concrete path to the parking lot, Mary took Hannah's hand. "Did you have fun at work today?" Hannah asked.

Mary chuckled. "Sure, Bunny," she said. "I had fun." Without a high school diploma, Mary's job prospects were limited, but she had been able to secure a position working at the front desk of a very nice hotel in town, the sort populated by wealthy older couples and soon-to-be-divorced businessmen. "Lots of people checked in. Everyone's visiting family for Christmas."

It would be the Chase girls' first holiday in their new apartment, which was on the bottom floor of an old white house that had been converted into a handful of small dwellings. It was on the outskirts of town on a street called Boosk Avenue, which was inhabited mostly by immigrants from Mexico. Mary soon found out that the residents of the town called the people who lived there Bookers, and she would occasionally hear the name shouted out of the window of a passing car at one of the dark-skinned men with grass-stained sneakers or their wives who worked as nannies. Mary looked at Hannah's too-small purple coat and wondered if she could have made more of their stay with the Dackards. If she could have been smarter.

At the hotel, Mary was able to make extra money the way she had become accustomed to making extra money. By being observant. By being fearless and fast, by relieving gentlemen of their wallets, by slipping into cars, hotel rooms, and homes to see what she could find. And so she and Hannah had gotten by, living frugally and nimbly, as they had during those months on the road. But what had seemed like a choice on the road now felt like a necessity. And throughout their first fall, Mary felt tense and caged by the confines of a place. She would often lie in bed at night with Hannah by her side and imagine waking her sister up and getting her in the car and driving until they no longer knew where they were or where they had come from. But she knew that Hannah needed a different sort of life. They weren't the same, the Chase girls. They shared Diane's blood, but there was more to their making. And on those nights when Mary felt like an animal gnawing at its tether, she would close her eyes and wait for the feeling to come, that feeling of falling. That feeling of no longer belonging to the earth. Only then could she sleep.

Putting the shifter into reverse, Mary backed the Blazer up, cutting the wheel sharply. "Hey, Bunny," she said, nodding toward the glove compartment. "Look in there. I got something for you."

Hannah pressed a button and the glove compartment fell open. With a gasp, she said, "Oh, my gosh." She reached in and pulled out a pair of furry white earmuffs, then brought them to her chest and stroked them as she looked at Mary. "They're so soft," she said, her voice high and light.

Mary shifted into drive, then straightened the wheel out, her smile full and pure. "Try them on," she urged. Hannah pulled them apart and placed them on her head, mussing her hair as she did so.

Mary chuckled. "You look so pretty, Bunny," she said, as Hannah pulled down her visor and tried to make out her reflection in the dim light.

As they came to a stop sign, Mary said, "What do you say we go for a little drive before going home?" Mary flipped on the turn signal and made a left out of the parking lot, away from their own home toward Northton Avenue.

The girls were both quiet as they drove, tired from their days and content to look at the lovely homes around them, with their garland-wrapped columns and shiny black doors. Then, without a word, Mary turned onto a side street and quickly looped around, putting the truck in park. They were only two blocks away from the stone house that they had driven by on their very first day in town.

Mary looked at Hannah. "I'm just going to check on something, Bunny." Then she pulled the handle of her door, pushed it open, and stepped out.

Walking around the front of the truck, Mary crouched next to the Blazer's rear right wheel, then twisted the gold cap on the tire's valve until it came off. Placing it between her teeth, she pulled a screwdriver from her pocket and stuck it into the open shaft, letting the air from the tire rush out. As she listened to the hiss of the release, she looked up to see Hannah staring out the window, the tip of her nose against the glass, fog from her breath forming a cloud beneath her nose.

"How're you doing, Bunny?" she asked.

"Good," answered Hannah.

"I'm almost done, okay?"

"Okay."

When the tire started to compress under the weight of the car, Mary put the screwdriver back into her pocket, took the cap from her mouth, and screwed it back into place. Then going around the front of the truck, she opened the driver's-side door and got back in.

"So you like your earmuffs?" she asked.

Hannah nodded, bringing her hands up to stroke them.

"Good," said Mary, remembering the little girl who had left them behind when her grandparents had brought her for tea at the hotel. They had come back looking for them, but by then, they were already tucked deep inside Mary's bag. *I'm so sorry; we haven't seen them,* she had said. *But if you'd like to leave your number, we can certainly call you if they turn up.*

Mary put her foot on the gas and the Blazer lurched forward, bucking unevenly due to the deflated tire.

"The truck feels weird," said Hannah.

"I know," said Mary, her gaze focused forward. "It's going to."

They drove a block in silence as Hannah's small brow tensed, feeling the bumps and jerks from the ride. When Mary came to a stop sign, she turned onto the wide and lovely Northton Avenue, and almost immediately, the stone house came into view, glowing and warm and looking like it had been waiting for them. Mary took her foot off of the gas and let the Blazer coast into the driveway, then she flipped on the truck's hazard lights and looked at the house. In the front window, she could see a tall tree strung with white lights and the movement of figures inside. Ahead of her in the driveway were cars that hadn't been there during her many previous drives past the house. And Mary felt her heart begin to thump wildly, as if operating independently from her mind, as if answering to a different master.

She opened her door and turned to Hannah. "We have a flat tire, Bunny," she said, then she extended her hand toward her sister, who took it. "Let's go and see if these people can help us." Hannah slid across the seat and hopped down on Mary's side, her skirt and coat catching as she lowered herself to the ground.

Mary looked down at Hannah, who was still wearing her earmuffs and purple coat, along with a black velour dress Mary had purchased at Goodwill and stockings that now had a hole in the knee. "You look cute," she said.

With Hannah's hand in Mary's, the Chase girls made their way up the long driveway to the house, which, they could see, bustled with the movement of family and visitors and holiday festivities. Mary saw Hannah look nervously ahead, apprehensive about entering a world that was not her own. The girls were noticed before they arrived when they stepped onto the stone path that led to the front door, tripping the motion detector and flooding themselves in light. In the wide front bay window, a group of blond women holding wineglasses paused their conversation and lifted their heads, trying to make out the figures walking up the path. Mary adopted an apologetic smile and waved. Mary and Hannah climbed the steps and pressed the button for the bell.

Inside, Mary heard, "Stefan, honey, can you get that?" through the conversation, through the glass clinks of laughter. And again her heart spasmed. If it had been a story Mary was telling, this would have been the culmination, the moment before all was set right again — the righteous recognized, the thrown secure, and prosperity befalling the kingdom.

Then the door glided open and he was there, framed in the warmth and the light of the place from where he had come.

Eleven

1982

I T HAD BEEN SEVERAL YEARS since they had seen each other. And then it was for only a night. But he knew her at once, his eyes widening as a smile burst on his face, memories of Mary playing in rapid succession in his mind. "Mary," he said.

Mary's brow wrinkled as she pretended to search for his name. "Stefan?" she asked tentatively.

His laugh was open and generous, a thunderclap of good fortune. "What are you doing here?"

Mary smiled crookedly, as if seeing him were still too much to trust or understand, then she gestured behind her. "Our car got a flat tire," she said. Then she laughed, her expression confused as she rested her hand on Hannah's back. "We just wanted to see if we could call a tow truck. What are *you* doing here?"

At that moment, one of the blond women Mary had seen through the window approached the door, her heels clicking on the shiny marble floor. "Stefan, honey," she said, as she rounded the corner. Her German accent still held a commoner's lilt. "Do these girls need help?"

Stefan's eyes didn't leave Mary. "They, ummm," he started. His skin was tan and his hair still sun bleached at the ends, as if he still existed in the summer of Mary's mind. Another solar flare of a smile. "They have a flat tire."

The woman, whom Mary already knew to be Martina Kelly, gave her son a look. *And why is that funny, Steffie?* Then she turned to Mary. "Well, come in, come in," she said, all grace and charity as she ushered the Chase girls inside. They stepped over the threshold, and Martina pushed the door shut behind them. "It's freezing out there," she said, crossing her arms and rubbing her hands over her thin silk blouse. "Stefan, honey, can you take a look at their car?"

"Oh, I don't want to trouble you," protested Mary, glancing briefly at Stefan. "If we could just use your phone."

Martina made a sound. *Tsk-tsk.* "Oh, no, no," she said, then she looked at Hannah and gave her a warm smile. "This little one looks cold."

Hannah, who resembled a Victorian street urchin with her tattered stockings, ill-fitting coat, and stolen earmuffs, turned to Mary for corroboration or direction.

Mary tilted her head, suggesting reluctant accord. "I think she is a bit chilly."

"Well," said Martina. "Let's get you something warm to drink while Stefan sees to your tire." She waved for the girls to join her, leading them past the expansive French doors, beyond which several of the other women sat craning their necks and offering their vanilla smiles.

Mary and Hannah followed Martina into the kitchen, with its hunter green walls and glimmering copper pots. "Let's see," she said, opening and closing cabinets, looking for something. When she found it, she emitted a pleased cluck. "Do you girls like hot chocolate?"

"Oh, I'm fine, thank you," assured Mary.

"What about your sister?" asked Martina.

Hannah looked from Mary to her hostess. "Yes, please," she said, her voice not more than a thimbleful.

"Good girl," said Martina, as she pulled a white packet from a box and marched over to the sink. She pulled a mug from a shelf and set it on the counter, then, giving the packet a brisk tear, dumped its contents inside. Positioning the mug under a small faucet, she pulled a lever, sending in a steaming rush of water. "Alright," she said, as the cup filled. "One hot chocolate coming right up." Pulling a spoon from the drawer, she stirred as she walked back over to Mary and Hannah.

"Careful, sweetie," said Martina, as she set the mug on the counter. "The water from there is very *hot*."

Mary gave Hannah a sidelong glance and an instructive nod.

"Thank you," said Hannah immediately, as she took her seat at the counter.

Martina turned to Mary, giving her a warm smile. "Now you, big sister," she said. "Would you like something else? A glass of wine?"

Mary's hand halted the offer with a polite wave. "Oh, no, thank you."

"No?" said Martina, the bottle already in her hand, gauging Mary's interest. Martina's words carried the easy warmth of drink. "Oh, well," she said, setting it back down. "I'm from Germany. We don't let anyone come to our house during the holidays without offering them wine."

Mary emitted a polite chuckle.

"Alright, well, why don't you girls stay here," she said, turning to leave the room. "We'll see what Stefan has to say about your car."

Mary watched her go, then took the seat next to Hannah. "Don't worry, Bunny," Mary whispered, seeing Hannah's nervous eyes. "Everything's okay." With her hand on Hannah's knee, she glanced around the room. Framed family photos were positioned on the walls and shelves—elegant professional shots of two handsome boys, of a beautiful mother and a dignified father.

"Stefan!" Mary heard Martina call from the front door. *"Was denken Sie?"*

After a few moments, the front door clicked shut and Stefan's voice echoed through the foyer, with its high ceilings and hard floor. *"Die Mädchen waren richtig. Es ist eine Reifenpanne,"* he said. *"Wir sollten den Abschleppdienst rufen."*

"Can't you change it for them?" asked Martina, switching to English.

"They don't have a spare."

"You were right, girls," said Martina, reentering the room with her handsome son trailing behind her. He found Mary immediately. And Mary let her eyes hang on to his for one long moment before looking back at his mother. His face was the sort that lent itself to stone—sculptural and timeless. "We need to get your car to a repair shop," Martina said. She then turned suddenly to Stefan. "Honey, are there going to be any open tonight?"

"Uhhhh . . . ," he said, running his hands through his hair and trying not to look at Mary. "Spillane's over on Cross should still be open."

"Really?" asked Martina. "Even during the holidays?"

Stefan gave his mother an amused smile. "Yeah, Mom," he said. "Even during the holidays."

She clucked her tongue and turned toward Mary. "He's teasing me. He thinks his mother is *clueless*," she said, trying on the word. Mary could see why she was so often described as charming. *Martina Kelly, the charming wife of businessman Patrick Kelly.* "Stefan," she said, her attention back to her son. "You will help the girls? I'm going to check on our guests."

And Martina was out of the room again, off to update the

other wives who would listen — rapt and concerned — to the happenings in the kitchen. *Poor little things.* It was easy to feel charitable toward Mary and Hannah. It was like taking in two little kittens.

As soon as his mother was gone, Stefan turned to Mary. And in the glorious serendipity of their chance meeting, he lifted her out of her stool. "What are you *doing* here?"

"Well, I don't know if you heard, but I have a flat tire," Mary teased, as he set her back down on her feet. She was at her most lovely in front of the boy who sailed his white boat into Sandy Bank.

"I mean in town?"

Mary let her hand rest on Hannah's head. "My sister and I live here now," she said, twisting a finger through one of Hannah's blond curls. "We moved here after our mom died."

Stefan's face fell. "I'm so sorry," he said.

Mary nodded, conjuring up emotion that wasn't entirely feigned. "Thank you," she said. "Hannah and I are doing alright, though."

Stefan turned to Hannah. "Hannah?" he asked, confirming her name. She looked at Stefan with her big eyes and messy blond hair. "It's nice to meet you," he said, extending his hand.

Hannah glanced at Mary, who nodded once, prompting her to take it. "It's nice to meet you, too." And as they looked at each other, Hannah and Stefan, Mary felt a burst of joy so intense that it caught at the back of her throat, slicked her eyes. She blinked it away and smiled.

"So . . . ," started Mary tentatively. "Is this where you live?" Mary knew the answer, of course.

"Yeah, well . . . no. I mean, I grew up here. It's my parents' place. I'm just home for the holidays."

Mary's eyes narrowed, as if looking into the distance of memory. "I wish I had known that you were from here," she said. Then she smiled at him, poking his foot with hers. "I might have looked you up." After all, it had been so long ago. And Stefan couldn't understand what he meant to her.

But he just smiled. "Well, it's good to see you," he said. The Kellys, after all, were a family to whom fate frequently delivered the fortuitous, the serendipitous.

At that moment, Mary heard a different voice from behind them. "Stefan?" She turned, and it was another generically pretty blond woman, this one younger. Her eyes skipped from Stefan to Mary, reading the space between them, all the things that hadn't been said.

"Oh," Stefan said, disoriented but pleasant, as if pulled from a lovely dream. "Hey, Beth." He straightened and swept his hand toward Mary. And she remembered how much she liked the confident ease of his voice. Of his gestures. "This is Mary."

Mary stood and extended her hand. "Mary Chase," she said. Beth looked at it for a moment before taking it. "Beth," she said, her lips in a polite curve. "It's nice to meet you."

"You two know each other?" asked Beth, a false lightness in her voice, a barely detectable helium high.

Stefan pointed as if gesturing down the coast. "We met a while ago. That summer I sailed down to Virgin Gorda. I spent a few days in Sandy Bank."

Beth's eyebrows lifted, but she kept her slim smile. Sandy Bank was a down-market little tourist trap, its heyday having passed in the 1920s. No one went there anymore but high school kids and blue-collar families with fat kids and Jersey accents. "Oh, how funny."

"And her car got a flat outside . . ." Stefan and Mary looked at each other, Stefan's smile more restrained in the presence of Beth. "So, we were just catching up."

The pleasantries finished, Beth turned to Stefan. "Your mom just wanted me to tell you that the Terrells are on their way." It was a subtle urge to move things along, get the girls on their way.

"Okay. Thanks."

Beth gave Mary a final smile. "Good luck with your car," she said. Then she looked at Hannah. "Merry Christmas, sweetie."

Stefan watched her go, then turned back to Mary, sobered but reluctantly so, brought back to the duties and obligations of the evening and his family.

Mary smiled, her eyes kind. "We should probably call that tow truck now," she said.

"Right," he said, remembering why the lovely Mary from Sandy Bank was sitting in his kitchen. He pulled out the yellow pages and flipped quickly through them, then he picked up the phone and dialed, leaning against the wall behind him, crossing an arm across his broad chest when a voice came from the other end.

As he gave the information and instructions, Mary turned to Hannah. "How's that hot cocoa?"

"It's really good," whispered Hannah. She seemed to weigh the benefits of speaking again before adding, "I like the marshmallows."

Mary whispered to Hannah while Stefan was on the phone, talking to her about their plans for the holidays, making everything seem wonderful, magical. *Tomorrow morning, you and I are going to make cookies. I got sprinkles and icing, and you can decorate them however you want.*

When Stefan hung up, he looked at the girls. "They're going to be here in half an hour," he said.

From the doorway came Martina's voice. "Everything is taken care of, Stefan?" she asked, as she leaned into the kitchen.

"Yup," he said. "It's going to be about thirty minutes."

Martina's eyes flitted cautiously to Mary, to whom she offered a less effortless smile. "Beth says that you know each other?" Charity was Martina's stock in trade, but a personal connection had not been bargained for, especially not with a girl from Sandy Bank.

Stefan smiled. "Yeah, Mary and I are old friends."

"Well, why did you not tell me?" she said, a mock scolding for a son she clearly adored. Martina looked at Mary and Hannah. "You girls must come join us, then," she said. "While you wait for the tow truck."

In the living room, Mary and Hannah took their seats on tufted chintz chairs as Martina Kelly's friends welcomed them, their manicured hands wrapped around wine stems, their berry-colored lips curled into welcoming smiles as they asked their questions. *A flat tire, is it? And you know Stefan? And where did you say you were from?*

Mary gave the room a lovely smile before speaking, mournful but brave. "We moved here only recently from New Jersey. After our mother died."

The women offered a collective gasp, their hands covering their hearts. "So it's just the two of you?" asked Martina, so willing to be won.

Mary nodded.

Another woman, who was seated next to Beth, leaned in. From the similarities in countenance and appearance, Mary took her to be Beth's mother. "And where is your father, dear?" she asked, her chin lifted, her words as elongated as a snake's tongue.

Mary's eyes snapped to hers. "London," she answered, without pause, the challenge not entirely wrung from her face. "But we don't see him. His wife prefers her space." If she noticed Hannah's confused expression, she didn't acknowledge it.

Some of the women exchanged glances, intrigued by the turn the conversation was taking and relishing reports of the selfish whims of later wives. Beth took a sip of her wine, her foot slipping out of the back of her heel. And Mary decided that Beth was the perfect name for her, with her slightly upturned nose, ambivalent eyes, and hair like spun white gold. She could be a Blair or a Blake. But Beth was perfect.

"Well," said Martina, clapping her hands, ready to right the conversation and steer it toward topics more jovial. "You girls must attend the Christmas concert at the Streinbach." The Streinbach was the very well-regarded performing arts center in town. "They do all the old carols."

Stefan, who had been leaning against the door frame into the foyer, looked at the ice in his tumbler and gave it a gentle twirl. "The arena also has ice skating on Christmas Eve," he said. "We used to go every year."

"We have to go to Willow's while we're home, Stef," said Beth, leaning back in her seat and speaking only to him though he stood across the room. "They do that *amazing* torrone this time of year."

"See this?" joked Martina, looking at Beth's mother. "We have to drag these two back from Boston for the holidays even though they are filled with nostalgia for their home!" As her wine deepened in effect, Martina's English became less natural.

After the room shared in a requisite charmed smile, Beth's mother turned back to Mary, the arm holding her glass of wine resting on her knee. "So what brought you to Northton in *particular?*" she asked, wanting to know more about the beautiful girl who seemed so acquainted with Stefan. "Do you have friends here?"

"Well, not exactly," said Mary, giving a self-conscious downward smile. "But my father used to live here."

From the doorway, Stefan looked up.

"Your father?" asked Martina.

Mary nodded. "Yes," she said. "He grew up here."

"What's his name?" asked one of the generic blonds, her lips slick and eager.

It was impulse that throbbed through Mary then, a reflexive response to a challenge. "Robert Mondasian." She said it without knowing she would. She said it without thought of consequence.

No one emitted a sound, but the shock pulsed through the room. Robert Mondasian was Northton's demon son. Revered and reviled and known for being charming and abusive and brilliant and narcissistic. He moved to Europe when he was kicked out of his elite boarding school and found his way into the gossip sheets for indiscreet dalliances with lesser royalty. A known womanizer, he used his first wife's family money to begin purchasing interesting art and was soon reputed to have one of the keenest eyes in the world for emerging talent. The town of Northton was fascinated with him, and the local paper often reported on his doings, though his parents were now dead and he had never returned. Mary had first encountered his name in a magazine of her mother's. She had read the article over and over, fascinated by him. And when she found out that he and Stefan were from the same town, well, to a girl like Mary, so prone to the quixotic, the grandiose, it all felt somehow preordained.

Finally, it was Beth's mother who spoke. "I didn't know Robert had any children," she said.

"He and my mother weren't married," replied Mary.

"Well" was all Martina could manage. She looked at Mary, whose almost unsettling beauty did have something of Robert Mondasian to it. "Your father is certainly an icon in the art world," she said, recovering. "He has a terrific collection."

For the remaining time that Mary and Hannah sat in the Kellys' living room waiting for the tow truck, the women treated Mary with reverence and caution. It was as if they had discovered the kitten that they had been batting about was actually a tiger cub. Stefan looked on, silent and curious. *Robert Mondasian's bastard daughter.*

When the conical lights of the tow truck finally shot through the night outside, all the women stood, like hens at the coop door, extending their hands and wishing Mary and Hannah a Merry Christmas. Stefan walked the girls outside and down the driveway to where the driver was inspecting their Blazer, assessing how best to get it up onto his truck. His hands were sunk into his pockets, his breath was white and vanishing. He and Stefan exchanged a few words, and then tow cables were attached to the Blazer. There was the mechanical noise of gears grinding and moving as the Blazer was slowly hoisted up onto the flatbed.

Mary and Stefan stood facing each other in the streetlight-lit darkness. "So, it was really nice to see you," said Mary.

"How are you going to get home?"

"We can ride in the truck and then walk from there," said Mary, tilting her head toward the cab of the tow truck. Boosk Avenue was only a couple of blocks away from Spillane's.

Stefan smiled at Mary. It was a warm thing, his smile. It was a nearby star. "I'll drive you," he said, his words near and quiet. "I'll take you past the ice-skating arena. Show you where it is."

Mary bit at her smile. "Okay," she said, then she rested her hand on Hannah's back. "What do ya say, Bunny?" she asked.

"Bunny?" asked Stefan, questioning Hannah's unusual nickname.

Mary's face was soft when she spoke. "That's what I call her," she said. She and Stefan looked at each other, their breath finding pace. "Ever since she was a baby."

As he drove the girls back to Boosk Avenue, Stefan offered commentary on the town, pointing out the best place for omelets and the hill where you could sit on the Fourth of July and watch fireworks burst in the sky, their booms following moments later. "My dad used to take us here," he said. "Right after dinner so that we could get a good spot."

"Was your dad at your house tonight?" asked Mary.

"No," said Stefan. "He's away for work." Through the

windshield, he glanced up into the sky, as if his father were hovering around them somehow. "He and my brother Teddy are actually flying home from Tokyo right now." Mary knew that the elder Kelly brother had gone to work for their father while Stefan, apparently, had resisted that path. "They've been over there for a month."

When the trio pulled up to the apartment on Boosk Avenue, Stefan took in the peeling structure. There were a half-dozen beat-up old cars in the gravel parking lot, and some of the tenants had wrapped Christmas tree lights around the insides of their windows. It was a dismal-looking place, especially for someone unaccustomed to dismal-looking places.

"It was really good to see you, Stefan," said Mary, skilled at letting her stare linger.

"Yeah," he said. "You, too."

Mary reached for her door handle and gave it a pull. "Come on, Bunny," she said to Hannah, who was watching quietly from the back.

"Here," said Stefan, joining the girls in opening his door. "I'll walk you in."

The girls got out, and Stefan crossed around the front of the car to join them. When they reached the stoop, Stefan glanced back at Hannah, who had been trailing just behind. "So you're going to be okay?" he asked. "You can get to Spillane's in the morning?"

"It's just a few blocks. Hannah and I can walk over there."

Stefan nodded, then glanced at the dented mailbox unit.

"Thanks for everything tonight, Stefan," said Mary, as she slipped the key into the front door and pushed it open with her hip. She ushered Hannah in ahead of her, flipping on the kitchen light, then turned back to Stefan. "It was good to see you again."

Stefan nodded. "Yeah, you, too," he said. And suddenly he

looked to Mary like a man who was about to let it all crash against the rocks for her.

"Good night," she said, moving to step inside the berth of the door and push it shut. But Stefan rested his hand against its glass, stopping it.

"Hey," he said suddenly. "What are you doing tomorrow?"

Twelve

1982

S TEFAN CAME IN THE EVENING. He wore a camel-colored coat and smiled under the porch light. Mary opened the door, feeling the cold rush past her, breaking the apartment's stale, warm seal. It had snowed that morning, and the brittle blades of grass stayed powdered with snow as crystalline ice floated lazily through the dark.

Stefan held her gaze before speaking. "Fancy meeting you here," he said.

Mary smiled, her lips apple red, her black hair spilling over her white sweater.

Then Stefan leaned past her to get a glimpse of Hannah, who was standing behind Mary's hip. "I'm told there are a couple of ladies here who've never had the pleasure of dining at Willy's." Willy's was a Northton institution, a family restaurant that Stefan had suggested, intuiting perhaps that babysitters weren't in Mary's budget or her plan.

She nudged Hannah up in front of her. "What do you think?" she said, looking down at the top of her sister's head. "You ready, Bunny?"

Hannah was wearing a red-velvet dress that Diane had

bought on clearance years ago knowing she'd grow into it. She looked up at her sister, then at Stefan, and nodded — her eyes wide, her lips tight.

"Alright," said Stefan, with a smile. "Let's go."

As they made their way down the concrete path windswept with snow, Stefan asked Hannah questions about Northton Elementary, where he had also gone to school.

"So you're in kindergarten?" he asked, reaching to open the rear door to his car.

Hannah nodded as she slid in, nestling her hands beneath her bottom. "I have Mrs. Murphy," she said.

Stefan groaned in sympathy. "Oh, man," he said. "The *Murph*. She's still around? Stealing joy from the hearts of children?"

And Mary watched Hannah's face brighten as she looked at Mary, pleased that they now had a comrade in their dislike of the teacher.

He slid into the driver's seat. "The Murph's a legend," said Stefan, buckling his seat belt and throwing his car into reverse, looking over his shoulder as he negotiated his way out of the spot. "I think she must be a hundred and sixty-three at this point."

Winding from Boosk Avenue to Northton's elegant downtown, they pulled up to an old yellow colonial, illuminated and bright. Outside was a green and gold carved sign. WILLY'S TAVERN. FINE FOOD AND SPIRITS. PRIME RIB. LOBSTER. CHOPS.

Stefan threw the car into park, looked at the sign, and smiled, his brow creased, realizing that he may have oversold the experience of Willy's. "It's kind of old-school. But it's been around forever. And I grew up sawing through their prime rib every Sunday."

Inside, Willy's was dimly lit with floral wallpaper interrupting the dark-stained wood trim. It had the bustle and din of a well-attended pub, and everything seemed coated in a thick varnish of time and spilled drinks. Men sat at the bar in starched shirts, sleeves rolled up to their elbows, sipping from napkin-wrapped rocks glasses under Tiffany-style lights. There was a wonderful shabbiness to the place, a grand old rot that Mary had come to identify with the truly rich. The gentleman at the maître d' stand had a generous belly that stretched the confines of his blue-and-white-striped button-down shirt. He looked up from his seating chart and brightened as he saw Stefan.

"Master Kelly!" he said, fiddling with his cuff links.

They clapped each other on the shoulders, and pleasantries were exchanged. Stefan was urged to say hello to his parents. The maître d' was assured Stefan would.

When they took their seats at their table, leather-bound menus in hand, Stefan turned to Hannah. "Do you like Shirley Temples?" he asked.

Hannah looked at Mary, who said, "I'm not sure you've had one of those, Bunny."

"We'll get you one," he said to Hannah, with a wink meant only for her. "My brother and I used to get them here all the time." And Mary noticed the way his voice became quieter, if only by a shade.

The waitress came and went and brought a delighted Hannah her Shirley Temple, followed by a beer for Stefan, a club soda for Mary. And as Stefan took a sip, he looked at Mary. The restaurant hummed around them; waitresses in black aprons balanced food-laden trays as they wound through the tables. "So," he said, as if that single word summed up the beauty and improbability and wonder of sitting there with her.

"So," replied Mary.

And Stefan smiled, his eyes focused only on her.

"So you're living in Boston?" Mary asked.

"Yeah," he said. "I'm in law school."

"And Beth," Mary asked, as if she weren't quite sure she recalled the girl's name. "She's there, too?"

Stefan nodded. "She lives in Beacon Hill," he said. "I'm in Cambridge." It was an elegant way to let Mary know that whatever he and Beth were, they weren't living together. "But what about you?" he asked, forearms on the table, leaning closer to her. "What have you been up to these last"—he shook his head—"*six* years?"

"Going to school, working at the motel." Mary's eyes drifted to her sister, who was coloring on a photocopied children's menu. "Helping my mom with Hannah."

"I'm so sorry to hear about what happened." His voice was low and intimate. "Was it . . . sudden?"

Mary let her eyes move to her drink. "It was a car accident."

"And are you guys entirely on your own now?" he asked, making a subtle reference to her father.

Mary picked up her soda. "So it would seem."

"Do you still have the motel?"

Mary shook her head. "We're doing alright, though," she said, looking at Hannah. "It's actually easier to *not* have it."

"I'm glad you're here," said Stefan. "In Northton, I mean. Besides the Murph, the schools are good. Or so I'm told." He chuckled, leaning back in his chair, his arm slung across his chest, his hand nestled in the crook beneath his arm. "Everyone here is so fixated on that kind of thing."

Their entrees came, and as they ate, they talked about law school and Mary's job, always circling the topic of their meeting, always lowering their voices when it came near. Their chairs moved closer and closer to each other's around the circular table until they were beside each other, looking out at Hannah.

"Did you ever make it down to the islands?" asked Mary,

her head drifting to one side as she leaned into her chair. Stefan's presence relaxed her, warmed her to her bones.

"I did," said Stefan. "Had to sail through a nasty storm, but I made it."

Mary smiled, rested her cheek on her hand. "I knew you would."

"I was a mate on a racing boat that summer. Sailed in the RORC for this insane Frenchman. It was a great experience, but I got a late start coming home." Stefan pushed his empty beer glass forward, then looked at Mary. "I'm happy to be seeing you again."

And Mary shifted in her seat, letting her knees drift to the side, resting lightly on Stefan's thigh.

Dessert was ordered and the bill was paid, Mary offering to split it while Stefan chivalrously ignored her and Hannah sunk her spoon into an ice cream sundae. "Forget it, Mary," he said. "This is my treat." And they got back into the car, Hannah yawning in the backseat.

"You tired, Bunny?" Mary asked, turning to look at her.

Hannah nodded.

"We'll get you home," Stefan said.

Jazz played softly over the radio as they drove, Mary sinking into the leather passenger seat. It was so unusual to not be the one driving. And she let herself watch as the town rolled past. She watched the big front windows filled with evergreens strung in white lights; she watched the garland-wrapped streetlights, the stately old homes. They passed by her like memories, like flashes of present moving to past. "It's beautiful here," she said. And Mary felt that if she was capable of truly making any place her home it would be Northton.

Hannah was asleep in the back by the time they returned to Boosk Avenue, her head flopping awkwardly to one side, her skirt up above her white-stockinged knees.

Mary opened the rear door and unfastened Hannah's seat belt, then bent down to scoop her up. "You sure you got her?" Stefan asked, as Mary gingerly coaxed her arms under Hannah's body.

"I got her," replied Mary, as her sister's weight shifted and fell against her chest.

"Do you have the keys?" Stefan asked. "I'll get the door."

"They're in my pocket." Mary smiled and tilted her head down to her coat. "If you can get them."

And Stefan reached inside, the warmth of his hand filling the thin lining of Diane's old tweed, the intimacy of the touch a palpable thing. "Got 'em," Stefan said, his voice quiet.

He walked with her, bursting ahead to prop open the door as Mary made her way up the path with Hannah, a concerned expression on his face. The walkway was slippery. And Mary's steps were tentative as she moved with her sister in her arms, her breath clouding then vanishing in front of her face.

Mary stepped in ahead of Stefan and brought Hannah to their small bedroom. "I'm just going to set her down," she called behind her.

In their room, the nightlight was on, casting stars about the room. She placed Hannah in bed, took off her shoes and stockings, then pulled up the covers.

"Night, Bunny," Mary whispered, her hand skimming her sister's forehead.

She walked back through the apartment, knowing Stefan would be there, knowing he would wait. And when she rounded the corner to the tiny kitchen, she saw him leaning against the wall, his arms crossed over his chest. The lights were off, and the only illumination came from the streetlamps outside, the blinds on the windows casting a ladderlike shadow on the wall.

When he saw her, he walked across the room without a word

and stopped in front of her. They stood there for a moment facing each other, the space between their bodies creating something that had its own physical presence, its own charge.

He brushed the hair off of one of her shoulders, exposing the moon-white curve of her neck, and took a breath, admiring this one small part of the creature that was Mary. Moving his hand to her lower back, he pulled her toward him. And still they stared at each other. Then his head inclined and his lips moved against hers and Mary closed her eyes, feeling Stefan open her mouth with his own. She loved him already, of course. She had loved him since the night she had lain down under a swath of stars, feeling his weight on top of her and the sand below. She'd loved him since he pushed inside of her and crimson ran out, as if he'd pierced her heart.

Thirteen
1976

MARY WALKED QUICKLY, HUGGING THE ROAD but keeping to the sand, which shifted under her steps. A car whizzed by and she tucked her chin, the wind whipping a strand of hair across her face as it burst out of the darkness. She was out of range of headlights, but everyone in town knew her. If they saw her out alone, they'd call Diane.

The dunes were to her right, and beyond them, the ocean churned and crashed, barely distinguishable from the black sky. She always loved the beach at night. When it was empty and ungoverned and wild.

He told her that he'd meet her at the Perkins Break near the lifeguard chair. He had some beer. They could drink it. The older kids in town always drank on the beach, sitting in quiet circles and passing joints, Budweiser cans between their crossed legs. The first time Mary joined them, the police came with spotlights that sent the group scattering, tripping and stumbling with pounding hearts as adrenaline surged into their fingers and toes. Only Mary stayed still. She simply leaned back with her hands planted into the sand and stared into the bright light. After that, Mary's presence, which seemed to inspire fear or deference or both, was never questioned.

She had met the boy that day. He had come to the Water's Edge to use the pay phone. Mary had been sitting at the front desk reading *Carrie*. She didn't look up as the bell on the door chimed.

He waited for a moment, with a dollar bill in his hand, to get her attention. Then he playfully cleared his throat. "Excuse me," he said. "Can you change this?"

Mary took a slow breath, then looked up, revealing nothing of what she felt the moment she saw his face. Like a chemical reaction, her attraction was instant and unadulterated. He had a regal look to him despite his wild sun-bleached hair. And in his eyes there was a pulsing life that Mary had come to identify with intelligence. Whether it was a girl's fancy or some deeper intimation of things to come, she saw lives unfold before her. And so it was that her young, ferocious, and flawed heart began to splay itself open.

She dog-eared her book, set it on the desk, then licked the tip of her finger and took the bill from him. "What do you need?" she asked.

"Dimes," he answered, the single word already sounding flirtatious. "For the phone."

Mary turned the key that sat sunk into the wooden desk drawer where they kept the on-hand cash at the Water's Edge and pulled it open. She counted out ten dimes, then dropped them smoothly into Stefan's hand.

Stefan paused, looking for a reason to linger in front of the beautiful girl at the front desk. "Hey, how much are rooms here?"

Mary cocked her head. "Well, they're actually extraordinarily expensive. This is one of Sandy Bank's finest motels."

Stefan dropped his chin and laughed, then extended his

palm full of dimes, his expression roguish and playful. "Will this do it?"

Mary smiled, unleashing her full capacity for charm. "That's plenty," she said.

Stefan never did make his phone call. He and Mary talked, his elbows resting on the ledge in front of the desk, she leaning back in her chair. She soon learned that he was sailing alone down the coast to the Caribbean and back, that he was taking the fall semester off from college to do it. He would be working on a racing boat this summer.

"How old are you?" she asked.

"Nineteen," he answered. In his eyes was a playful challenge. "How old are you?"

She hesitated for only a moment. "Seventeen," she replied.

Stefan smiled. "When do you get off of work?"

A single shoulder lifted in a shrug. "I can leave right now," she said.

With her dog-eared copy of *Carrie* in her purse, Mary locked the door to the Water's Edge front office and followed Stefan to his boat. It was May, the true start of the tourist season still a few weeks away, and so the marina was comfortably quiet, the weathered gray boards of the dock groaning beneath their feet.

"Here she is," said Stefan, as they approached a trim, elegant boat, its white mast extending into the bright blue sky. On the transom, in stately gold letters, was written LÄUFER, NORTHTON, RHODE ISLAND.

Mary stopped. "What's *Läufer?*" she asked.

Stefan stopped and brought his hand to the back of his neck, rubbing the salt-soaked tanned skin. "My mom's German," he said. "*Läufer* means *runner*. But she always liked that it sounds like *loafer* in English." He smiled, grabbed the boat's silver railing, and ably pulled himself aboard, then reached back for

Mary. "She says that describes me perfectly." Mary took his hand and he pulled her up, resting his hand on her hip as she stepped down. "American and German. A loafer and a runner."

They stayed on the boat all afternoon, lying on the bow under the late-spring sun. Mary pulled up her T-shirt so that the rays could warm her belly, and she noticed the way Stefan's eyes found it, that soft expanse of skin. Mary was used to men wanting her. But the boys she had let touch her had spasmed with pleasure, wasting themselves and collapsing on top of her with damp breath and quivering bodies before much of anything happened. They'd cup their now-limp penises and whimper their apologies until she pushed them off of her, feeling as though whatever it was that she possessed had the power to decimate, to deny her pleasure and give others more than they could endure.

So when Stefan's hand slid over to her stomach, when his fingers slipped just under the waistband of her jean shorts as he told her about his route down the coast, when he didn't convulse and then spend himself from simply touching her skin, Mary wanted him all the more wholly.

"When did you start sailing?" Mary asked, letting her head roll toward his as they lay side by side.

His position mimicked hers. "I was a kid," he said. "I used to go out with my dad. Then I started to take his boat out without his permission." He smiled. "Used to piss him off."

And as they spoke, Mary noticed that his mother's classifying him as a loafer seemed flawed, as Stefan had very little about him that seemed complacent. "I want to sail around the world someday," he said. "Follow the trade winds. Go across the Atlantic." His finger traced through the air, as if he were following a map. "Then through the Mediterranean and down the Red Sea. Then across the Indian . . ." His voice trailed off and he looked at Mary, lifting his head to rest his free hand under it, and he gave the waist of Mary's shorts a light tug. "You can harness the currents. Go fast." He squinted at her. "You never really have to stop moving when you're in the ocean."

And never before had anyone spoken such perfect words to Mary Chase.

For the rest of the afternoon, Mary and Stefan batted about their desire, finding ways to touch each other under the scrutiny of daylight. Mary would press the side of her hip against his as she spoke; Stefan's fingertips would brush over her breast as he pointed toward this or that, their youth allowing them the honesty of their desire.

Finally, as the sun began to sink, Stefan rolled back onto his side, and with a depth to his voice that masked nothing of his intention, he asked, "Can I see you later?"

Mary nodded.

When Mary returned to the Water's Edge, Diane was in the office. "Where the *hell* have you been?" she asked, slamming down the brown phone receiver as Mary pushed open the door. "You were supposed to be at the front desk!"

"There's only like six people even staying here right now," Mary retorted, with an unperturbed shrug.

"That is entirely beside the point!" said Diane. "You were supposed to be working the desk. You cannot go gallivanting off anytime you please!"

Mary met her mother's eyes and saw that there was more there than anger. "Where were you anyway?" asked Diane, worry lining her words.

"I was at Lisa's house," she said. "She needed help with her math."

Diane held Mary's eyes for a moment, then, as if a string had been cut, her shoulders slumped forward and her head hung down. "Mr. Pool said he saw you walking home from the marina," she said.

"I stopped there on my way home from Lisa's," said Mary. "To see if any of the summer people had come yet."

Diane and Mary would sometimes hand out coupons for the Water's Edge to the summer people. *Tell your friends!* Diane would say.

Diane shook her head. "Just stop, Mary." Without looking up, Diane went on. "I can't take it anymore. I punish you. I yell at you. Nothing works. You disregard everything I say. Why don't you tell me what it is you're trying to prove running wild the way you do and we can be done with it?"

And if it were only that simple, Mary certainly would have.

Mary was grounded, told that she couldn't go out for three weeks. "You know I'm supposed to go out with Barry tonight," Diane said. "How am I supposed to do that, Mare?" she asked. Barry was one of the few men Diane had dated since having Mary. "How am I supposed to sit there and smile when the whole time I'm wondering what the hell my daughter is doing?"

Mary looked at her mother blankly. "Why don't you call Mrs. Pool?"

Diane shook her head with disappointment, but that's exactly what she did. She called Mrs. Pool and told her that she had a date with Barry. She glanced at Mary and lowered her voice before continuing. "And I just don't feel comfortable, Alice, leaving Mary here alone."

It was only after Mary's grandfather had died that Diane started looking for a husband. Someone to take care of her, to share the responsibility of Mary and the Water's Edge. Barry was divorced but childless, and he owned a carpet-installation service out of Shore Haven. And that night, Diane put on her stiff maroon polyester shirtdress, and she walked out to the office, where Mary and Mrs. Pool were sitting on the itchy brown couch. Diane fidgeted, her expression showing just how nervous she was, just how eager for their praise. Mrs. Pool, who indulged everyone, but especially Diane and Mary, let her hands come together with a gentle clapping. "You look gorgeous, Diane."

"Yeah, Mom," said Mary, who, at the sight of her mother's too-heavy blush, at the smell of her too-heavy perfume, felt a stab of something she didn't quite recognize. Something that pained her. "You look really pretty."

And that night, after Barry came to the door and escorted Diane to the car, Mary scooted up to the television set and, with her finger on the channel selector, said to Mrs. Pool, "What do you want to watch?"

Mrs. Pool smiled, the skin beneath her chin soft. "Whatever you want, dear."

Within the hour, Mrs. Pool had fallen asleep, her head resting on the back of the couch, her mouth open while her hands remained folded in her lap. Mary tiptoed out of the office and back to her room. She ran a brush through her long hair, changed into new white cotton underwear, and slipped out the door to meet Stefan.

He was standing right where he said he'd be, under the lifeguard chair, the waves battering down on the sand, then retreating quickly. "I didn't think you were coming," he said.

"Were you about to leave?"

"No."

Without another word, Stefan pulled her into him, setting the pace of their kiss, the pulse of it. "Do you want to go to the boat?" he asked, the question whispered into her mouth.

His fingers moved up her back, under her shirt. Behind her, the wind moved through the dune grass. In front of her was her ocean scattering the moon. "No," she said, wanting to feel the yielding sand beneath her, wanting to hear the steady drum of the surf. "Let's stay here."

They lay down where they were, moving as if toward the inevitable. Unlike the boys who had tried to be with Mary, Stefan was slow. Kneeling in front of her, he pulled off her shorts, then his own.

He laid her down, then rested his elbows on either side of her. They were eye to eye when he pressed himself in. And Mary gasped in pain, her body offering resistance, then release.

When it was done, he took her place in the sand and pulled her on top of him and ran his fingertips up and down her skin, his back in the sand, her hair riddled with it.

"You didn't tell me," he said.

She lifted her cheek from his chest and looked at him. "Would it have mattered?" she asked, her curiosity genuine and unmasked.

Stefan pulled her head back toward his chest, as if he didn't want her to see the answer on his face.

They lay there like that until Mary's eyes started to slip shut, until the blood on her inner thighs was dry, was dust. They lay there like that until Mary said, "I should get back." Then Stefan laid her on her back once again and slipped her shorts back onto her body, buttoning them gently, before his thumbs ran over her hip bones, before he helped her to her feet.

"I have to leave for Bermuda tomorrow," he whispered, holding her hand as they approached the Water's Edge. "I have to get supplies there. But I'll come back." He brought his other hand over to surround hers.

They took a few more steps, their movement synched. "When?" she asked.

"October," he said. "On my way home."

She turned to face him.

"Do you promise?" she asked.

Stefan nodded. "I do."

And then, from inside the Water's Edge, a light came on. Stefan dropped to his knee and kissed Mary's hand before disappearing into the night with his promise of a return. Mary heard only the rustle of grass on the dunes until, from behind her, she heard her mother's voice. *"Mary Catherine Chase!"* Mary turned to see Diane standing at the threshold, her face tear streaked, Barry's hand on her shoulder. "What the hell are you *doing* out here?" And Mary saw Diane search the night, sensing but not seeing another presence.

Mary looked at her mother. "I just went for a walk." She then looked at Barry, offering a polite smile. "Hi, Barry."

Mary would go back to her room that night, take off her clothes, and look at her body in the bathroom mirror while the bathwater ran. She'd soak in the hot water, then slip between her sheets, naked and damp and yearning for sleep. Her dreams would come quickly that night, bounding into her mind agile and swift. In them, she became a creature, black and muscled and darting between trees. She came to a calm pool and saw the reflection of her yellow eyes. She woke with a gasp, hearing her heartbeat in her ears as if it were a roar. Then she walked over to the window and stared into the parking lot. In the dawn light, she saw Barry's car, as still and silent as it had been when she had tiptoed past it, her hand in Stefan's, only the night before.

Fourteen

1983

MARY WAITED AT THE DOOR to the apartment on Boosk Avenue, watching for Stefan. He was coming down from Boston, as he did most weekends. She'd gotten off of work at the hotel, put Hannah to bed. And now there was only waiting.

She felt herself lift when she saw his car, felt her body rise as if floating. She stood on her tiptoes but was otherwise still as she watched him get out of the car and pull his bag from the trunk, as she watched him walk quickly to her door, a smile crystallizing on his face as soon as he saw her. She opened the door and he stepped inside, dropping his bag on the kitchen floor and pulling her into him. It was full of his schoolbooks, the bag. And under the yellow fluorescent light, his unshaven cheek catching on her hair, his hand firm on her back, he held her, as if she were something vital and life-giving. As if she were air.

She stood there facing him, letting him run his hands over and over her body, her eyes closed, her hands gripping the counter. She had changed much in the years since they were first together. She was younger than he knew then and was so still. But she had come into herself.

He and Mary had sex on the living-room floor while Hannah slept in the bedroom. Then they lay together, their limbs intertwined on the worn brown carpet, listening to the clatter of pots and pans and the lilting conversation that carried through the thin walls from the apartment next door. When Stefan was around, the apartment felt like a charming pied-à-terre rather than a shitty one-bedroom that smelled constantly of cigarette smoke and mold.

"Can I ask you something?" Mary said, her face against his chest.

"Hmmm?" said Stefan. As his fingertips circled Mary's shoulder, she could have asked him anything.

"Did you come back? To Sandy Bank? When we first met?"

Stefan drew in a long unhurried breath and pulled her closer. "I did," he said sleepily. "You weren't there. There was a sign on the motel saying, CLOSED FOR THE SEASON."

And Mary knew that everything she had done to bring them back together had been worth it.

Mary soon became not only a fixture in Stefan's life but also in the Kellys', Martina embracing nearly anything adored by her son. Beth had been disposed of quickly without discussion. Only once, when Martina had thought Mary was out of earshot, did Mary hear Martina say, "Steffie, you should really call to check in on Beth. You two have known each other since you were little. There's no reason that you can't still be friendly." It seemed that whatever fledgling romance there had been in Beth and Stefan's relationship had been extinguished the moment Mary arrived.

But despite her concern for Beth, Mary knew that Martina loved that Stefan had taken up with her — the lovely girl with the interesting past. And sometimes Martina would ask about the man Mary said was her father.

"Do you think your father will come for a visit?" Martina asked one day, as she and Mary stood at the sink cleaning up after brunch. She was running a plate under the water streaming from the faucet.

Mary adopted a wounded expression. "I don't think so," she said, as she set a glass in the rack of the dishwasher. "We don't really communicate much." And not for the first time, Mary wished she hadn't made mention of Robert Mondasian.

Martina turned to Mary and, with a damp hand, reached for one of hers. "I'm so sorry, sweetie . . . ," she said, always looking to help, always looking to heal. And in those moments, the affection that Mary felt toward Martina was genuine.

It was Patrick Kelly who expressed wariness toward Mary. She noticed it in the slowness of his smile as he greeted her, in the glances he'd give her when no one was watching. Mary suspected Patrick would have preferred a more conventional match for Stefan. A girl with a similar upbringing. A girl who would join the Junior League and decorate with chintz. Though Stefan was younger than his brother by five years, it was clear that he was the favorite son. Stefan was a better debater than his brother — quicker and more agile. And when Stefan and Teddy would circle the ring over politics and policy, it was Stefan who landed more hits.

"The country's already starting to see the benefits of fiscal discipline," Teddy would say, Claire, his wife, resting her hand encouragingly on his knee.

Stefan would lean back in his seat. "Discipline? As a percentage of GDP, the national debt is higher now than it ever was under Carter!"

Patrick would force a smile and wipe his mouth with a white cloth napkin, seemingly amused by his sons' rivalry. "Will the gentlemen cede the floor?" he would say — a distinguished call for conclusion. Then he'd drop his napkin back on the table, giving Stefan a final glance, acknowledging the victor. It was Stefan, of course, who should have been granted the keys to the kingdom. Patrick had known this since they were small. He had also known that it was the traits he found most admirable in Stefan that would keep him from joining him in business. And Patrick Kelly, above all else, was lauded for his instincts.

"Did you ever figure out how you girls got that flat tire?" Patrick had once asked, not long after Mary and Hannah had first arrived at the Kellys' door.

He held Mary's gaze before tilting a bottle of cabernet and filling his glass. Mary shook her head. "You know what?" she said, as if the thought had just occurred to her. "I didn't."

The memory of that conversation would return to Mary unbidden from time to time. It did so now, as Stefan sat on the floor in front of her, his back resting against the tweed sofa that the last tenants had left, his head reclined against the cushion. He had arrived last night and stayed until his eyes started to drift shut. Then he gathered himself up and went to his parents' to sleep. He hadn't ever stayed the night with Mary and Hannah. Mary let her finger slowly twirl through his lion-colored hair as he held his book elevated and open. Hannah was playing Barbies on the floor next to Stefan, whispering a scene quietly enough that no one could make out the words except for her.

Mary let her fingertips trace their way down his neck. Stefan took a breath and closed his eyes. "We should really get you packed," he said.

It had been decided that the apartment on Boosk Avenue was unsuitable for the Chase girls. And no sooner was it deemed so than Martina Kelly spoke to someone who spoke to someone who happened to have a nice little condominium in a recently construction development. They would love to rent it to Mary and Hannah. And when the question of the rent came up, Martina named an impossibly low sum. *They're just glad to have nice tenants, sweetie.* And just like that, it was done. Such was the ease that came with being close to the Kellys. In their new condo, the Chase girls would have a dishwasher and a laundry room. They would have new carpeting and a bathroom mirror surrounded by globelike bulbs. The Chase girls would even have two bedrooms, but for Mary, the idea of sleeping separately from her sister was unthinkable. She decided that maybe they could use the second bedroom as Stefan's office, so he could have a place to study when he was down from Boston.

Before Hannah even spoke, Mary sensed that she was about to. She looked first to Mary, but then addressed Stefan. "Stefan," she said, her eyes concerned and determined. "I don't want to move."

Stefan put his book down. "What?" he said, reaching over to tickle her belly. "Hannah Banana, your new place is going to be great!"

Hannah squirmed away from his touch.

"Bunny," said Mary. And Hannah's eyes found her sister's. "You didn't tell me you didn't want to move."

Hannah's face remained serious; she didn't like to cause trouble. "I like it here."

"I like it here, too, Bunny," replied Mary, realizing that Hannah's attachment to place was one of the very many marked differences between the Chase girls. *If I didn't know better, I wouldn't even think you were related*, Diane had once said, while looking at a picture of a toddler Hannah and a teenage Mary. "But we're not going far. You'll be at the same school. You'll even ride the same bus."

"But it'll be a different house."

Mary was silent for a moment. "We don't have to go if you don't want to," she said, shaking her head. "We can stay right here. We don't have to move."

Stefan cocked his head but remained silent. Mary remained focused on Hannah.

Hannah held Mary's gaze for a moment, then she dropped her chin. "No," said Hannah. "It's okay. We can go."

"I think," said Stefan, straining to stand up from the floor, "that moving will sound a lot better after a peanut butter and jelly sandwich." He didn't realize that Mary meant it when she said they didn't have to go. He didn't yet know the lengths Mary would go to for Hannah. Mary watched his calves as he walked to the kitchen. They were a sailor's calves: strong, sinewy, and tanned. "Hannah Banana!" he called, as Mary heard the cupboards in her shabby little kitchen open, then bang shut. "You want grape or strawberry?"

And later, as Mary stood at the sink washing the plates they had eaten on, she heard Stefan and Hannah in the living room. She knew that they were lying where she had left them: with their heads at opposite ends of the small couch, Hannah's socked foot pressed against Stefan's bare one. Hannah liked him more than she had ever liked a man before. He bought her books and showed her maps. And there was a steadiness to him. A constancy. "You're gonna be happy at your new place, Banana," Mary heard him say. "There's a great big yard for you to play in."

"And it's not far, right?"

Stefan shook his head. "Nah," he said. Mary pictured him lifting Hannah's foot higher using his own. "It's not far."

"And we're just going to move once. It's not going to be like before," she said, letting herself find comfort in Stefan's reassurances. Letting herself believe him. "It's not going to be like after the swamp."

Mary shut off the water. She was in the doorway as Stefan asked, his eyes narrow with amusement, "What swamp?"

And before another sound could be uttered, Mary said, her expression as smooth as stone, "So, should we start packing?"

That night, after Stefan had gone home, Mary climbed into bed next to Hannah.

"Bunny," she whispered, stroking Hannah's hair away from her forehead. "Wake up."

Hannah's eyes opened for a second and then slipped shut again, as if her lids couldn't manage under the weight of sleep.

"Bunny," said Mary again. "I just want to tell you that I meant what I said." Mary looked around the dark room. The Chase girls' few things had been put into cardboard boxes and stacked in the corner. In black marker Mary had written the contents on each. TOYS. CLOTHES. BOOKS. It was comforting to Mary to see how little they had accumulated. "We don't have to move if you don't want to."

Hannah's eyes opened and stayed that way this time. Then she propped herself up on one elbow and seemed to think for a moment, the wheels of her mind starting to turn slowly after slumber. She looked at Mary. "Why does Stefan think we should?"

"He cares about us," answered Mary. "He wants us to have a nice place to live."

Hannah let her head fall back onto her pillow, and she stared at the ceiling, her arms at her sides atop the white sheets. She watched as lights from a passing car moved like a spotlight through the room. "I remember where we used to live." It was the first time Hannah had mentioned the Water's Edge in months and months. "With Mom."

"I do, too," said Mary.

"Do you think we'll ever go back there?"

Mary studied the curve of Hannah's profile. "I don't think so, Bunny," she finally said.

"We never go back to places once we leave. We stay there for a while and then we never go back." Mary knew that Hannah was talking about their time on the road.

"We're not going to do that anymore."

"Promise?"

Mary paused for a moment, realizing the gravity of what she was about to do. Hannah is the only person for whom she would try to hold to her word. "I promise," she said, nodding.

Hannah watched her sister, then took a breath and seemed to settle down deeper into their mattress, letting her eyes slip shut. "Hey, Bunny, one more thing," said Mary. And Hannah's gaze was once again on her. "You know some stories are just for us, right?"

Hannah's nod was slow and small.

Mary leaned in and kissed her forehead. "I know it can be hard sometimes. To remember what's what," she said. "But it's going to get easier. We're not going to have to tell so many stories. We're just going to have to remember the important ones."

"Mary?" asked Hannah.

Mary pulled back to find Hannah's eyes. "Will you tell me about Princess Mary and Princess Hannah? Until I fall asleep?"

So Mary did. She took the princesses to a castle on a mountain with a spire that rose through the clouds, where the evil queen couldn't find them. Where they could hide forever if they wanted. And when Stefan asked Mary about what Hannah meant when she was talking about the swamp, Mary smiled knowingly. "Sometimes Hannah just makes things up. She's at that age, I guess."

Fifteen

1976

MARY HAD ALWAYS UNDERSTOOD her duality, which began at the moment of her conception. Her mother was young and unwed. Her father was a phantom or a devil, or some earthly incarnation of the two. She came into a place and a time where her existence was scandalous, but her beauty was revered. Mary was lovely and terrible. Mary was a blessing and a tragedy. Mary was capable of great love, but only toward a very few.

In the months before Hannah was born, she had nothing to moor her to Sandy Bank. Her affection for her mother was real, but it was muffled by her adolescent anger that was like a roaring in her ears. And when Diane announced that they would be leaving in September, that she couldn't endure the speculation and rumors that would soon be slithering around Sandy Bank — not again — the longing for the road that was cocooned in Mary's heart finally unfurled its wings. And Mary decided that she would leave.

She would go as far south as she could and then go farther still. She would find the boy in the white boat on his sandy island, the boy who could take her anywhere, and they would be together. She wouldn't be in Sandy Bank in October when he came back. So she would go to him.

But Mary needed money.

And so on the sort of evening in August when the humidity was so thick that she would watch the graying sky, waiting for the opaque thunderheads to roll in like chariots, Mary set out for the Pools' little house, her feet bare on their buckling sand-strewn back walk, and went up to the potted geranium plant. Tilting it carefully to its side, she revealed a brass-toned key. Alice kept it there, Mary knew, for those nights when Stan forgot his set on the boat. Mary was accustomed to taking what she wanted, snatching this and that, lifting a bill here or there to pay for little niceties for herself. But not from the Pools. She wasn't used to stealing from the Pools. She hesitated for only a moment before lifting the key from the soil-dusted brick. Circumstances, she thought, were extenuating.

Mary propped the screen door open with her hip as she slid the key into the knob and turned. With the side of her body, she pushed against the swollen back door. It offered only a moment of resistance before yielding. The Pools' kitchen was small and tidy, like the rest of the house, with white ruffled curtains and a blue speckled countertop edged with metal. In the corner was the small table-and-chair set that Mary had sat at countless times while Mrs. Pool made fried bologna sandwiches or mended a hole in her sweater. She knew this house as well as she knew the Water's Edge. She knew the rattle and roar of the fan in the wood-paneled bathroom. She knew the yellow stain on the doily that lay on top of the television. She knew the closet full of books saved for children who were never born, books of fairy tales with thick spines and leather covers. And Mary also knew the small metal box in the drawer of the Pools' bedside table. Mr. Pool kept the cash from his fishing charters there. Right underneath the Holy Bible and beside his bottle of TUMS.

It was a Thursday evening and Mrs. Pool played bridge on Thursday evenings. Mr. Pool had taken a group out fishing and wouldn't be back for hours. Mary had already made her way to the Pools' bedroom and slid open the drawer when she heard Alice's voice at the front door. "Don't say things like that, Marjory." Her words came gentle but true, a reprimand more forgiving than firm. "She's had an awful hard time."

The front door opened with a groan; Mrs. Pool only ever used that entrance when she had a guest.

"Well!" Mary heard a voice she recognized as Marjory Porteiski's. "I will say that she brings a good deal of it in on herself!" Mrs. Porteiski was a joyless busybody with the same physical softness as Alice Pool but with none of her kindness.

"You don't know how bad things have been for her. But by the grace of God——"

"*Go I.* I know my scriptures, Alice."

Mary knew without seeing that Mrs. Pool was scuttling around the living room, hoping to make her guest feel at home. She was lifting the lid on her candy bowl. She was setting out a tray table that she'd place a plate of cookies on. Stepping carefully to avoid the floorboard that squeaked, Mary collapsed one of the louvered doors to the Pools' bedroom closet and stepped inside, feeling Mr. Pool's flannel shirts on her back, Mrs. Pool's church dresses. More than even the Water's Edge, the Pools' house held the smell of the ocean. It was unadulterated there. Undiluted.

"It is a shame that we didn't get to play tonight," said Mrs. Pool, trying, Mary thought, to steer the conversation in a more pleasant direction. "I hope Shelley feels better."

"Shelley is a hypochondriac," said Mrs. Porteiski. "It's a condition. Donohue was talking all about it."

Mary heard Mrs. Pool mumble in both assent and interest. "Can I get you a drink?" she asked.

"Can you make a Tom Collins?"

The doors to the oak liquor cabinet in the Pools' living room opened and closed. "Let's see . . . well, I do have gin . . ." Bottles clinked and clanged.

"Just a scotch is fine, Alice," said Mrs. Porteiski. "Neat."

Mary heard the glugs of liquor being poured. A few moments later came Marjory's voice again. "Good Lord, Alice!" she scolded. "That's plenty!"

"Well, you don't have to finish it, Marjory!"

After a brief pause, Marjory Porteiski continued her previous line of questioning. "So who is it this time?"

"Hmmm?" asked Mrs. Pool. "How do you mean?"

"Who's the father of the baby *this time?*" The disdain in Marjory's voice was unmistakable.

"You mean Diane's?"

Mary heard Mrs. Porteiski huff. "No, I mean mine!" she said. "Of course I mean Diane! Who'd she get knocked up by this time?"

"You know who the father is, Marjory. It's not as if Diane is running around all over the town!" It was as firm a defense as Mrs. Pool was capable of.

"So, it's that Barry?"

"He doesn't want a thing to do with her since he found out."

"Well, of course not! That's what happens when you give away the milk for free. No man wants to buy the cow!"

"For goodness' sake, Marjory!"

"You mark my words; she'll never find a man now. Not with two children born out of wedlock. It's a real shame."

Mary could almost see the lifting of Mrs. Pool's vast chest with a sigh. "It is."

At this, Mary felt a well of anger burst inside of her. She slipped carefully out of the closet and lifted the metal box out of the still-open drawer before gently shutting it. Mrs. Pool and Mrs. Porteiski were on the couch. Their backs would be to the wall. They wouldn't see Mary as she slinked out of the bedroom, down the hallway, and out the way she had come.

Mary moved without footsteps, without sound or breath, the box pressed against her stomach, until she reached the back door. She hadn't intended to take it all, but her rage begged for retaliation, however misdirected. Mary turned the knob with a slow, steady hand, then opened the screen door in front of her. Stepping across the threshold as if she were stepping off of a ship, she pulled the wood door closed and, with a straight arm, kept the screen door propped open, feeling the tension in its springs. She pressed it until the springs groaned in pain, then she let go. And the clatter broke the silence like a slap.

Mrs. Pool came quickly, her thick thighs rubbing at each other as she bustled down the hall, her eyes wide and anxious behind her glasses. With Marjory behind her, she'd step out onto the walk and look all around. But Mary would be nowhere in sight. *What do you reckon that was?* Mrs. Pool would ask her friend. *Do you think someone was trying to get into the house?* Mary would be nearly to the dunes by the time Mrs. Pool and Marjory would decide it was nothing and head back inside.

IT WAS LATER THAT EVENING that Diane came into the office of the Water's Edge, where Mary was on the couch watching television. Diane was wiping her hands on her apron; she had been in the kitchen. "You know, I was thinking that maybe getting away from Sandy Bank is going to be nice." She looked at her daughter, perhaps sensing that something had changed. Perhaps sensing that somewhere a bag lay packed, that plans lay made. "I always hated the fall here," she said. "It's so depressing. Everyone's gone and it's always so gray. Florida's supposed to be beautiful then. Silver linings, right, Mare? That's how we have to think about it."

Mary gave her mother a glance. "Sure," she said, her eyes back on the screen. "Silver linings."

Diane moved tentatively toward her daughter and sat down beside her. "I know you're mad at me," she said, staring between her legs at the tweedy couch, at the spots where the threads had been rubbed bare. "But I don't know what else to do, Mare." She shook her head. "I just don't know what else to do."

Diane reached for Mary's hand, and Mary let her hold it for a moment, just a moment, knowing that by tomorrow she would be gone. She'd be on her way to the boy with the boat. Then she pulled her hand away. Mary needed to hate her mother tonight. She needed her anger to stoke her flight. Diane leaned in and kissed her daughter on her forehead, then stood. She walked over and shut off the television; the picture disappeared with a flicker. "You need to go to bed."

Mary sat on her bed in the dark, the slick bedspread sticking to the backs of her thighs. Her room was off of the hallway that led to the office then, right across from her mother's. It didn't have a bathroom of its own so Mary used Diane's. Her mother had watched her as she brushed her teeth, had watched her as she brought her face to the sink and filled her hands with cold water, drinking it down. Diane watched her as she went across the hallway to her own room. "You know, maybe we can move you into one of the guest rooms," Diane said. "After the baby comes. So you can have a little more space. Your own bathroom." Mary shut the door behind her. Diane waited until she heard the lock slide into place.

It was Sunday night, so Mary knew there would be weekenders heading back over the bridge until late. She'd walk to the highway and hitch a ride over to the bus station in Darby. She'd get on the late bus to the city. And then she'd be gone.

Mary waited until she heard Diane go out and lock the door to the office, flipping the sign to read CLOSED. She listened for the flush of her mother's toilet, and then she waited. And it struck her how well she knew her mother's routine, her waxing and her waning. She wondered if she might miss it someday.

Then at a quarter after ten, Mary stood, her backpack already slung onto one shoulder, the $892 from Mr. Pool's box divided between the pockets of her shorts, the inside flap of her bag, and the cup of her bra. With small silent movements, she slid back the lock to her room and opened her door.

She was guiding it gently back into place when her mother's voice came through the dark. "Hi, Mary." A light switched on and Diane was sitting on the couch in her pink polyester nightgown, her arms bare, a blanket on her lap. She looked at her daughter. "Alice called. She said she's missing some money."

Mary remained as still as stone, her hand on the knob to her room, her muscles tensed. The only part of her body that was in motion was her heart, which was thumping quickly inside her chest.

"But Mr. Pool doesn't get back until late."

"He's not the only one who knows where the box is, Mare."

Diane and Mary stared at each other until Diane finally spoke. "Where were you going?" Diane looked weary, her limbs seemingly weighted with effort. "Hmm? Just where in the hell did you think you were going to go?"

Mary found some of her anger. *"Away,"* she said.

"Well, we're going to do that anyway. Remember?" Diane rubbed her hand over her face. "Mary, what do you think? That I'm just going to let you go? You're my *child*. Do you know what that *means?*" Diane leaned forward, her elbows on her knees. "Do you have any idea what that means?"

"I don't want a sister," said Mary.

Diane let out a chuckle that sounded like a sob. "Mary Catherine Chase," she said, meeting her daughter's eye, her head starting a slow shake. "I don't want you to have one."

Mary drew back at the truth of it. She looked at her mother; behind her was only a smooth pane of glass and then the limitless night beyond.

"I need you to stay with me," said Diane. "*Promise* that you won't leave me."

If Mary's life came down to only a handful of decisions, a smattering of choices directing the lines of her life, this was one of them. Finally, she looked at her mother. "On the way down to Florida," she started. "Can we go to the swamp?"

Diane settled back against the couch and lifted her chin toward the sky, her body and mind spent, her hand resting on the belly that had once born Mary. "You don't know what it is to be a mother, Mary" was all Diane could say.

Sixteen
1983

MARY LET HER ARMS LIE LIMP above her head as she stretched out on the bow of the boat in her bathing suit, warming herself in the sun. The space behind her eyelids glowed orange as if heat were a visible thing, as if she were turning into light from the inside out. The Kellys' summer party was that evening, and so she, Stefan, and Hannah had left early to spend the day on the boat. She could hear Stefan and her sister now as they leaned over the railing, spotting the fish that floated over the green and brown pebbled bottom of the marina, their voices distant and close all at once. "Did you see that, Hannah Banana?" Stefan asked. "I think that one was a shark."

Hannah's laughter came trilling up like bubbles, and Mary's lips curled into a Pavlovian smile at the sound of it. "It's not a *shark*," giggled Hannah. "It was a *minnow*."

"Alright, you make sure it doesn't attack," Mary heard Stefan say. "I'm going to go sit with your sister." With her eyes still closed, Mary felt his steps, sure and solid, make their way toward her. He sank down next to her on the bow, and Mary brought her hand to his back, letting her fingertips slide underneath his shirt, letting them run up and down his skin, her center finger on his spine. "She loves you," she said.

Stefan looked down at Mary, his head cocked to the side, his hair sun-bleached and salted with summer. "What about her sister?"

Mary smiled, and it felt as if ripples were moving through her body. "Her sister thinks you're just okay."

They stayed on the boat all afternoon: Mary, Hannah, and Stefan, on their own buoyant, moveable world. As the sun started to sink toward another ocean, making a slow exit from its vast blue sky, Stefan turned to Mary, and whispered, "We better get going." Mary could imagine the catering trucks lining the driveway and the florists unloading arrangements from their vans as Martina whisked around the house in her robe offering her particular brand of polite, precise German instruction to the various staff. Mary reached above her head and stretched, the sun having sapped her motivation. But Stefan straightened up, dutiful though reluctant. He pulled off his T-shirt, balled it up, and threw it toward the duffel bag that sat slumped on the deck. "Everyone will start getting there soon."

By the time Mary, Stefan, and Hannah arrived, the first wave of guests had been welcomed to Northton Avenue. Even among the privileged, the Kelly family seemed charmed. In a different era, Mary could imagine throngs of common-ers lunging and grasping just to touch their hems in hopes of some transference of good fortune. Mary could hear the buzz of their laughter-spiked conversation rise through the air to mix with the music from the brass band that played from the gazebo. The sky was washed in a watercolor dusk, and Mary reached for Hannah's hand as they made their way up over the thick carpet of grass. An atmosphere seemed to hover over the Kellys' property like a pleasant hallucinatory haze. There, anything unlovely or troublesome seemed to cease to exist.

"Is this a wedding?" asked Hannah, her voice quiet and unsure.

Stefan laughed. "Not that I know of," he said. And Mary understood his lingering smile.

They walked past long buffet tables laden with food and surrounded by guests who feasted like unwitting peasants. Eyes brightened as they alighted on Stefan and hands covered overstuffed mouths. But Stefan simply nodded politely and kept moving toward the back of the yard and the rose garden, where the Kellys stood like reigning monarchs — Martina, the benevolent queen, and Patrick, the shrewd king. Teddy was there with Claire — all excellent posture and white smiles.

Pair by pair, guests would make their way over to the Kellys. A hearty handshake would be exchanged, shoulders would be gripped, and cheeks would be kissed on each side. They had just finished such an exchange when Martina caught sight of her son. "Stefan, honey!" exclaimed Martina, waving him forth. "Come say hello to the Carlsons!"

She saw Teddy meet his brother's eye and subtly tap the face of his watch, his face reproachful. And Mary heard Stefan take a breath before he adopted a smile, rested his hand on Mary's back, and led the three of them into the breach. *Nice to see you. The pleasure's mine.* And when Mary was introduced, eyebrows flitted up in recognition. This was, after all, the girl they had heard about. She fit into the story of the Kellys so well: the girl on the doorstep, the handmaiden turned princess. *Is Hannah your father's daughter as well?* Martina had once asked. And Mary just shook her head. *No,* she said. *She's not.*

Finally, after several introductions, Martina linked her arm through Mary's. "I'm stealing the girls for a bit," she said to Stefan, and she led Mary and Hannah off, leaving Stefan standing shoulder to shoulder with his father, watching them.

And as they wove their way through the crowd — Martina clasping Mary clasping Hannah — they drew stares of envy and intrigue and every point on the continuum between. Mary saw Beth in her floral sheath and her French twist, standing with her mother, her eyes searching about for Stefan. And she felt a temporary pang of pity for the girl, who thought her backseat blow jobs and inner-circle status would be enough to keep Stefan. Theirs was a polite, tentative romance, one that ended before it really even began. Beth would never understand the part of him that Mary did, the part of him that would sail across an ocean to find her. The part of him that could fall to his knees and promise a girl that he would come back. The part of him that would follow Mary to the bathroom of a restaurant, hike up her skirt, and back her against the wall while his family waited for their crème brûlée.

Martina put a wineglass in Mary's hand and had the bar make a Shirley Temple for Hannah, who sucked it down until her lips were the artificial red of maraschino cherries. And laughter came like breath, unbidden and unconscious. And as they stopped in front of the gazebo, watching the black men in white shirts play golden instruments, Martina leaned her head toward Mary's, her eyes still on the band. "I don't know if Steffie ever told you, but my mother got Alzheimer's when she was very, very young. I had to take care of her and my little brothers while my father worked. And we were not rich. My father was a teacher." She reached for Mary's hand and gave it a single squeeze. Mary waited for her to continue. "I know it's been difficult," Martina said, in her melodic *Sound of Music* voice. "Both raising your sister and having your job at the hotel. And I see what a hard worker you are. But . . ." She looked at Mary and smiled. "You're not going to have to worry about that much longer. You're going to be able to do anything you want." Then Martina looked back at the band, and her head once again began to sway with the music.

Then Mary felt a hand wrap around her waist from behind. "Hey you," Stefan said, his breath near her ear. Martina let out a cluck of approval, and her hands came together in a single clap as she smiled, as she saw just how nicely Mary and Stefan fit together.

MARY HAD HAD A FEW GLASSES OF WINE by the time Martina took to the gazebo, inching her way in front of the band, then clinking a salad fork against her goblet. "I just want to thank you all for coming," started Martina, her accented English becoming more charming with drink. Patrick stood by her side, smiling and mute, but impressive all the same. "We love nothing more than to be surrounded by family and friends, and so you all do us such an honor by joining us for this every summer." Martina clutched her heart and nodded at the faces she looked onto from her perch. "And because I always must lead us in a toast" — Martina raised her glass as her eyes searched the glowing dark — "this year I would like to honor our wonderful sons, Teddy and Stefan, who are making us so very proud." Martina's eyes found her sons, and Stefan nodded graciously toward his mother. "Cheers, my loves," she said. And Mary felt her skin tingle; she felt the warmth of adoration as glasses were raised and the sound of goodwill rose through the sea of guests to honor the man her heart had claimed. And Mary pulled Hannah close to her, wanting her to feel it, too.

"You know," Mary said, leaning down so that only Hannah could hear, her voice like wind. "Someday I'm going to tell you everything, Bunny."

Hannah looked back at her sister, and Mary smiled, her eyes wild and twinkling things. "It's such a good story," Mary said, just as the crowd echoed a thunderous "Cheers!" and Mary stood and drained her glass.

And after Stefan's hand was shaken and his back patted, Mary linked her arm through his and held Hannah's hand with her other, and the three of them whirled through the crowd under a ceiling of starlight. And perhaps it was the feeling of motion, of movement, that emboldened her, that dulled the dexterity with which she usually wove her tales, or perhaps it was the wine, but Mary's stories came spilling from her mouth without thought of repercussion. Perhaps, for that one evening, Mary believed them. *Oh! I love Paris*, she said. *I spent some time at the Sorbonne.* And *Yes, I met Princess Diana once with my father.* Hannah squeezed her hand, a silent plea to stop, as Stefan gave her glances of amused confusion.

And only when she heard Hannah's gasp of recognition, the tiny intake of breath through her sister's lips, did fantasy and reality fall apart as if cleaved by a blade. When Mary followed her sister's eyes and saw through the shifting crowd the face of a ghost, her feet turned leaden, and all that lay in her wake seemed not distant but far too close. For one moment, they stared at each other, as the sea of bodies that had parted flowed together once again. "I think I need to go home. I don't feel good," said Mary, her eyes not moving from the spot where he had been, sensing his presence like scent. Because Mary had told enough tales to know the narrative of a fall, enough to know that on either side of an apex lay a steep slope down. That all someone would have to do was push.

STEFAN TOLD ONLY HIS PARENTS that they were leaving before taking Mary to his car. "I had too much to drink," she said, as he led her over the lawn, her steps unsteady.

"Hannah Banana, how are you doing?" called Stefan, as Hannah walked behind them. Mary glanced back at her sister, and Hannah met her eyes, her face serious, intuiting that she should say nothing about who was there but not knowing why.

"I'm okay," Hannah finally answered, her dress dragging on the grass as she walked.

"We're gonna get your sister home, okay?"

And Hannah nodded. "Okay."

Mary was silent as they drove, her head against the cool

glass of the passenger's window of Stefan's car as it glided over Northton's smooth black roads. And when they pulled up to the condo, Stefan got out without a word and began to walk quickly across the front of the car to Mary's side. Mary turned back to Hannah, her chin on the seatback.

Mary stared at her for a moment before speaking. Her face always softened when looking at Hannah. "Did you have fun tonight?" she asked.

Hannah nodded. "I thought I saw someone," she said. "I can't remember his name."

"Shhhh," she said, her voice like wind through grass. "It was no one, Bunny." Then she turned back to the black windshield just as Stefan opened her door.

"Thanks, Stef," she said, taking his hand as he helped her out. "I think I just need to lie down. Hannah, can you get yourself ready for bed tonight?"

Hannah nodded again.

In her room, Mary got undressed, pulled on a thin white tank top, walked over to the bed, and pulled the phone cord from the jack in the wall with a tug. She climbed into bed, gathering the loose white covers up around her. Her teeth began to chatter, but not with cold.

Hannah soon joined her, and so did Stefan later, bringing with him cushions from the couch. He arranged them on the floor next to Mary's side of the bed and pulled off his dress shirt before lowering himself onto them. On her other side, Hannah laid limp with sleep. Mary kept her eyes closed, but Stefan reached up and stroked her arm until his movement slowed, then stopped. It was the first night that he had spent with the Chase girls. And when all was quiet around her, Mary opened her eyes and stared at the square patch of ceiling that was illuminated by the lights outside. "I'm sorry," Mary said. Though spoken quietly, her words penetrated the room.

She heard Stefan give a ragged intake of breath as he rolled to his side and repositioned himself. "It's okay, Mare," he mumbled. And Mary looked down at him, feeling an almost unbearable weight on her chest. "You just got a little looped." Her stories, their sudden departure—Stefan blamed them on the very good gewürztraminer that Martina was serving. And Mary thought that perhaps it was all for the best, that the grace of the Kellys couldn't change who she was. That our natures brought with them inevitability. That we were all blindly hurling toward our own like a boat barreling toward the falls.

Throughout that long night, as Mary lay on her back with one hand reaching down toward Stefan, the other over Hannah, she felt the specific regret of a creature that had mistaken its opponent. And when sleep finally did overtake her, she dreamed of a long open wound in her leg. She dreamed of licking and licking and licking it clean.

In the early hours of the morning, when her eyes opened with a jolt, she knew he was there. And Mary Chase lifted herself carefully out of bed and climbed over her sister. She left the bedroom quickly and took a blanket that she wrapped around her body like a cloak. Then she went down to the foyer and sat in the stairs, her leg bouncing as she waited for him. She stood before the bell rang, opening the door as soon as she sensed his presence, the hinges moving silently.

"Hi, Tim," she said.

And his smile is one that she would never forget.

Seventeen
1983

T IM DACKARD STOOD BEFORE HER, his eyes red-
rimmed, his lips cracked. It appeared as though he
had been up all night, if not for days. "I wish I could
say you were a hard person to find." His eyes were eager, wanting Mary to ask how, how he knew where she was. When she
didn't, he offered it. "My dad hired a detective after you left.
To make sure you were really gone. I read his report."

Mary leaned against the door frame, the pristine white tile
aligned perfectly beneath her feet, her skin visible through the
loose weave of the blanket. "What are you here for?"

Tim's head fell back in a gaping but silent laugh, and Mary
noticed the rash of pimples on his neck where his beard was
coming in. When he looked at her again, she saw the delight he
would take in this, in finally having power. "Are you serious?"
he asked, with equal measures of hostility and amusement.

Mary waited for his answer, her face impassive.

With his arms crossed in front of him, Tim let out another scoffing laugh, then rolled his head to look around at
the neighborhood. Squinting against the light, he let his eyes

settle on the rustling leaves of one of the young oaks that stood in a neat curbside row. "It's nice here," he said, almost to himself. "Classy." Then he turned back to Mary. "So where's your sister?"

A ferocity swelled inside Mary like a rush of blood to the head, but she answered Tim plainly. "Sleeping," she said.

"And your boyfriend?"

Mary didn't feign shock. Since he was here, of course he would know about Stefan. "He's sleeping, too."

"Well, this will be cozy," he said, as he went to step over the threshold.

Mary moved her body in front of his. "You can't come in," she said.

"I can, Mary," he said quietly, all his wild, pulsing teenage anger radiating from him like something nuclear. Then from his back pocket he pulled out a Polaroid. She recognized it at once. Her face looking foreign and grotesque with feigned pleasure as Ron Dackard nuzzled her neck. "I absolutely can."

"Stefan knows I've seen other men, Tim," she said, her voice emotionless.

Tim's eyes narrowed and she could see the eagerness of his lips, the wet anticipation of his threat. "Does he know you *blackmailed* them?" he asked. "Something tells me a family like the Kellys would frown on that sort of thing."

Mary shrugged, as if brushing away a mild concern. "It wouldn't matter," she said. "You wouldn't be able to prove anything."

Tim leaned close until his lips were almost at hers. She could feel his stale breath, the warmth of it, when he said, "I wouldn't have to." Then he pushed past her and stepped into the foyer, looking around as he took it all in, as his eyes swept from ceiling to floor. "Nice carpet," he said, letting out a single quiet laugh as he looked at the living room beyond.

It was true, of course — any proximity to such scandal would be enough to sully her in the eyes of the Kellys. Mary felt her heart begin to pulse. "What do you want?"

Tim smiled. "Not much, really," he said. "A place to stay, to start." Then he turned toward the hallway and began walking down it, tracing his fingertips down the white wall. "My parents kicked me out," he explained, as Mary followed him. "Old Ron got tired of having me around."

"Do you have any money?" asked Mary, as they stepped into the kitchen.

"I did," he said, stiffening as he turned to face her. She noticed the red thread-thin lines of blood vessels rimming his nostrils. "But I ran out."

"Do your parents know you came here?"

Tim let out an angry laugh. "No," he said, crossing his arms in front of him and leaning against the counter. "Not yet."

From the stairs, Mary heard footsteps, the halting sort that marked Hannah's one-by-one descent down the stairs.

"You can't stay here, Tim."

Tim's eyebrows drew together in feigned hurt. "That's not very cousinly."

Hannah was in the hallway now, and Mary felt the beat of her heart begin to build, but her voice was a flat line. "You need to leave," she said.

Tim shook his head, crossed one ankle over the over, and wriggled his haunches against the counter, settling in. Behind him, light poured in through the window that looked out to the other units and their identical rear decks. "I'm not going anywhere," he said, relishing the taste of the words in his mouth, letting them linger. And she imagined waking Stefan up, begging him to come with her and Hannah, begging him to leave. She imagined the three of them just driving, driving, driving. Because Mary knew that she and Tim were the same sort of creature. That she could see through to his bones, and he to hers. That she knew what Tim was capable of because she was capable of it, too.

From behind her, she heard Hannah's voice. "Mary?"

She let her eyes remain on Tim for a single exhalation that came up through her throat like a silent roar. Then she turned. Hannah stood at the threshold of the kitchen, her curls matted on one side with sleep. "Come here, Bunny," Mary said, the blanket falling from her extended arm like it was a wing.

Hannah just looked at Mary.

"Oh, *that's* what you call her," Tim said, nodding with recognition. "I couldn't remember."

At the sound of Tim's voice, Hannah shuffled to Mary, resting her cheek against her belly as she took in Tim. "You said he was no one," she whispered, looking up at her sister.

And Mary felt Hannah's words sink down to her stomach like an anchor drifting down through a dark sea. "I was wrong," she said.

"I'm your cousin," said Tim, cocking his head to see around Mary. "Remember?"

Mary and Hannah both looked at him until Mary pulled Hannah's attention back in. "Did you sleep okay?" she asked, lifting Hannah's chin so that all each of them could see was the other's face. So that everything else was in the periphery. So that it always would be.

Hannah nodded. "Stefan's still sleeping."

Mary looked at Hannah and managed to smile. "Let's let him," she said. And she felt relief begin to rise inside her like a tide.

BY THE TIME STEFAN CAME DOWN, Mary was at the stove making breakfast. She was silent as she prepared the meal, feeling the peace of inevitability. She remembered how a calm came over her grandfather during the last months of his life. He would look at Diane and smile, and Diane would burst into tears. *Don't worry, my girl,* he'd say. *Don't worry.* And Diane's cries would escalate. But that was the time that Mary liked her grandfather best, just before he died. When there was no fear on his face, just the detritus of the past. When what was coming seemed no more optional or exceptional than the turning of the earth.

Mary had heard Stefan's steps as she cracked the eggs, swiftly sending six plump yolks sliding into the glass bowl. Looking to the doorway, her eyes met his for a moment before she said, "Bunny, can you get me the milk?" Without a word, Hannah leaped up from the chair she was sitting in and walked over to the refrigerator, then tugged on the handle.

"Hey, Mare," said Stefan, the question thick in his voice. With the smallest of movements, he nodded toward Tim. "What's going on?"

Mary took the milk from Hannah and set it on the countertop, then wiped her hands on her white tank top. And as Mary looked at Stefan, she knew that she would love him through the long stretch of her life. "Morning, Stef," she said. The blanket was in a pile on the floor now, and Mary stood in her underwear. "How'd you sleep?"

She heard Tim clear his throat. Stefan glanced at him but kept his face turned toward Mary, letting his eyes run briefly down the body that stood so bare in front of another man. "Who's this?" he asked, nodding more explicitly this time to Tim.

Tim raised his hand and waved, a mocking, hard-jawed smile on his face. "I'm Tim," he said.

"He's a cousin of ours," said Mary. "He surprised us."

Stefan jerked his thumb to the hallway. "Mare, can I talk to you for a sec?"

And Mary followed Stefan out of the kitchen. They walked in silence until they were in the living room, then Stefan turned around. "Who the fuck *is* that, Mary?"

Mary crossed her arms over her chest. "I told you," she laughed. "He's a cousin."

"Mare," said Stefan, looking into her eyes as if unable to get the right view. "He looks like shit. He's sitting there at the table grinding his teeth. He's clearly on something and he's in there with Hannah. And you're standing there in your *underwear*." Stefan extended his hand, as if waiting for Mary to place a retort in it.

As Mary felt her eyes begin to burn, to well up, to reveal everything she didn't want them to, she dug her toes into the carpet. Then she turned her huge glimmering yellow brown eyes up to Stefan, and said, "I know. He's got some problems. I just wanted to help."

Stefan took a single step forward and pulled Mary into his chest. He cupped the back of her head with his hand. "Come here," he said. "You have such a good heart, Mare." And Mary felt something that was very close to remorse.

When they went back into the kitchen, Mary was wearing Stefan's T-shirt, which he had pulled off and helped her into, gently guiding each of her arms through the sleeves. Hannah watched the two of them enter the room as if they were feuding parents who had excused themselves as to not disagree in front of the children.

"Tim," said Mary, with as much politic as she could muster, "I'd like you to meet Stefan." Mary smiled from Tim to Stefan. "Stefan, this is Tim."

Stefan promptly strode across the room with a firm outstretched hand.

Tim stuffed each of his hands under his armpits and gave Stefan a nod of acknowledgment. *"Charmed,"* he said, with no small amount of disdain.

"So you're Mary and Hannah's cousin?" asked Stefan, making the sort of small talk that Martina would make.

"Of sorts," answered Tim.

"On which side?" asked Stefan. "Their mother's or their father's?" Confusion passed over Tim's face before it slid into delight. There was only one side of the family, of course. He swiveled his head toward Mary, and said, with his brows raised, "What an *interesting* question."

Mary's gaze was unwavering. "My mother's," she said, before she turned, picked up a whisk, and, with quick rotations, began beating the eggs into yellow.

"Are you making *real* eggs?" Tim asked, angling his head to better see Mary's preparations. "Gail only uses fake eggs now. The real ones are supposed to be bad for you."

After they all ate their scrambled eggs and toast in a stiff silence broken only by the clank of fork to plate, Tim leaned back in his chair, resting his head against his laced hands. "So, Stefan," he said. "I'm dying to meet your parents." Then he smiled. "I've heard so much about them."

Eighteen

1983

I T WAS A TESTAMENT TO STEFAN'S UPBRINGING that he invited Tim to his parents' house that evening. *Mary and Hannah are coming. Why don't you join us?* And so, after sleeping most of the day, Tim rose in his rumpled clothes and rode with the Chase girls to the house on Northton Avenue. With his feet up on the dashboard of the Blazer, he wore a sneering, half-cocked smile as he watched the town pass.

When they arrived at the Kellys' and the car pulled into the driveway, Tim tilted his head thoughtfully as he regarded the beautiful stone house, which he had first seen the evening before. "I've got to hand it to you, Mary" was all he said.

Mary put the Blazer in park and let her shoulders round forward. "If you tell them anything, then we both lose," she said. The Kellys' finding out any of the number of truths that Tim could tell about Mary would mean that he wouldn't be able benefit from their benevolence either.

Tim's eyes narrowed in consideration. "I guess that depends," he said. "On whether or not we're playing the same game." Then he pulled the handle and got out of the car.

Mary, Hannah, and Tim made their way up the path to the Kellys'; it was early evening and the day had just spilled the last of its gold. Tim hung back as they reached the door. "Go ahead, Bunny," Mary said, nodding toward the bell, her voice carrying with it an inevitability. Hannah looked back at her, a worried expression on her face, before pressing it.

Martina answered and her eyes flitted nervously to Tim. Stefan would have warned her, of course. *He has some problems.* "Hello, sweetheart," she said to Mary, leaning in for a kiss on each cheek. "How are you feeling today?" Martina always smelled like perfume, her cheek always felt slick and smooth.

Mary managed a smile. "Better," she said. Then she stepped aside, directing Martina's attention to Tim. "This is my second cousin. Tim Dackard."

Tim extended his hand. "So nice to meet you," he said, his saccharine greeting just subtle enough to pass for sincere.

"You as well," she said, with a genteel nod, her hands clasped in front of her.

Martina led her guests back through the house through the kitchen. "So how long are you in town, Tim?" Martina asked.

"Dunno," replied Tim, his voice light and casual, his eyes running over the Kellys' things, everywhere but in front of him as he walked. "Could be a little while."

"Well," said Martina, managing a smile. "We certainly hope you enjoy it. Northton is so lovely this time of year."

As they reached the French doors to the deck, Martina turned around and again faced her guests.

"You have a lovely home," Tim said, with a polite smile. "Very elegant."

Martina clucked in gratitude, pleasantly surprised by his flash of manners. "Thank you," she said. "We certainly enjoy it."

"My mother prefers that whole nouveau thing," replied Tim. "Her place is very Barbie Dream House."

Martina glanced at Mary, not knowing how to respond, then pushed open the doors to the wide bluestone patio, where Stefan and his father were standing, beers in hand. "We have company!" she called.

Stefan strode over to greet Mary while Patrick appraised his guests, then followed his son more slowly. He tousled Hannah's hair, took his turn kissing Mary's cheek, then turned to Tim. "Patrick Kelly," he said, with his boardroom handshake, his sharp eye.

Tim, to his credit, didn't shrink from it. "Tim Dackard," he replied, one hand hooked across his side.

The group soon took their seats outside around a low-slung coffee table, and Martina brought out trays with beautiful hors d'oeuvres.

"Wow, this is gorgeous, Martina," Mary said.

"You would not believe how much food we had left over from last night," Martina replied. "The caterers are making me look good."

But Mary knew the effort that she was putting into the evening was a sign of her affection. They sat for a few moments, recounting the highlights from the evening before. *The band was exceptional. The florists did a wonderful job. And wasn't it nice that Gregory and Melissa Dunks made it?*

"So, Tim," said Patrick, slicing off a bit of blue cheese. "I hear you're up from Miami." Around them, the crickets trilled in a call and response.

Tim dunked a shrimp into cocktail sauce, then bit into it. "Yeah," he said, pushing the shrimp to one side of his mouth as he tossed its tail into a bowl. "My dad owns LubeTime."

"The oil-change chain?" asked Patrick.

"Yeah," he said. "Thirty minutes or your lube job's free." Tim rolled his eyes. "Totally crass, but that's sort of Ron." He then looked over at Mary, letting their eyes hang together. "Right, Mary?"

Mary smiled and let her gaze fall to the table. She leaned back and rested her head in her hand, her foot bouncing in front of her as if it were all a silly little joke.

In the periphery, she saw something flash on Patrick's face, whether suspicion or curiosity she could not say. "How many locations are they up to now?" Patrick leaned forward, his forearms resting on his knees.

Tim squinted with thought. "I think like forty-five or something. But most of those are franchises."

"How long ago did he start franchising?"

"Like forever ago. I think they're opening ten more in the next year."

Patrick's jaw moved, as if grinding the numbers. "Annual revenue well into eight figures?"

"Tim," interrupted Martina, with a good-natured smile, "you must forgive my husband. He is *obsessed* with business." Then she gave Patrick a sidelong glance, effectively calling him off his line of questioning.

Stefan stood and walked over to the ice bucket that was set on a nearby table. "Can I get anyone anything to drink?"

Tim raised his hand. "I'll take a beer," he said. Stefan and Martina exchanged a brief look before Stefan read the label of the bottle in his hand. "Sam Adams okay?"

Throughout the evening, Stefan seemed eager to find ways to remove himself from Tim's company, whether playing Frisbee with Hannah or manning the grill, but Mary stayed near until Martina said, "Mary, sweetie, can you help me bring some dishes out."

Mary smiled, her eyes catching Tim's. "Of course," she said.

In the kitchen, Martina pulled a foil-covered bowl from the fridge. "He is close to you, your cousin?" Martina asked.

Mary shook her head. "Our mothers used to be," she said, though Diane only ever felt jealousy toward Gail, never kinship. "But I don't know Tim very well. I'm sure Stefan told you that his visit was unexpected."

"Not in so many words, but . . ." Martina looked at Mary, her eyes soft and affectionate, as if she were her own daughter. "Well, we cannot choose our family, can we?" she asked. Turning back to the fridge, she took another bowl from a shelf and handed it to Mary. "Here, let's get a good meal in everyone's belly and then off to bed."

Mary glanced outside and saw Patrick and Tim facing each other, Tim's back to the house. The sun had sunk even farther in the sky, and Mary noticed how much darker it seemed as she looked out from the light of the bright, cool kitchen. Martina pushed open the door and let the humid night rush in, the air warming Mary's skin. And as Mary followed Martina back to the table and the meal and everything that was lovely, Tim's voice came like the cackle of a crow. "A flat *tire?*" he asked Patrick. And Patrick's shrewd eyes met Mary's for just a moment before Mary looked away.

Dinner was consumed in strained silence, Martina volleying the conversation to and fro between her family and guests, searching for subjects on which to engage and linger. *I do love Miami's architecture. When was the last time you were there, Patrick? Steffie, what is that restaurant with the crabs?*

When they finished the meal, the Kellys stood, walking their guests to the door together. Patrick stood at the threshold, his hands in his pockets, looking at Tim. "You know, I'd like to speak with your father," said Patrick. "About his business."

Tim smiled. "Among other things, I'm sure," he said. Mary's eyes snapped to Tim's. Tim held her gaze for a moment before turning back to Patrick. "It seems like you have a lot in common."

Stefan followed Mary home that night. He didn't say so, but Mary knew that he didn't want her alone with Tim. In the front seat of the Blazer, Tim stretched his legs, relaxing into what he assumed to be an imminent victory. She heard him chuckle quietly to himself. In the rearview mirror, Mary glanced at the headlights of Stefan's car behind them.

When they pulled up to the condo, Mary put the truck in park but made no move to leave her seat. "Bunny," she said, turning to her sister, "why don't you run back and get Stefan." Mary watched as Hannah walked on the streetlight-lit sidewalk to Stefan's parking space a few spots down. She was still watching her when she spoke. "All you've got are pictures, Tim," she said. Then she opened the door and closed it behind her. It was only much later that she thought perhaps she should have given him a chance to respond.

Mary didn't look at Tim again that night. Once inside, she put Hannah to bed, keeping Stefan close by her side. *Hannah loves when you read to her.* And so the three of them lay on the Chase girls' big white bed, Mary's head on Stefan's shoulder as he read a story about a stuffed rabbit that a child loved so much that it became real.

"Will you stay with me?" asked Hannah, when the story was over. "Until I fall asleep?"

She was asking only Mary, but Mary gripped Stefan's hand. "We'll stay with you," she said.

Mary waited until Hannah was asleep and Stefan's breath had started to go shallow, until his eyes closed and she heard the breath at the back of his throat. Until he was at the precipice of sleep but not over it. Then she extracted herself from her position, went to the bathroom, slid down on the tile — so bright white in the dark — and began to cry.

She thought of Diane, saw in slow motion her limp, unconscious body thrown forward at the moment of impact, saw the soundless shattering of glass. She thought of her grandfather, thought of the inside of his body, the empty black cavities the disease had eaten through. And the tears came quickly. She let them come without fight or restraint. Let them stream down her cheeks, finding their way into her mouth, her hair. She let the sobs break up through her chest, let them rip into the air. Until the bathroom door opened, and Stefan's face appeared.

"Oh, baby," he said. And in a moment, he was on the floor next to her.

As he pulled her into him, Mary climbed and clutched him as if she were drowning. His fingertips found the back of her head, her wild black hair. "What's wrong?"

She took a breath as if readying herself to speak, but only ragged breath came out, as if her grief stayed buried until it was needed.

"*Shhhh,*" Stefan said, his lips to her forehead. "It's okay. It's okay."

Mary swallowed, gasping, seeing her mother again and again.

"Mary, baby, what is it?"

She breathed in and out until she was steady enough to speak. "It's Tim," she finally said, moving her face back and forth against Stefan's shoulder, wiping her eyes.

She felt Stefan tense, protectively, reflexively. "What about him?"

"After I . . . After my mom died . . . I went to stay with Tim's parents." She paused, felt Stefan's hand slide down to her back, pull her closer. "Tim's dad . . . at first he just seemed so nice." She felt the broadness of Stefan's body, the constancy of it. "I thought he was just being sweet, you know? It was Christmas. He bought me and Hannah these necklaces. His wife went to bed and he offered me some wine." She felt her tears come again, genuine and true. "There are pictures, Stefan. Tim has them. He thinks . . . I don't know what he thinks, but I left the next day. I didn't know what to do. I don't know how it happened or why I let it. But now he says he's gonna show you the pictures. Show your family."

Stefan's hand made its way up and down Mary's back. *Shh-hhh. Shhhhh.*

Stefan stayed with Mary in the dark bathroom until her mind drifted into unconsciousness, where the line between what was real and what was not was a fluid, lovely thing.

She woke the next morning beside Hannah, the sheet pulled up to her waist. He must have carried her to bed. She got up and looked out the window. Stefan's car was still there, parked under a crab apple tree, its fruit growing red and heavy on its low-reaching branches.

Padding down the soft carpeted stairs, she expected to hear voices, confrontation, but she heard only quiet. In the kitchen, Stefan was alone at the table, drinking a cup of black coffee. When he saw her, he pushed his chair away from the table, the legs groaning over the floor, then he patted his lap. "Come here."

Mary went to him, her arms wrapped across her chest, her T-shirt slipping down over one shoulder. He wrapped his arms around her waist as she stood before him, resting his head against her smooth pale belly. "Don't worry," he said. "He's gone."

"What?" gasped Mary. "How?"

"I told him that he had to go."

Mary lowered her chin to her chest and squeezed her eyes tightly, feeling them grow wet, feeling her cheeks burn red. It was as close as Mary Chase came to mourning what she was. "I'm so sorry, Stefan."

"There's no reason to be sorry."

She lowered her head to his, brought her hand to the back of his neck. Stefan was goodness and righteousness. Stefan was the light to her dark.

"He's flying back to Miami in a couple of days. He's going to stay in a hotel by the airport until then."

"Where is he now?"

"A car came for him an hour ago."

Mary found Stefan's eyes. "Where's he getting the money?"

"Don't worry about that," he said.

Mary searched Stefan's face for a sign that he had seen the pictures. "Did he show you the . . ."

"No," he answered quickly.

And Mary became lightheaded with relief. "Thank you," she said, lowering her lips to his head, breathing the words into his hair.

They stayed like that for what felt like several minutes, Mary feeling the ebb of adrenaline, feeling the nearness of the escape. Tim was gone. She had outmaneuvered him. She and Hannah were safe.

And when her limbs could move again, she sat down beside Stefan and he poured her a cup of coffee. Hannah puttered down soon after, asking for orange juice. "I got it, Banana," Stefan said.

They watched cartoons that morning, the three of them on the couch, Mary and Stefan's eyes meeting over Hannah's head as she giggled. Outside the sun was bright and high and fearless.

"It's too beautiful," Mary said, her head resting against the back of the couch, her gaze rolling toward the window. "I'm going to go get ready. We should go do something."

And when she reached the top of the stairs, she looked behind her to see the door to the guest room where Tim had stayed—a white rectangle set against a white wall. She walked toward it, the carpet quieting her footsteps. Inside, the room was empty. The bed was made, the shade pulled up, the closet door closed. All signs of Tim were gone save for a white note folded and left atop the comforter. MARY was written on the front. Inside, it said only YOU'RE WRONG.

Nineteen
1983

OVER THE NEXT COUPLE OF DAYS, Mary felt Tim's presence in the periphery, lingering just out of sight. He was there when she was alone, as she unloaded the dishwasher, as she lay in bed awake, the words a whisper in her ear. *You're wrong.*

But what was she wrong about? She pressed Stefan for the details of their conversation, but he simply held her, brought her head to his chest. *Don't worry, Mare,* he said, though Mary couldn't see his eyes. And she knew Stefan's impression of her had started to fray around the edges.

It was five nights after Tim's departure that the phone rang. She looked at Stefan, who was lying on the couch reading. Hannah was asleep in bed. Stefan glanced up at her. The phone rarely rang in the condo; no one called Mary save for Stefan and Martina. Without a word, Mary stood, instinct making her alert, tensing her muscles. She went to the kitchen to take the call, stepping out on the deck and closing the door behind her. Pulling up the antenna on the handset, she answered. "Hello." She already knew it would be him, but for a moment, there was only silence. Until Mary's own voice spoke to her.

I'm at the B & M Diner. Right by the Miami Herald.
You're going to meet me here in three hours with ten
thousand dollars in cash.

It took her a moment to realize what she was listening to,
how it was possible that she was hearing her voice. Her mind
rewound rapidly, her life playing in reverse until she recalled
with cinematic clarity the phone call she made from the pay
phone on that street in Miami. She remembered Hannah's
face in the window of the diner, she remembered the morning
sun's heat against her skin, and she remembered the Dackard's
answering machine clicking on before Ron answered.

It was Tim's voice she heard next. "Remember that, Mary?
Gail plays it for Ron sometimes. When he's acting like a dick.
She wouldn't let me have it at first." He waited for a moment
for Mary to speak, but her voice had left her. "What's wrong?
Cat got your tongue?"

"I can get you money, Tim."

Tim snickered. "I don't need money, Mary."

"Your parents kicked you out."

"Ron doesn't call the shots anymore. I'm back in Miami.
Gail says hi."

Mary was silent. She could picture Tim's face, his thin-
lipped sneer.

"Anyway, I'm going to give Patrick a call tomorrow. He gave
me his number, remember? So my dad could call him about his
company." Tim was smart to go directly to Patrick. He knew
that Stefan could be manipulated by Mary. But not his father.

"Tim—"

"And you thought all I had was pictures." His voice was
venom when he spoke again. "You thought you were so fucking smart, Mary. You thought you had everyone fooled. I knew
the whole time what you were doing. I knew the whole fucking time. I was watching you, Mary. I was *watching* you." And

whether he was there or not, Mary pictured Tim crouched outside Ron Dackard's office that night, peering through the slit in the doorway. "Everyone's gonna know what you are," he said.

Then the phone went dead.

She stood outside for several minutes staring at the empty illuminated decks of her neighbors against the indigo sky, their duplicative sameness like a hall of mirrors. She felt her heartbeat start to quicken, her breath turn shallow as she looked at them. There was no variation in their presentation, no exit. No egress. The Kellys would know what she had done. Tim had won. By the time she went back inside, that certitude had burrowed inside her like ice into rock — a trickle finding its way into a fissure then expanding.

In the living room, Stefan was still on the couch. "Who was that?" he asked, a book on his chest, the room illuminated only by the lamp beside him.

She looked at him for a moment, at the solidity of his form, then she crawled on top of him, rising up the length of his body on the couch. "That was nobody," she answered. "Just someone selling something." He dropped the book to the floor and moved his hand to her lower back.

Mary angled her head to look at his face. "Stef," she said. "Can we go to the boat tomorrow?"

Stefan's hand slid up Mary's back into the tangle of her hair. "Sure. We can do that."

"Let's go all day. Let's go early then spend the night."

"We can do that," he said, not understanding what he was saying. Not knowing what would come next.

Twenty
1983

THE SUN HADN'T YET REACHED CENTER SKY when the Blazer beat over the crushed gravel of the long road that led to the marina. The truck crested a hill and the ocean burst into view, its waters dotted with white boats, its shoreline anchored with tastefully grand homes.

"Look at how pretty it is here," said Mary, as her eyes lingered over the sapphire blue bay, her elbow resting on the open window. She felt the sun on her skin, felt it warming her hair. "It's like a fairy tale."

Mary slid the Blazer into the spot next to Stefan's and looked out through the windshield. Stefan was on the boat already, his feet moving nimbly over the vessel as he prepared for a day at sea. He lifted his hand and waved at the girls, and Mary gave him a radiant flash of a smile, raising her slender arm in the air to return the gesture. Then she turned to Hannah. "Come on," she said. "It's going to be such a pretty day."

She walked around to the back of the Blazer and opened the tailgate, pulling out a small tote bag that sat next to large overstuffed black duffel bag whose presence was like a vacuum, something with the power to devour. She wondered when Tim would call Patrick. The onslaught of the truths would be like relentless waves, knocking and knocking and knocking her down the moment she found her feet to stand back up.

"Hannah Banana!" she heard Stefan call from the boat. "I need some help over here!"

Mary slammed the tailgate, letting her fingers linger on the metal. "Go help him, Bunny," she urged.

If there was a day made for sailing, it was this one. The wind blew steady and sure from a cloudless sky. Mary closed her eyes and turned her face toward the sun, feeling the spray from the shimmering sea as the boat charged through it. And she realized how much she relished this distance from land. How much she loved the boundlessness of water.

"If I died today, I would die happy," said Mary, her eyes still closed, the skin of her bare back sticking against the cushion of the seat.

In front of her, Stefan stood at the wheel. "Don't say that, Mare."

"I'm just saying that I love this." She opened her eyes and reached for him, the flash of his figure against the sea and sun.

Stefan looked back at her, then his eyes moved to Hannah. "You think you can be the captain for a second, Banana?"

Hannah stood and cautiously made her way up to Stefan. "Here you go," he said, holding the wheel steady as she put her hands on it. "Just like that. Nothing to it."

Stefan sat down next to Mary, keeping his eyes on Hannah as the thrill of being at the helm of a boat turned her face to sunlight as she glanced back to Mary and Stefan to make sure they were watching her.

They stayed at sea until the sun started to sink below the sky, throwing its arms up into pools of color. The boat slid into its slip just as the last bit of light was wrung from the day. That night, the three of them sat with their legs splayed open on the bow of the boat, eating bread and cheese and tomatoes and green beans, snapping off the tops and throwing them into the water. Stefan opened up the lid of his red cooler, tossing Hannah a Coke and Mary a beer. "Can I have a soda instead?" asked Mary, as she passed it back.

And when the sky was an inky blue, Mary and Hannah lay with their heads on Stefan's stomach as they looked up at the pavé stars.

"You can see why humans used to believe in deities," said Stefan.

"Used to?" said Mary. She remembered driving through those small southern towns, watching women in pastel dresses and men in light gray suits funnel into morning services, fanning themselves with the photocopied program while greeting one another. "Lots of people still do," said Mary.

"What's a deity?" asked Hannah.

Mary rolled her head toward Hannah and found her eyes. "A god," she said. "Something all-powerful." Mary shifted, brought her hands beneath her cheek.

Stefan and Mary waited until Hannah was asleep in the berth, wrapped inside a thin towel in the cool evening air, before they laid a blanket below them and had sex under the stars, their bodies moving and churning like the sea, their breaths like waves. And when they were finished, Stefan's fingers ran through strands of Mary's hair as they talked about a past and future that didn't exist. Mary would start taking classes at the state university in the fall. She'd study art. They'd spend Christmas in Paris. Mary loved it there. She had been once.

And when Stefan drifted into easy sleep, his back against the hard boat, his head resting on a foam cushion, Mary stood up, her body bare under the moon. She walked to the railing of the boat and rested her forearms against it, staring at the dead-calm water, at the boats that swayed silently in the night. And she thought about what lay before her and what lay behind. She thought about the road and the ruin. Then she walked back over to Stefan and pulled on his shorts, rolling them over and over again at the waist until they held, feeling the weight of his wallet against her hip. And she pulled on his T-shirt, breathing in his scent as it passed her nose. Then, with silent steps, she descended the stairs below deck. For a moment, all she did was look at her sister.

"Bunny," she finally whispered, squeezing her sister's toes. *"Bunny."*

And Hannah sat up, one eye open, one eye still stuck with sleep. "What?" came Hannah's quiet, disoriented voice.

Mary let out a low shush. *"Shhhh . . .* We have to be so quiet, Bunny."

"What is it?"

"We have to go," said Mary, her voice as low and smooth as a horizon.

"Why?"

Mary extended her arm to Hannah. "It's time."

Hannah blinked and let her gaze fall to the sheet. Then she looked back to Mary. "Is Stefan going to come?" she asked.

The sisters' gazes hung together like garland. "Not yet," Mary finally answered. "But he'll meet us soon." She then extended her hand out to Hannah. "Come on."

The girls walked silently from the boat, the rock of the boat hiding their footsteps, the night a cloak of cover. Neither spoke a word as they went, but Hannah slowed as she passed Stefan and looked down on him as if she were passing a casket.

Mary took the step from boat to dock first, then she turned to reach across for Hannah. "You're such a good girl," said Mary, as she helped her down. "Such a good girl." Then Mary bent down so that her eyes met Hannah's. "Go to the truck," she said, with a smile, her black hair blending into the dark, the moon behind her head like a crown. Then she held out the keys and dropped them into Hannah's hand. "Start it up. I'll meet you there."

Mary watched as Hannah headed for the Blazer, her small tired feet shuffling along the dock. Then Mary turned back to the boat and, with a swift, elegant pull, was back on board. From the pocket of the shorts she was wearing, she pulled Stefan's wallet, removed eighty dollars in cash, then dropped it on the deck beside his feet. Then she dropped to her knees and, with careful, graceful movements, crawled over his body.

When her mouth was above his, she breathed his name. *Stefan.* His eyes opened and she smiled.

"Hey, baby," he said, bringing his hand to her back, letting it rub up and down the thin T-shirt that he didn't realize was his.

"I need you to do something for me." she said.

He looked at her. *"Hmmm?"* he asked, his mind still thick with sleep.

"There's a letter in the bottom of your bag," she said. "You have to read it." Mary watched as consciousness started to fill Stefan's eyes. "And no matter what else you hear about me, know that what it says is true." She took his hand, then released it just as quickly. "I'll call you soon. I promise."

Stefan started to sit up, but Mary's movements were too quick, too stealthy. By the time he stood, she was off the boat. By the time he was off the boat, she was in the Blazer. She heard her name echo through the dark. *Mary!*

She flipped on the headlights, and Stefan's form became flooded in light. Her eyes met his through the vast night between them for just a moment before she jerked the truck into reverse, the tires spitting rocks in their haste. And as she pulled quickly away from the marina, looking only once in the rear-view mirror, she said to Hannah, "Hey, Bunny, why don't you try to fall back asleep, okay?"

Twenty-one
1983

MARY DROVE QUICKLY THAT NIGHT, feeling the comfort of the vibrations as the truck raced over smooth black roads like a horse lunging south. The dashboard glowed with its soft light, and Hannah was asleep beside her, her head on Mary's lap. Mary drove for twenty-four hours straight, from night into day into night again, radio stations coming in and then fading out as she crossed the territory of their signals. When she or Hannah had to go to the bathroom, she'd pull to the side of the road, and they'd squat next to the car, watching the streams of urine pool on the asphalt between their feet. And when they were hungry, they'd find a gas station or a diner or a drive-through. And the hours that passed on that trip felt like something other than measures of time. Each was a decade. Each was an instant. Each seemed to take them somewhere more profound than down the road.

They reached Bardavista just before midnight. And as they crossed the endless bridge that connected the barrier island to the mainland, Mary stared out to the black water looking for the glow of shrimp boats as they floated, their trawlers extended out like wings.

They took the single-lane road as far as they could. When they reached Ft. Rillieux, Mary put the truck in park and shut off the engine. If a vehicle could collapse from exhaustion, the Blazer would have. It would have gasped out a final roar and rolled on its side.

"We're here," said Mary.

Hannah lifted her head from her sister's lap and sat up. She could only make out the curve of the dunes, the swaying strands of seagrass. "Where?"

Mary smiled and looked at her sister. "The end of the earth." She then gently poked Hannah's rib. "Come on," she said. "Let's sleep on the beach."

Hannah crossed her arms over her chest. "How?" she asked, the word short and challenging. "We don't have anything to sleep on."

Again, Mary smiled. "Yes, we do."

The large black duffel contained their sleeping bags, their tent, and little else. Mary pitched it in the dark, her fingers running down the lengths of pole, finding the channels in the fabric as if from muscle memory. Hannah stood with her sleeping bag clutched to her chest as she watched Mary complete the setup.

"Remember when we bought this?" asked Mary, offering the memory a small sad smile.

Hannah nodded. "Before the swamp," she said.

"That swamp's not too far," she said. Then she nodded toward the Gulf, only apparent through the steady metronomic beat of its waves. "Remember how we threw the flowers into the water here?" she asked. "For Mom?"

Hannah looked out in the dark toward the sea, but not at it, saying nothing. And Mary's fingers paused their work while she watched her. "This is where you were born, Bunny."

"I don't remember it."

As soon as the tent was up, the girls crawled inside wordlessly, laying their sleeping bags on the sides they always slept on. As the wind lapped the tent with warm humid air, their bodies instinctively curved into each other. And Mary found a depth of sleep she had never known before and would never know again.

It wouldn't be until the next day that she would think about Northton, and everything that must have occurred there since she left. She would think of Stefan, crouched down in the berth, reading her letter with a flashlight over and over again until he felt like a madman, until he felt insane. Tim would make his revelations, and everything Stefan thought he knew about Mary would become inverted and twisted. But Mary hoped that Stefan would recognize the truth in her letter. That somehow he had known it all along.

Mary Chase bided her time in Bardavista, which was where she had become accustomed to biding her time. Two weeks after the Blazer had first sped over the bridge, she finally reached Stefan. She called him from a pay phone at a gas station illuminated by overhead streetlights. Standing barefoot, she watched the sand sweep over the black asphalt of the parking lot. It was night and the air had cooled. She had tried him several times already, spacing her calls by a day or so, hanging up when it was Martina or Patrick who answered. And that night, she sunk her quarters into the slot one after another. On the third ring, she heard his voice. She stilled at the sound of it.

"Stef, it's me."

He took a breath. "Mary?"

"There are things that I can explain, Stefan," she said, feeling the weight of all she had borne since Diane had died. "I need you to meet me."

She tried to picture him, his arm slung across his chest, his eyes closed as he fought away her memory. "Where are you?" he asked.

She looked at Hannah, who was asleep in the front seat, her mouth slightly open, her skin tanned from their ceaseless summer. "I'm far away, Stef." She took a breath. "But there's a place. We can talk there." And when she named it, he said not a word. "Next Tuesday. One week from today."

"Next Tuesday," he said. Then she heard him take a breath before hanging up the phone, as if each word cost him something dear.

Twenty-two

1983

T HE CHASE GIRLS ARRIVED at the Tammahuskee in late evening, cooking hot dogs on one of the camp-ground's grills as they listened to the family in the neighboring site sing songs in a circle as dusk bled like ink in the sky. Hannah talked in her sleep that night, muttering some concern—acute but incomprehensible—while Mary drew in the dark, her eyes finding enough light to see the black lines of her pen in the margins of the park's photocopied map. And as the sun first lifted above the cragged horizon, bleeding red over the water-covered earth, Mary, whose eyes had closed only briefly that night, turned to Hannah, her sleeping face vacant, her curls looking like they were coated with sea spray. "We'll see if he comes," she said toward Hannah's sleeping face.

Hannah made a gasping inhale and rolled her head away from Mary's words, as if she were being doused with water. Then she blinked, letting her eyes orient to the dim light in the tent.

"Morning, Bunny," Mary said.

Hannah rolled to face her, moving her tongue inside her

mouth. "Where are we going?" And Mary saw that Hannah's familiarity with leaving had returned, had perhaps never left.

"There are these trees," said Mary. "They're famous. But you have to take a boat there."

Hannah managed to summon a disdain that was beyond her years. "We're going to take a boat to go see *trees?*"

"They're called the Shrouded Trees."

Hannah rolled her eyes. "That sounds stupid."

"Bunny?" said Mary. "Only stupid people say *stupid.*"

Mary had read about the Shrouded Trees when she and Hannah were last in the Tammahuskee. They made up a grove of oaks that circled the perimeter of a small island in the middle of the swamp, their roots digging down so deep that they extended like fingers into the earth, gripping it and holding on, bracing themselves against wind and storm. From their branches dripped long dust-gray swaths of soft Spanish moss. "Anyway. People go there just to see the trees. There are tour boats that take people there like every half an hour."

Mary had planned it out carefully, knowing about the boats when she called Stefan, remembering them from last time. They departed on the hour, and Mary always imagined them like those slender vessels that ferried beings across the River Styx. On that island, she would be guaranteed enough time to plead her case before the boats once again boarded their passengers and slowly paddled back out into those silent dead-calm waters. On that island, the world would be reduced to a small circle of earth. On that island, she could make Stefan see that all that mattered was her and him. And Bunny.

Hannah and Mary took an early boat that they shared with an elderly couple whose eyes lifted heavenward as they smiled and looked for some of the swamp's rare birds. Their guide was a man who wordlessly worked the oars with smooth, clean strokes, his muscled ebony-colored arms well practiced. His eyes didn't settle easily on their destination but remained alert and vigilant, darting to any movement around them.

Mary stared at him as he paddled. "What's your name?" she asked, when she had his eye.

He let go of one oar and, pointing to his ear, shook his head. He was deaf.

From her jacket pocket, Mary pulled out her clear plastic pen, the end of which was broken off, leaving the ink tube exposed. On her hand, she wrote her name, *Mary*, and she held it up for him to see. He nodded once and Mary gestured toward Hannah, who had been half watching their exchange, half pretending not to. *Hannah*, Mary wrote.

The old birdwatchers had now noticed the silent conversation, and Mary saw elbows press into sides as they looked at the girls and the man, and smiled.

"He's deaf," Mary said. "So I was telling him our names."

The older woman pressed her hand to her chest and smiled. "I'm Ethel," she said, then looked at the deaf man and mouthed her name, as if the absence of sound would somehow bring clarity.

"Here," Mary said, handing her the pen. "You can write it."

And so on their mottled hands they wrote *Ethel* and *Joseph*, the names lifted up and offered to their guide. Finally, he nodded toward the pen and Mary handed it to him. Their guide once again let go of the oar and, with a slow and steady hand, wrote *John*, the ink nearly disappearing into his brown skin, before handing the pen back to Mary.

As they approached the island, John's stroke became more nuanced, as he turned the paddle and let it cut through the water in beautiful sibilant curves. The canoe slid up tightly against the small dock that ran from the island, neither bumping it nor giving it any undue space. And with a turn of the paddle, the boat stopped.

John hopped off the canoe first, standing on the dock and

extending his hand to help Ethel and Joseph off, then Hannah, and finally Mary.

"Thank you, John," she said, meeting his eye. Hannah stood waiting, but her eyes were on the trees. Even in the swamp, she had never seen anything like them before. She couldn't have. John gave Mary a respectful nod before she took Hannah's hand and followed Ethel and Joseph onto the island. Halfway down the dock, Mary looked over her shoulder and saw that John, with one foot in the boat, one on land, was still looking at her. And not the way that men normally did. Not with lust or longing or disbelief. But with concern. Each of his hands formed what looked like a peace sign and he stacked one on top of the other and moved them in circles toward his body. Mary knew it must be sign language, but she didn't know what it meant. When she turned, the end of the dock was nearly upon her and she heard herself gasp as she stopped short to avoid falling. One day, she would find herself in a small town inside a vast state. She would see a small girl nearly step onto the street, her eyes lifted toward a solitary cloud. "Careful!" her mother would say, while making that same motion. *Careful.*

"Watch your step, girls," said Ethel, looking over her shoulder as Mary, then Hannah, stepped onto land.

"This is so cool," whispered Hannah, as she looked up at the giant oaks that stood like cobweb-covered sentinels in an almost perfect circle around the island.

With their clasped hands, Mary tapped Hannah's side. "I knew you'd like it," she said.

For the first hour, Mary and Hannah walked around the island, looking up at the giant oaks and finding a unique and finite world underneath each of them. Moss hung from their branches to the ground, so that Mary felt like a child hiding underneath the skirt of some regal gown-clad mother.

In the center of the trees was a clearing, and Mary understood that this was where tour guides would begin their lecture on the history of the Shrouded Trees. The trees were brought in as saplings and planted on the island during the early days of the Underground Railroad by a group of free blacks who hoped to provide escaped slaves with some protective cover so they could make it north to a more organized network. Those who knew about the island said the trees grew quickly there, quicker than they would have naturally, as if the oaks knew they had to link their great arms together in protection. It was said that they reached a height of eighty feet in fifteen years, rather than in forty. That the moss was thicker and longer than on any other trees in the swamp. That the trees helped to provide shelter and rest to thousands of souls, warding off not only search parties but also gators and bears and all manner of threats. It was said that no harm came to anyone on the Island of the Shrouded Trees.

"Let's watch the boats come in," Mary said to Hannah.

Hannah reached for Mary's hand. "I want to walk around more," she said.

"Okay," replied Mary, as she lowered herself onto the earth. "I'll be right here."

Hannah's brows drew together as she looked at Mary. It seemed the freedom that Hannah increasingly longed for wasn't quite so appealing when offered on Mary's terms. She hesitated for a moment, and then she wordlessly set off, looking back over her shoulder at Mary as she did so.

As Hannah began her tentative exploration, Mary leaned back on her elbows and waited for new boats to glide steadily toward the island. It wasn't long before Hannah rejoined her, before she wordlessly took her place again next to her sister. And so together they sat studying the faces on each boat as they arrived, though Hannah didn't understand why.

"Did you know Princess Hannah and Princess Mary were once lost in a swamp?"

Hannah turned toward her sister. "They were?"

Mary nodded. "Not a swamp like this one. It was a cursed swamp. The water seeped poison, and the princesses had to cover their mouths with their skirts. And even then they were gagging and coughing; the air was so terrible they couldn't breathe."

"How did they get out?"

"Well," started Mary, her voice transitioning into storytelling mode. And she spoke of the magical creature who lived there. Who was as black as night, but whose eyes glowed white. "He found the girls near death," said Mary. "But he lifted them with his mouth, then tossed them onto his back and *raced* them to his underground lair."

"Could they breathe there?"

"Yes," said Mary, her eyes focused on another boat that was now visible on the still waters. "But not until he placed his mouth over theirs and breathed fresh air into their lungs."

"And then they were okay?"

"Well," replied Mary, with a tilt of her head. "Then they could *breathe*."

"Did he take them out of the swamp?"

"He couldn't leave the swamp. If he did, he would die. But he put them on his back again and raced them to its edge, and then lowered his head and let the princesses slide down his neck onto the ground. They rolled back and forth coughing and gagging from not having been able to breathe on the ride out of the swamp, but once the fresh air entered their lungs, they were fine."

"What was the creature's name?" asked Hannah.

Though her head remained static, Mary's eyes lifted slightly as if the answer were written in the air above her. "I don't know," she mused, her voice lifting with curiosity.

At noon, Mary pulled out two sandwiches she had packed, and the girls ate them under one of the trees, taking shelter from the bright, high sun, but Mary kept her eyes toward the dock.

"Who are you looking for?" asked Hannah.

Mary hadn't realized Hannah had been paying such close attention. "No one, Bunny," she said. "I'm just watching the boats."

And as the sun started to lean toward the west, Mary noticed the glances from the tour guides who were now on their tenth recitation of the history of the Shrouded Trees. Hannah was growing restless; John had guided his canoe back and forth a total of six times now.

"Are we going to go back soon?" she asked.

Mary unscrewed the top of their canvas-covered canteen, took a deep draw of water. "Soon," she said, as she offered the bottle to Hannah.

Hannah's body heaved with protest, but all she said was "I'm gonna go walk around again" before she pushed herself up off the ground.

Mary watched until the last of the boats arrived. It was late in the afternoon, and the tours stopped running at four. A small family arrived — a mother and father and two sons. But no one else was with them. Stefan hadn't come.

Mary stared at the sun feeling it burn her eyes, seeing it blur her vision as the eclipse of its heat made her see only light. She hadn't realized how much of her believed that he would be there until he wasn't. She remembered the way the words had felt coming from her lips, the receiver slick in her hand. *The Island of Shrouded Trees in the Tammahuskee Swamp.*

Mary knew that if Stefan didn't come, then what she had told him, what she had written down in black and white, what she had spilled on that page like blood, was taken for a lie. And Mary vowed, for the second time, to never speak of it again.

The girls were quiet on the canoe ride back, Hannah from fatigue that was physical, from the hours spent in the sun. And

Mary from the exhausting hours of waiting and watching and feeling hope recede further away with each boat.

They rode back from the island in silence, the heavy orange sun beginning to sink in the sky. The canoe docked, and John extended his hand, helping Mary back onto land. Though Mary took it, she couldn't meet his eyes. And as the Chase girls walked back to the Blazer, Mary opened her mouth to speak, but the words stayed deep. She closed her mouth and tried again. "Just so you know," she said. "If when you're older and you wonder, I wanted Stefan to meet us here."

Hannah looked up. "I know," she said.

Mary stopped, dust from the dry dirt forming clouds around her feet. "How did you know?"

Hannah looked at her and gave a small shrug, her eyes sad and wise. "I just did."

Twenty-three

1977

THE DOOR WAS OPEN, the hall light all that breached the darkness of Mary's room, when Diane's form appeared at the threshold. "Mary," she barked, her voice hoarse. She cinched her robe tighter around her waist as she squinted at her daughter. "What are you doing with her?"

On her bed, Mary lay on her stomach. Beside her was Hannah, whose small hand gripped Mary's finger as her legs kicked excitedly at the air. Mary was looking at Hannah's tiny fingernails, at her tiny knuckles, marveling at the perfection in miniature. "She woke up," said Mary, her gaze unmoved.

"No, no, no," said Diane, shaking her head. "It's a *school* night." She took a steadying breath, her face lined and exhausted, then she stepped into the room. "You shouldn't be waking up with her," she said, as she bent down and slid her hands between the shiny bedspread and the baby's small body. "That's my job. You have a math test tomorrow." Diane brought Hannah to her chest, and Mary finally looked at her mother.

"You don't hear her right away."

Hannah started to cry and Diane brought her upright, holding the back of her head as she began to bounce and shush. "No baby needs to be picked up the second she wakes up. She'll be fine if she has to fuss for a bit," scolded Diane. "She might even go back to sleep."

Hannah's cries escalated with the new upright position.

"She doesn't like to bounce," said Mary.

Diane's shoulder slumped, exhausted. "Mary," she started slowly. "This is just . . ." She stared at Mary for a moment, deciding how much to reveal. "Look, I know that you've been skipping out on school to come home, telling the nurse you don't feel well. Mrs. Pool said you were home before noon yesterday and you went right in to get the baby."

"I know everything they're teaching. I don't need to be in class."

"But you do need to be a kid," retorted Diane. "You don't hang out with your girlfriends. You just come home and hold Hannah!"

"Because I *want* to," said Mary, her body tense, her black hair falling over her shoulders.

"Mary, I'm sorry," she said. "But you don't get long to be young. God knows, I didn't. And I swore to myself that Hannah wouldn't be your responsibility."

"You wanted me to love her."

"Yes. I wanted you to love her. I didn't want you to live for her," she said. "I didn't want you to have to."

Mary and her mother looked at each other until Diane began to nod. "We're going to have to figure this out," she said, her hand still on the back of Hannah's head.

"What do you mean?"

"I mean maybe Mrs. Pool will have to start watching Hannah at her house. Or maybe we could even find a day care. But we need to make sure you're not neglecting school. You can't just play baby doll, Mare."

Mary felt rage surge inside her like a wave, but she revealed none of it. "Fine," she said. And if Diane hadn't been so very tired, if she hadn't been running the motel and raising two daughters, if she hadn't been working part-time at the casino to help make ends meet, she might have seen a warning in Mary's easy surrender.

"I'm going to bring Hannah back to my room. And if she wakes up again, just let her be. We can talk more about this tomorrow." And with that, light from the hall filled the space where Diane had been, then the door closed and Hannah's cries became muffled.

Mary had already decided what she would do by the time she heard Diane's door close, though she lay on her bed for another half hour, her muscles stone-still. Hannah's cries dwindled then ceased, and when only the silence of sleep was in the air did Mary get up and begin her preparations. Many of Hannah's clothes were already in her room, ferreted away from Diane's and tucked neatly into drawers. There was a stack of diapers on her dresser, and the stroller was in the office. It had started to rain earlier, and Mary saw the fat drops hit the glass of her window then slide down, leaving their glistening trails.

She turned her backpack upside down and let her schoolbooks fall out of it, let them lay splayed and contorted on the floor. Then she began to fill it with what they would need. She pulled up a corner of the carpet in the closet, lifted out the $263 that she had kept there, and slid it into the back pocket of her jeans. Then she took a coat—the one that had been her grandfather's—from a hanger and pulled it on. It nearly came to her knees, but it was warm and thick, and water beaded on its heavy canvas fabric and then ran right off. She took a baby blanket from her bed and rolled it tightly, cinching it with a shoelace, and then she hooked it to her belt, where it would stay dry under the jacket. She put on the backpack that was filled with clothes and diapers, leaving enough room for the formula and bottles that she would get in the kitchen.

The stroller was in a closet off of the office and Mary set it up, unfolding it quietly, straightening the bar between the wheels. When everything was ready, she went to Diane's room. She cracked the door only slightly at first, peering at her mother who was lying above the covers, her bathrobe still on, her arms crossed over her chest as her head lolled back. Her mouth was open and her breath sounded wet and thick. Mary opened the door just wide enough to slip through, then she walked silently and quickly to Hannah's crib and leaned over.

Hannah was awake and on her back and looking at the mobile that hung above her bed. She grabbed her feet, covered with the pink flowers of her onesie. When she saw Mary, she smiled.

"Hi, Bunny," Mary whispered, beaming back at her.

Then she reached down, scooped her up, and was out the door before any sound could disrupt Diane's leaden sleep.

"We're going on a trip," she cooed, as she held Hannah tightly against her chest. "Just you and me."

In the office, she set Hannah into the stroller and fastened the straps. Then she unlocked the door, propped it open with her hand, and wheeled Hannah out. The cold rain hit Mary's face immediately, and she blinked against it, adjusting the cover to the stroller to shield Hannah. "Don't worry," she said, her voice gentle as she tucked a thick blanket around her. "It's just rain."

With her hood up, Mary lowered her head against the wind as she walked, charging down the sidewalk without looking up. She saw the blinding brightness of headlights as cars approached, heard the splash of their tires against the wet street as they passed. It was a little more than a mile to the bus station. There would be a bus leaving just after one in the morning.

Mary walked quickly, and the calves of her jeans were soon soaked with water, making them stiff and cold. She thought about where she would go, what she would say once they were in the city. There were shelters, Mary knew. She could say they needed help. She could say that they had no place else to go.

When they were halfway there, Hannah started crying and Mary stopped the stroller, lifted her sister out, then zipped her into the inside of her coat, where she held her with one hand, pushing the stroller with the other. And against the dry warmth of Mary's chest, Hannah found comfort.

They arrived at the bus station with less than an hour to spare, and Mary unzipped her jacket and lifted Hannah out as she looked around for a bathroom; she needed paper towels to dry off the stroller. The yellow cinder-block walls were made yellower still from the humming glow of the fluorescent lights overhead, and faded posters of destinations hung crookedly. Sedona. Las Vegas. Miami. After they got to the city, they could go anywhere. Mary caught the ticket agent's eye through the Plexiglas he sat behind.

"Is the 1:05 on time?" she called. The few other passengers waiting for the bus looked up as they sat on plastic chairs that were bolted to fixed metal bars.

He nodded, regarding Mary from behind his spectacles.

"Where's the bathroom?" she asked.

Without a word, he pointed toward the hallway that ran parallel to his perch.

"Thanks," Mary said, as she started toward it. "We're going to get everything nice and dry," she whispered to Hannah. "So that you can just sleep on the bus."

In the bathroom, Mary took a paper towel and rubbed it over her wet face. She took another and wiped down the vinyl of the stroller while balancing Hannah on her hip. Then she walked back out to the waiting room and up to the clerk.

"One," she said, reaching into her back pocket. "For the 1:05." Then she tilted her head toward Hannah, adjusting her weight to better balance her. "Plus a child."

"Child's free," said the clerk, as he licked his finger and reached toward a stack of tickets.

Mary took one of the many empty seats and put Hannah on her lap facing her. She brought Hannah's hands to her cheeks and smiled, feeling her cool fingers on her face. Then she clapped Hannah's hands together. *Patty cake, patty cake, baker's man.*

She would miss Diane, of course. She did love her mother. But Diane was condemned by the effort she put into raising Mary. By her desperate tactics. By the threats and punishments leveraged to try to rein in a willful and wild daughter. Diane was condemned by being a mother. But Hannah . . . Mary loved Hannah boundlessly.

"We can pretend we're princesses," whispered Mary, bringing her nose to Hannah's. "Whose castle and fortune were stolen. We can pretend we used to dress in silk and diamonds."

The station's waiting room all but emptied when the bus boarded. The driver helped Mary stow the stroller in the under-bus compartment, then Mary took the black rubber-treaded steps up. She took a seat at the very back of the bus next to the bathroom, watching the other passengers settle in, watching them let their heads sink back. Both the girls slept on the way into the city, Mary's head resting against the cool glass of the window, Hannah's body warm on her chest. The bus's interior was dim and quiet, and the roads were empty as they glided over the interstate, the speed bringing Mary peace.

Mary and Hannah were the last to disembark at the terminal, to make their way down the bus's long center aisle. They were the last to see the two police officers waiting at the bottom of the steps, one of them lifting his radio the moment his eyes made contact with Mary's.

It wasn't long after the bus first set off that Diane had woken up. And after thirty minutes of searching on foot, she had called the police. Mary was memorable and so she was easy to find. The clerk at the ticket window had given her up before the bus had even reached the turnpike.

Diane would meet them at the police station, still in her robe as she sat in the waiting room, her hair still wet at the roots from walking around in the rain. Mary would meet her eyes and Diane would bring her hands to her face and she'd weep—huge aching sobs shaking her shoulders. And Mary would want to go to her, but she'd resist and she'd hold Hannah tightly until her mother looked up at her and with swollen eyes, nod. *Fine,* she'd say. *Fine.*

Soon after, Diane would switch her shift at the casino from afternoons to nights. She'd spend the day with Hannah at the motel, then she'd turn her over to Mary, kiss them both on the forehead, and leave.

Twenty-four
1989

WHAT CAME AFTER MARY AND HANNAH left the swamp that second time was this: years. Vast expanses of time that sped by like the flat empty land where they were spent. They passed those many days in the middle of the country, in towns that rose up out of the yellow horizon like islands, isolated and hours from the next.

As Mary drove between those towns, she used to watch the storms gather in the sky, their opaque gray clouds churning, bending earth and air toward them. They called them twisters in those parts.

The girls would stay in a town for two months or maybe three. Mary would find temporary work washing dishes or cleaning rooms or doing whatever work for whichever business needed an extra hand. Sometimes Mary would take money for other things. She wouldn't talk about what those were, but neither was she ashamed of them. The things she did to survive were automatic, reflexive, and once they were done, they were no more than dust in her tracks.

She liked the Midwestern boys, with their awestruck professions of love, with their earnest, down-on-one-knee senti-mentality. She liked their pale backs and strong tanned arms. She liked their simple minds. She always chose the docile ones. The tame ones. The ones who would do anything for her. Or, rather, she let them choose her. Mary's instincts were keen enough to steer clear of the ones with dark eyes and matching hungers. When she encountered one of those, it was time to leave.

Mary marveled at how many towns there were in this swath of the country, how many that seemed just alike. It was a safe place for her to have Hannah. The authorities didn't bother much with truancy, and their homeschooling laws were lax to nonexistent. These were places were kids grew up work-ing on farms, not sitting in classrooms. But Mary was diligent about Hannah's schooling, and they would often spend their evenings scratching out equations or reading whatever Mary could find. She taught Hannah algebra by the time she was eight. They'd find owl pellets in fields and dissect them, orga-nizing and identifying the rodent bones. And at night they'd sit together reading the same page in the same novel, Mary waiting for Hannah to finish before she went on to the next.

Hannah grew up during those years. Grew taller and leaner, her fledging breasts just starting to become visible under her T-shirts. Her sense of privacy blossoming with her body. They were staying in a trailer in an RV park where Mary was help-ing out for the summer when Mary opened the bathroom door without knocking.

"Hey!" Hannah yelled, bumping her hip against the open door, but not before Mary saw her pull her shirt down. Hannah had been looking at herself in the mirror.

"Bunny," scolded Mary. "*Relax.* It's not like I've never seen boobs before."

Hannah pushed her way out of the bathroom, mumbling something unintelligible and storming out of the trailer.

"Pretty mature!" Mary called after her, the door clanging, then swinging wide open. "Keep acting like that, and those boobs are going to crawl right back up into your chest!"

She watched the back of Hannah's form as she stomped over the dry dirt, then Mary went back into the bathroom.

"Jesus," she moaned, when she saw the state of it. Her makeup was spread all over the counter and her razor was in the sink still covered with shaving cream. "It's not like you have any hair yet!" she called to the sister who couldn't hear her. "Come on, Bunny," she muttered to herself, rinsing the razor clean. Hannah had been getting into her things more and more, slicking on lipstick and splashing on the Jean Naté that some boy had bought her in some town.

They'd be leaving the park in the morning. Mary hadn't yet told the owners, but the tourist season was nearly over; there was no longer any reason for them to keep her around. After she cleaned up the bathroom, she began packing. She had done it so many times and they had so wonderfully little, it was a mechanical act. They had clothes and shoes, they had sleeping bags and coats. Mary had makeup, a hairdryer, and some books that she kept. Hannah had Barbies and some stuffed animals. Their lives were containable and transportable. Home wasn't a place.

When their backpacks were packed and fully zipped, Mary set them beside the thin metal door of the trailer, then went to go find Hannah.

It had been a dry summer so the grass was sparse—ragged yellowing clusters holding to the dry dirt. The park was starting to clear out, only cinder blocks and bare earth marking the spots vacated by the summer people's RVs. Mary wondered if there was a place on the planet that didn't have summer people.

She walked to the small aboveground pool where she could usually find Hannah, taking the steps up to the wooden platform. Helen was in the water. Helen came up from outside Oklahoma City every summer. All day long, she'd glide from one end of the pool to the other like some huge pelagic mammal. "You looking for your sister, honey?" she asked, drawing closer to Mary like a surfacing walrus.

Mary nodded, then she brought her hand to rub the back of her scalp. It had been hot in the trailer. "Have you seen her?"

Helen reached the edge of the pool by Mary's feet, turned and pushed off again, her pale thighs powering her off the wall. "I saw her walk by a little while ago," she called behind her. "She was walking toward the fields."

"Thanks," said Mary. She paused before heading back down the steps. "Have a good swim," she called behind her.

"You, too, honey," replied Helen, as she absent-mindedly dunked underneath the water.

The park was surrounded by thousands of acres of slender green stalks of corn. Mary and Hannah had walked in those fields a few times, their eyes following the lines of the plants up toward the blue sky above, knowing that they were concealed by the terrestrial. In another month or so, the combine harvesters would descend on that land like massive churning beasts, leaving nothing but yellow ankle-high husks.

When Mary reached the field, she walked along its edge. Hannah was mad at her, as she had been more often lately. There were some kids at the park Hannah had become friends with. They would leave together when Mary started work and run in a pack all day long. Mary would see them at the pool, she'd see them at the playground, she'd see them sitting on the ground by the shady side of the trailer, their backs in the dirt, their heads on one another's bellies. It was Hannah, another girl, and a boy. Hannah, Kim, and Shawn. Kim had left a week ago and Shawn, just the other day. The night he left, Mary had lain next to Hannah in bed and listened to her crying and fiercely wiping her eyes in the dark, letting out only nearly inaudible high-pitched whines. That was when Mary decided it was time to go, time to push on to the next place.

It was getting close to suppertime, and Mary turned around and headed back to the park; Hannah would be getting hungry soon. She pushed open the door to the trailer, feeling the tinned warmth hit her. They kept the windows open, but the late afternoon was always insufferable. "Bunny!" she called from the threshold, not wanting to go inside. In reply, there was only silence. But on the floor, just beside the door in a neat little parallel, sat Hannah's dingy white canvas sneakers. "Bunny, I know you're home," called Mary, kicking off her own shoes, feeling the dampness of her soles. "I see your Keds!"

There was no real answer, but from the bedroom, Mary heard a muffled cry of frustration. It was just like Hannah to go to the trouble of hiding only to reveal herself with orderliness.

Mary pushed into the bedroom, and her eyes scanned the empty room. "Where are you?" she asked.

From below the bed where Mary and Hannah's sleeping bags lay, Mary heard Hannah's voice. "I'm not leaving."

"Bunny, come out from under there."

"*No.*"

"Bunny . . . ," Mary started. Then she got down on her belly and lay on the floor next to Hannah. With her hand in between her cheek and the worn industrial carpet, Mary looked at her sister. Hannah was facedown, resting her forehead against the back of her hand. Mary looked at the chipped and faded pink nail polish on Hannah's fingers. Hannah had picked out the color earlier in the summer, and Mary had painted them for her. "Why are you hiding?"

"I'm not leaving tomorrow. I don't want to go."

"Summer's done," said Mary, her voice gentle. "Everyone's leaving here soon. Your friends are already gone. Kim and Shawn are gone. There's no reason to stay, Bunny."

Mary watched the side of Hannah's face redden, watched her eyes tighten, listened to a high, steady whine come from the back of her throat. "Kim and Shawn *had* to go," she said, her words an accusation. "They had to go to *school*."

"Bunny, what are you saying? You want to stay here and go to school with the eight farm kids who live here all year long? You want to live in an unheated trailer this winter?"

Hannah sniffed and rubbed her eyes hard against her hand. "No," she said, her face still down. "I want to go to a school like the one I used to go to."

Northton, on the few occasions it came up, was never mentioned by name. "We can't go back there," Mary said.

Hannah finally turned to face her, the whites of her eyes shot with red, her lashes slick and moist. "Why?" she asked.

"We just can't."

And Hannah turned back to the floor. "I knew you'd say that."

For a long time, the Chase sisters lay next to each other in silence, Hannah under the bed, Mary on the floor beside it. They lay there as the sun began to sink, until the light through the window was yellow gold, until their hair was wet with sweat. They lay there as all the towns and all the time and all the boys since they left Northton took their turn in Mary's mind. They lay there until Hannah spoke, her voice weak. "I don't want to drive anymore, Mary."

Mary reached under the bed and put her hand on the back of Hannah's head, feeling her damp curls, feeling the dip at the base of her skull. "I know, Bunny," she said. "We don't have to anymore. This'll be the last time. I'm gonna find some place better for us. Some place where we can stay."

The next morning, they drove for hours before they reached the interstate, through endless stretches of corn that covered the Midwest like a landlocked sea. The only signs of humanity came by way of the occasional silo or farmhouse, silhouettes against the early-morning sky. They didn't talk during the first stretch of that drive. And as Mary let her head rest against the seatback, she thought of the infinity of miles she had traveled in that truck. The Blazer that was still running due to minor miracles and boys who knew how to rebuild engines and change timing belts. Its passenger's-side door didn't open anymore, rust had eaten away a small hole in the floor of the truck bed, and the exterior was spray-painted a matte black, but the Blazer still ran.

Next to Mary sat Hannah, slowly eating a donut from a box, picking off one piece at a time.

"What kind is that?" asked Mary, though she could see it was chocolate glazed. She just wanted Hannah to talk.

"*Chocolate,*" answered Hannah, as she stared out the window, her forehead against the glass.

"Pass me one."

Hannah's limbs suddenly seemed leaden, and the effort of retrieving the box of donuts from her feet, taking one out, and extending it toward Mary seemed calculated to look tremendous.

"Thanks," replied Mary. She took a bite, a large green sign for the interstate coming into view. "The highway's coming up soon," she said, her mouth half-full.

"So?" grumbled Hannah.

"I just thought maybe you'd want to know where we were going."

Arms over her chest, Hannah looked out through the passenger's-side window. And not for the first time, Mary tried to divine her sister's features. To determine which parts of her came from whom. She listened to the car's tires thud against the road, waiting to see if Hannah would take the bait. Waiting to see if Hannah would ask. But Hannah remained silent.

And when the on-ramp for the highway came and the Blazer curved smoothly to the right, Hannah immediately looked at Mary.

"West?" she asked.

Mary smiled and nodded. "We're going to Utah," said Mary. "We're converting to Mormonism. We'll learn how to make Jell-O molds."

Hannah shook her head and gave an artful roll of her eyes. "Seriously, Mary."

Mary chuckled, her hands on the wheel. "Alright, Bunny," she said, her voice quiet. "We're going to California."

"California?" asked Hannah, a smile forming at the corners of her mouth. "Where in California?"

"A town up north. Right on the ocean. There's a famous hotel there."

"And we're going to *stay* there?" Hannah asked, her words a test.

Mary nodded. "Yeah, Bunny. We are."

"And I'm going to go to *school*."

"You're going to go to school." Mary felt the rhythmic bumps of the road underneath her tires. "But you know, since you haven't been in a while, you have to start over again in kindergarten."

"Shut up, Mare," said Hannah, with her arms crossed over her chest, but the smile was still on her face. Throughout all of their travels, the Chase girls had never been to California. Mary extended her arm out to her sister who knew nothing so well as the curve of Mary's side. And after a reluctant moment, Hannah folded into it, resting her head on Mary's shoulder.

THE GIRLS DROVE ALL DAY UNTIL the land started to hint at the massive mountains that broke out of the earth in the distance, hiding behind the cloak of cloud and sky. They ate donuts and unwrapped American cheese singles, sandwiching them between slices of white bread. When they had to go to the bathroom, they'd pull off to the side and squat next to the Blazer with the door open.

"*Shit,*" Mary said, as she peered down at the slick red-brown oval staining the lavender cotton of her panties. She hung on to the door handle with one hand for balance.

"What's wrong?" Hannah asked.

"Pass me down my purse."

Hannah reached for the beat-up bronzed leather bag that Mary had carried forever. Since Miami. Since before. "What's wrong?"

"I got my period."

Mary saw Hannah cock her head inquisitively and crane her neck to better see her squatting sister, the curiosity of the uninitiated. "Just give me the bag, Bunny," Mary snapped, and Hannah quickly passed it down, then faced straight ahead, her cheeks flushed. As Mary reached inside and pulled out a thick maxi pad, fixing it over the stain, she realized that while there was little she hid from Hannah there was also little she fully explained. Mary pulled her jeans up and stood in one swift motion, then she got back in the truck, and staring at Hannah's profile, she pulled the door shut. "Sorry," she said. "I just didn't want to sit there bleeding everywhere."

After many, many more miles, Mary nodded to a sign. "Look," she said.

Hannah followed the direction of her sister's attention. "What's the Continental Divide?" she asked.

The last time they had crossed it, that great spine where the earth heaved up and split North America, Hannah had been much younger. The West was outside of Mary's natural range. "It's a line," said Mary. "Of mountains. On one side, everything leads to the Atlantic. On the other, everything leads to the Pacific."

"You mean all the rivers and streams and stuff?"

That divide always seemed profound to Mary, something with a significance greater than hydrological. "I mean everything."

Hannah looked at the land around them, and Mary suddenly wished that they were taking the high road, the difficult road. The road with the grand views and dramatic vistas. They were passing through the Great Basin, where the mountains bowed away, letting high arid land create the pass the early settlers used to travel when the country was untamed and loosely mapped. She imagined the white curves of their covered wagons like gaping mouths, a visible symbol of their propensity for hardship and error.

Mary leaned forward so her fingers touched the glass of the windshield as the Blazer sped past the sign. "Crossed it first," she said, smiling at her sister.

But Hannah looked at Mary as if she were getting too old for these games. "So we're going to the Pacific?" she asked.

Mary nodded. "Yeah, Bunny," she said.

After the sun bled out into the enormous sky, after its color was leached by night, after a star-speckled blanket replaced all that was above them, after Mary's eyelids began to feel weighted, the Chase girls pulled off the interstate and found the warm lights of a small motel set near the side of the road.

Mary stretched her arms, pushing against the resistance of the fixed steering wheel. "I'm glad we're stopping," she said. "I think I need a bed."

Hannah looked at the sign, with its movable black letters advertising the room rate. "Thirty-nine dollars a night," she said, her voice hopeful. "That's not bad." Hannah always preferred motels to camping and knew the disappointment of pulling back out of the parking lot when Mary deemed an establishment too expensive.

Mary felt a yawn overtake her words. "Yeah," she said, talking through an open mouth. "It's not too bad."

In the room, Mary dropped her backpack onto the floor just inside the door. "I'm taking a shower," she said. "I feel disgusting."

Hannah followed her in and more gingerly placed her own bag at the foot of the double bed. "I'll have a bath when you're done."

Mary turned on the water and let it run hot for several minutes as she sat on the toilet naked, the still water below. She let the room become hot, let her skin start to bead with sweat, then she drew back the vinyl curtain and stepped over the wall of the tub into the water's stream. Mary always luxuriated in showers like this, in warm water washing over her body in a place that was someplace other than where she had been that morning. It felt like a baptism. A rebirth that could happen again and again.

She drew her hand between her legs and washed herself clean, rubbing her hands over a slick wet bar of peach-hued soap, then letting them slide up and down her body, under her arms, up to her neck.

When she turned off the water, her fingertips were wrinkled and white. She turned her head upside down and dried it roughly with a thin white towel, put on a fresh pair of underwear, hand-washed the stained ones in the sink, then she opened the door and left the bright bathroom in a cloud of steam. Hannah was sitting on their bed, her back against the pillows, her knees angled up, and a notebook in her lap.

"Whatcha doin'?" asked Mary, as she reached into her bag and pulled out a T-shirt, putting it on over her head, the ends of her hair saturating its fabric.

Hannah didn't raise her head. "Writing a letter." The dim lamp beside her cast a wan yellow light through the room.

"To who?"

Hannah took a breath, annoyed either by the interruption or her inability to put words to page. "Shawn," she said.

"You miss him," Mary said, trying to mask her surprise as fact. There was only one boy Mary missed after he was gone. As she looked at Hannah, as she thought of how the childish lilt had left her voice, of how her pink pilled T-shirt stretched across her chest. And Mary felt a panicked urgency to better arm her sister for womanhood, to find out just how mature she had become. She sat on the edge of the bed.

"Is he the first boy you've liked like this?"

Hannah gave her an annoyed glance. "I never said I *liked* him," she mumbled, her gaze again on her letter. And Mary saw her flush.

"But you do."

Her brows tight, Hannah stared at her notebook.

Mary's voice was soft when she spoke. "You know about sex, right?"

"Geeze, Mary!" said Hannah, angrily closing her notebook. "Don't be disgusting!"

"It's important, Bunny."

Hannah grunted and, with her notebook clutched to her chest, made for the bathroom. *"I don't want to talk about this!"* The door slammed behind her.

Mary waited a moment. "Bunny," she called. When only silence met her, she rose and walked toward the thin, hollow bathroom door. "Bunny," she said again, her hand trying the knob, feeling it halt.

"I need privacy!"

Mary paused for a moment, looking at the blurred lights of the parking lot beyond the drawn ruffled curtain. "Mom never really told me about sex." She felt herself smile. "I think she was scared that she'd give me ideas. But we all want what we want, Bunny. We're all just animals, really." She felt Hannah's attention beyond their divide. "Just make sure you tell me before you do it. There's some stuff you need to do. To be safe."

And though Hannah didn't respond, though she wouldn't

come out of the bathroom until Mary was under the covers and the television was yammering in the background, Mary knew by Hannah's inability to meet her eye that she had heard her.

THE CHASE GIRLS STAYED THE NEXT MORNING until it was time to check out, lying on the bed and basking in the infinitude of being nowhere. The motel served Saran-Wrapped Danish, hard-boiled eggs, and oranges for breakfast, and Mary and Hannah ate them in their room, Hannah feeling the optimism of going somewhere, Mary feeling the relief of having left. The Chase girls were always happiest in those brief moments of in-between, when neither of them was sacrificing, neither of them being sacrificed.

When it was time to go, Mary stopped at the front desk.

"Enjoy your stay?" asked the woman who sat there. She had round features and a gap between her front teeth. She wore her thin blond hair pulled half back on her head and didn't look up from her book as she spoke.

"Yeah," replied Mary, setting the key in front of her, the room number written in masking tape and affixed to a brown plastic disc on a chain. "This is a nice place."

With their late start, Mary knew that she would have to drive into the night, and so when they stopped for gas that evening, Mary bought a large coffee, pouring it from a discolored glass carafe into a Styrofoam cup. She felt a man at the beer case staring at her.

"Thirsty?" he asked. She turned to face him. He was rat shaped, with thin limbs and a plump torso. His hair was long in the back. She could see that he had an erection, and he shifted his weight as he looked at her, his hand still holding open the glass door of the cooler.

"No, just tired," she said. "My medication makes me sleepy." It took all of her will to keep her face impassive.

"What kind of medication is that," he said, wanting to find the salacious in any and all details.

"My antipsychotics. I just got out of a mental institution." She waited for the statement to register on his face. Then she jutted her head forward, bared her teeth, and hissed — a wide-eyed, wet-fanged, unrestrained feline hiss.

"Jesus," he muttered, as he skittered away, glancing over his shoulder as he hurried out the door, leaving Mary to pour the cream into her coffee, smiling as she stirred.

As Mary walked back out to the truck, she looked around. All along the interstate, there were places like this, brightly lit truck stops with rows of gas pumps and glassy-eyed clerks who didn't look up as they counted out your change. "You should put your seat down," Mary told Hannah, as she got back in the Blazer. "Get some sleep."

"Aren't we gonna stop?"

"I think we should keep driving," she said, as she turned over the engine, set the gearshift into reverse, then rested her arm over the seat as she looked behind her. "We're making good time."

After another hour or so, Mary saw Hannah's eyes start to slip shut as the wide flat road skated by mountains that were shadows at the edge of the dark. Mary was looking at them, trying to make out their detail when up ahead she saw a figure slinking next to the road, four legged, black bodied, in relief against the night. She took a quick breath and sat up straighter just as it stopped and turned. Yellow eyes to yellow eyes, it looked at Mary, and just as quickly, the truck sped past; Mary looked in her rearview mirror, and it was gone.

"Bunny, did you see that?" Mary asked, without thinking; asked through quickened breath.

"What?" said Hannah.

"That animal," she said, with less urgency, questioning now whether she should have mentioned it at all.

"What was it?" asked Hannah sleepily, adjusting herself in her seat and curling to her right.

"I don't know," said Mary. "It might have been nothing."

Mary did drive all night, reaching the coast and following it south while Hannah snored lightly next to her. She drove on a road that hugged the line of earth and sea, curving where it curved, turning where it turned. Mary felt the pleasant weariness of travel in her arms as one hand loosely held the steering wheel, her left foot lodged up against the dashboard. Driving was now as reflexive and unconscious as breathing, its motions and demands were no more or less great than those of her own body.

She had passed through small sleeping towns, their windows lidded and black, and stretches of narrow road elevated above a dark ocean. She rolled her window down so she could hear it, the water's rhythmic churning. And as she let her hand slide through the thick night air, as she played with its resistance, she felt a dreamlike smile take her face; it had been a long time since she had been near the ocean.

When the sun first reached over from the east, it cast a yellow light on the water, drawing up droplets of the Pacific with its magnetic warmth. And it was through that mist that Mary first saw it. Her foot lifted reflexively from the gas, and the Blazer glided with the road. It was a grand old hotel, set on a bluff, looking both elegant and otherworldly, both of the moment and of the past, like a place from a tale. Like a place that might be home. And though Mary would later question her memory of that moment, whether the bath of golden light was a sleepless hallucination, at the time, it seemed like the Chase girls' own private manifest destiny.

Mary pulled onto the shoulder of the road. "Bunny, look," said Mary, resting her hand on the back of her sleeping sister's head. "There it is."

Jostled, Hannah opened one eye with a sharp breath and

downturned mouth. But as soon as Hannah's eyes found it, she stilled.

"It's pretty, isn't it?" asked Mary. Hannah, of course, didn't know why Mary had chosen this hotel. Hannah, of course, didn't understand its significance.

Hannah still only looked, blinking her way into lucidity.

Mary reached across and pressed a button, releasing the glove compartment, and pulled out a camera. The girls rarely used it since film and developing were so expensive.

"Smile," she said. And before Hannah could object, with her face innocent and lovely and fresh with sleep, Mary took her photograph, the hotel in the background. In a couple of weeks, the film would be developed. And Mary would stare at the photograph in a way that she sometimes did with pictures of Hannah. Then she'd do what she had done a dozen times over the past few years. She'd put it in an envelope, seal it shut, and write out an address she knew by heart. Because time could testify for what Mary couldn't. And anyone could see how much Hannah looked like her father.

Twenty-five

1976

A T FIRST, MARY DECIDED NOT to think about it. She decided to tightly fold up the facts in her head again and again. Mary could do that. Mary could lock away parts of her mind, of her heart. Mary could hide things.

But sometimes she'd lie in bed and stare up at her ceiling and listen to Diane laughing with Barry in the bedroom across the hall. And she'd let her mind unfurl itself, the inconceivable future spread out for her examination.

It was summer. The Water's Edge had paying guests. And Diane was in love. Or seemed to be. She was dressing nicely. She was dabbing drops of perfume behind her ears. She was pulling the loosening skin of her face taut and looking in the mirror.

Mary was out of school and spent her time helping her mother around the motel. Or, more often, not. More often, she'd walk down long stretches of beach, past where the tourists sat, with their umbrellas and coolers and distended flesh. She'd walk to the point where the beach became a state park that no one went to, where the dunes were roped off to protect the nesting sites of tiny shore birds that rushed the sand as the waves retreated and hurried back to the grass when they advanced. Mary would sit and watch them, holding still enough that they stopped avoiding her, that they didn't widen their berth as they went back to the safety of the blades. Mary would sit and watch them until they no longer realized she was there.

Once, without thinking, Mary grabbed one. Her hand moving independently of her mind, she took the little bird. Bringing her nose near its beak, she looked into its black eyes, which didn't register terror, as she might have expected them to. At first, the bird held still, then its legs bicycled around, and it let out a peep. "You have to be careful," she said. Then she set it gently back onto the sand, and with a fury of flutters, it was gone. "Now you have a good story," she said, over her shoulder.

She felt different; she knew she did. But it wasn't in any way she might have expected. She wasn't retching into the toilet in the morning. She wasn't suddenly craving pickles. Instead, she was simply hungry. Hungry and so tired that she'd fall asleep on the sand, her limbs angled out around her, her black hair hot from the sun.

"Were you at the beach all day?" Diane would ask, inspecting the red hue to her skin, the bloom of tiny freckles on her nose.

"Yeah," Mary would reply, letting her bag drop on the floor. "I went for a walk."

Diane would stop and square her hand to her hip. "Well, I needed some help getting the rooms cleaned up for check-in!"

Mary would roll her eyes. She'd walk right past Diane.

"Don't you think *I'd* like to spend *my* days at the beach?" And Mary would start down the hallway to her room. "You really are a piece of work, Mary Catherine Chase!" Diane would call after her. Adding, when she heard Mary's door shut, "What would your grandfather think, huh?"

If Mary knew that she was pregnant, it was an abstract

understanding. She wasn't panicked. Not really. The boy was coming back. He'd told her so. He'd return in the fall just as the winds changed and the earth was leached of green. He'd sail over the sapphire sea in his white boat. He'd come right to her. They'd whisper their plans, and she'd leave that night, her black hair waving in a sky as dark as pitch.

The day Mr. Pool had a huge catch of albacore at the trenches off the coast, Alice called over to the Water's Edge. Mary was lying in bed, pressing her hands into her belly, feeling the taut roundness that was forming there, pushing it from side to side, up and down. As if she could prove that it wasn't part of her. That it was something alien. Diane appeared in her doorway, her arms crossed in front of her. One of Mary's hands casually flattened against the plane of her belly; the other slid toward the book that lay beside her. But Diane hadn't noticed anything. Diane was looking at Mary's face.

"You have any plans tonight?" she asked. It was early evening, and she had her hair in rollers. Mary assumed that Barry was coming over, as he often did to spend time with Diane. She couldn't leave the Water's Edge, not really. Not in the summer.

Mary didn't look up. "No," she said, her knees angled up, her back against her pillow.

"No friends you want to see? Allison hasn't come over in a while."

"She's babysitting for the O'Nearys," Mary said, though she hadn't spoken with Allison in months. She turned to angle her back toward Diane, her open book in her hands.

"Well, Mrs. Pool just called," Diane finally said. "She said Stan got a bunch of tuna and the charter group he was with didn't want it. She's putting it up tonight. Wanted to know if we wanted some."

"Do we?"

"You like tuna," responded Diane. "I like tuna."

Mary remained silent.

"It's probably going to take Alice all night to get that fish canned. I'm sure she'd love some help."

Mary carefully folded down the corner of her page, running her finger along the crease. She knew that Diane was worried about her, was wondering why her teenage daughter slept all day and went for walks alone, why she didn't see her friends. Why she seemed to be putting on weight. "Okay," Mary said. She liked helping Mrs. Pool in her pale-blue kitchen. She liked the amicable silence. "I'll go over." And the relief on Diane's face was undisguised.

The processing was already underway by the time Mary arrived. She stepped into the warm humid kitchen, letting the screen door clatter shut behind her. Mrs. Pool was hunched over the white stove, the coil burner below the pressure canner glowing red. On the small kitchen table lined with newspapers were mountains of pink flesh, slick and shiny, and the fan overhead cast its whirling shadow around the room.

Mary stepped up beside Mrs. Pool. Without saying a word, she rested her hand on Mary's back and smiled.

"Mom said you needed some help."

"More like some company," she said. It was the great tragedy of Alice Pool's life that she could never have children and the great grace of Diane's, for it was the childlessness of the Pool household that created a void the Chase girls helped to fill.

"What should I do?"

Alice tilted her head toward the piles of fish behind them. "You can get it into jars. Get it ready." In a box on the floor were clean mason jars. On the table, a small cutting board and a knife.

Mary pulled out the chair and sat down. "Are you going to can all of it?"

"I think so," said Mrs. Pool, as she peered down at the gauge on her cooker.

"How full should I make them?"

"You can pack it right up to the bottom thread," Mrs. Pool replied. "Just get it into chunks first."

Mary took one of the large hunks of meat. It was still cool and smelled only of seawater. Then she brought her knife against it, and with an elegant stroke, the meat was severed in half. Mary didn't mind this kind of work. When she was younger, she used to go out with Mr. Pool on the boat, and he'd taught her to run a blade along a fish's spine, to remove all the bones and innards with a few deft slices.

They worked for more than an hour before either of them uttered a word. If Mary appreciated one thing about Alice Pool, it was her ability to stay quiet. When Mary was alone with Diane, Diane was on a constant quest for information. *How is math going? Is Angie Barclay's mother feeling better? Have you seen Kathy lately? Ann? Laura?* But Alice Pool didn't ask questions. Alice Pool just quietly hummed.

When she finally did speak, it was a statement. "Stan says that the Japs eat fish raw." Her voice was distant and light, as if lifting to meet a passing thought. "They don't even cook it first."

"Why?" asked Mary.

"Beats me," said Mrs. Pool. "They've got some funny ideas."

And with Mrs. Pool's back to her, Mary made a clean slice of fish and plucked it up with her fingertips. She brought it close to her face and turned it from one side to the other for inspection. Then she passed it through her lips whole and let it fill her mouth. She bit down and felt its cool, firm resistance. As she watched Mrs. Pool — the soft roundness of her shoulders, the dromedary droop of her neck — Mary felt the lovely slow-release pleasure of hiding something.

"Didn't Mr. Pool used to live over there?" Mary finally asked. Mary knew the answer but wanted to hear it again all the same. Though no one was aware of it, Mary had looked through Mr. Pool's photo albums, seen the picture of him in his sand-colored uniform, read the bundle of yellowed letters written by his parents, and by a young, besotted Alice.

"Mmm-hmm," replied Mrs. Pool. "After the war. He was stationed in Okinawa."

Mary had found Japan on a map, run her finger along the crescent nation. "I want to go there," she said. "Someday."

Without looking up, Mrs. Pool chuckled.

Mary and Mrs. Pool canned more than a hundred pounds of tuna that evening, enough to line the pantry shelves with a winter's worth of fish.

And after the last batch had been put into the pot, after Mary gathered up the wet piles of newsprint and brought them to the metal garbage can in the shed, she walked back to the kitchen and let the screen door again clatter shut behind her. She watched Mrs. Pool for a moment. "I guess I'll go," she said.

Mrs. Pool turned around and stepped toward Mary, pulling her into a hug. And perhaps it was the weariness from the hours of canning that made Mary forget. Or perhaps it was that Mrs. Pool's embrace came so naturally, without the shifting, cautious hesitation that had started to precede all of Diane's. But when Mrs. Pool rested her hand on Mary's back, when she gently pulled Mary's body into her own, that round hardness that had formed so insistently in her belly made its presence known—an orb between them. And before Mary could react, before she could sliver away, Alice Pool gave a small but certain gasp, then pulled back. With her hands on Mary's shoulders, Alice's frightened eyes probed Mary's.

"Well," said Mary, her face registering neither acknowledgment nor guilt. "I better get home." And she pushed out the door into the night. Mary didn't look back as she walked across the scrubby grass to the Water's Edge, but if she had, she would have seen Mrs. Pool standing on the brick walk watching her, her apron still on, moths circling the bright beam of the floodlight above.

Glancing briefly through the glass of the door to the Water's Edge office, Mary saw Diane and Barry sitting on the couch, white containers of Chinese takeout in front of them. The television was on, and Diane's foot was under the coffee table, rubbing Barry's ankle.

The bell of the door clanged when Mary pushed it open.

Diane straightened up, nudging Barry, whose eyes had been fixed on the television. "Hi, honey!" she said. "How'd it go with Alice?"

Mary assessed the spread of food in front of them. She was hungry. She was always hungry now. "Good. We're finished."

Diane clucked in amazement. "That's great. Right, Bare?"

Barry nodded. "Yeah, nice job," he muttered, before turning back to the television.

"Okay, well," said Mary, with a stony calm. "Good night."

"Night, hon!" called Diane.

And that night, as Mary walked back to her room, she knew it was all just a matter of time. That, really, it always was. Because, though Alice Pool had no children of her own, she would know the meaning of what she had felt in Mary's stomach. She had felt it before. She had been the first one to know about Diane, too.

Twenty-six
1989

T HE HOTEL BY THE OCEAN was called Sea Cliff. She had been familiar with it for some time. When she was little and her grandfather was still alive, he'd show her pictures of grand old hotels, images he'd clipped from magazines of venerated establishments, places that hosted royalty, movie stars. *Princess Grace stayed here*, he'd say. Or *They made a movie with Cary Grant at this one.* And Mary would sit on his blue-polyester-clad lap and stare at the pictures, at the colors that looked so bright they couldn't be real. And the girl who loved stories understood that hotels were their repository.

But she knew of Sea Cliff from elsewhere.

So after she and Hannah had first seen Sea Cliff, they drove to a beach nearby and parked the Blazer by the side of the road. With a blanket wrapped around her, Mary walked down the old wooden stairs to the sand. It felt cooler down by the water by a few degrees.

"I like it here," said Hannah, as she stared at the shore birds diving and calling overhead.

Mary blinked. The morning sun on the water made everything look faded, pastel. "Yeah," she said, her head nodding to one side with fatigue from the drive. "I knew you would."

Mary lay down and she slept, the sand working its way into her black hair. And Hannah walked knee-deep into the water, letting the frigid, foamy surf swirl around her legs, feeling it rock her back as it spilled onto the shore, then watching the sand change under her feet as the Pacific took another great breath in.

When Mary had dozed away enough of the drive, she sat up with red-rimmed eyes closed against the light. "We need to get some food," she said, to the air around her, having no knowledge of exactly where Hannah stood, only knowing that she was near. She was always near.

"We passed a place," answered Hannah. "It looked like a bakery."

"Are you hungry?" asked Mary.

Hannah watched as a ship moved slowly along the ink-blue horizon line. "Yeah," she said, reluctant to leave the water. "I guess so."

The Chase girls climbed the wooden stairs back to the street and drove to the bakery. Outside, they sat on the curb and ate their cinnamon buns, taking huge mouthfuls, not pausing to breathe or speak. Finally, Mary said, her mouth full of pastry, "I'm going to go to the hotel and get a job."

"Do you think they'll hire you?" asked Hannah. She was watching the cars pass, trying to hide just how much she wanted to stay there, in the town by the sea, where the sun sank rather than rose over the ocean.

"I don't know," said Mary. But right down to her bones, Mary knew that they would. Mary sensed some finality here, in this town. Some inevitability. A lovely trap, the door locked tightly. "But I bet they will. Hotels always do."

And when she walked into Sea Cliff and asked to speak with

someone about a position, she was ushered to a small conference room and offered a seat. As if her hair wasn't matted and sandy. As if she wasn't wearing the clothes she had put on the morning before. Human resources would be right with her, she was told.

And human resources arrived in the form of a portly man as pale as a poached chicken with thinning drab blond hair. He squeezed himself into the seat across from Mary, the thick of his thighs pressing against the arms of the chair.

"Bob Kossel," he said, extending his hand.

Mary took it, feeling its damp warmth. "Mary Chase," she said.

And the interview began.

"So have you worked in hotels, Ms. Chase?"

Mary gave him a solar grin. "All my life."

And she went on to tell him about the storied East Coast hotel she had grown up in, the one that had closed last year, the one her father had managed.

"Well," he said, his voice as wobbly as a top. He looked over what appeared to be a schedule, pushing his glasses up his nose. He was a man to whom things happened. A man whose choices were made for him. "I guess you came at the right time. Half the staff just went back to college."

"That's fantastic!"

"It's a front-desk position."

"Great!"

"Yeah, well . . ." He gave her a wagging finger—an attempt at authority. "You'll have to start with the night shift. The girl who works it now has been waiting to move to days."

Mary's smile came slow and genuine. "The night shift is perfect," she said.

Bob looked at her, his suspicion piqued. No one wanted the night shift. Not ever.

"I have a sister," Mary said. "She lives with me. I can sleep while she's at school."

THE GIRLS FOUND AN APARTMENT above a Laundromat in a building behind the town's grocery store. The landlord met them at the property the afternoon that Mary got her job at Sea Cliff. He watched Mary as she walked through the space, her hands clasped behind her.

"So utilities are included?" she asked.

"Gas, water, and electric. You have to pay for the phone. And cable if you get it."

Mary paid the first month's rent and deposit in cash. She'd done pretty well that summer and had managed to save a bit.

It was a small one-bedroom, smaller than even the trailer she and Hannah had lived in, but it was clean, or smelled so at least, with the warm scented air wafting up from the enormous metal driers that churned and spun all hours of the day. It would get hot, Mary knew, in the summer. But they had arrived in early fall, when fog rolled in from the sea and settled into the valleys, sapping the heat out of the nights.

Their first evening there, Hannah kneeled by the front window and peered out. She looked down to the metal slot through which the postman would slide their mail, down to the doorway that led to the stairs, down to the Dumpster, where they were told they would put their trash. "I like it," she said.

Mary sat down on the carpet behind her, but she didn't say a word, she just watched Hannah, watched her face become illuminated with the headlights of passing cars. And that night the Chase girls pulled their sleeping bags out once again and set them on the floor. They opened the windows wide, trying to lure in the ocean air. And as they lay beside each other, Mary spun her finger through one of Hannah's curls.

"It's going to be tight for a while," she said, feeling the beginnings of sleep start to spread through her body like a thin layer of ice on water. "Until I get paid."

Hannah nodded. She understood.

"And I'm going to have to be at work while you're sleeping at night. But I'll be home early. Before you leave for school."

Without seeing Hannah's face, Mary knew that joy had spread across it. And when Hannah spoke, her words galloped with anticipation. "Do you think the school here will have lockers?"

"Probably," said Mary. "Mine did."

Hannah inhaled. "That's so awesome," she whispered, the words rushing back out.

"We'll call the school tomorrow. I'll find out when you can start."

Then Hannah rolled onto her side and curled into Mary, laying one arm over her sister. She buried her face into Mary's sleeping bag, and her words were muffled when she said, "Thanks, Mare."

The next morning, from a pay phone in front of the grocery store, Mary called the local middle school. She had to speak with three different people and wait on hold for several minutes before the principal got on the line to talk about Hannah and her *situation*, as it was termed.

"And she's had no formal schooling?" His voice crackled over the line; the receiver felt slick in Mary's hand.

Mary leaned against the glass wall of the phone booth. "No, she *has*," she said. "She went to kindergarten. Since then, I've been teaching her myself."

There was silence on the line. "Well, she'll need to take placement exams so we can find the right spot for her."

"When?" Mary asked. "When can you do the exams?"

The placement exams were to be administered in a few days. The girls spent the rest of the day doing what little they could with the money they had. They bought some groceries. Mary put gas in the Blazer. They were coming back from the beach when they passed a house with two bikes out front. There was a cardboard sign on them. FOR SALE.

Mary pulled over.

"Look," said Mary, nodding toward the bikes. One looked like it would fit Hannah. Mary unfastened her seat belt and opened the truck door. "I'm gonna see what they want for it."

Mary knocked on the door. Two minutes later, she was pushing one toward the car.

"Get the back!" she called to Hannah.

Hannah scrambled out of the Blazer and pressed hard to pop the heavy tailgate of the truck.

"You like it?" Mary grinned as she reached the truck. "It's your new bike."

Hannah looked at the bike. It was metallic green, with long antennae-like handlebars and a big white banana seat. Hannah laughed, her hand running over the top of her head. "It's crazy."

"Okay, try and get it in the truck. I'm going to go get the other one."

"What do you mean?"

"It needed a sister," said Mary, without looking back as she marched toward the house.

As the girls drove away, Hannah watched the bikes bounce and shake behind her. "How much were these things?"

"I got 'em both for twenty bucks." Mary joined Hannah in looking at their new acquisitions in the rearview mirror.

Hannah leaned back in her seat, crossing her arms over her chest. "We should name them."

"No," replied Mary, patting the dashboard. "The Blazer would be jealous."

"You . . . are so weird," said Hannah, smiling.

• • •

WITHOUT A TABLE OR CHAIRS, the girls ate dinner that night on the floor, resting the once-frozen French-bread pizza on the torn-in-half box that it came in.

Mary took a bite. "Don't open the door," she instructed, wincing against the scalding cheese. "Ever. When I'm not here."

Hannah swallowed down a more diminutive bite. "I know, Mare." She had been through all this before. Hannah had been spending nights alone since she was six. "I'm not stupid."

Mary looked around the barren room. There was no television. No phone. Just two sleeping bags on the floor, a clock radio that had been left in the apartment, and some of the girls' paperbacks. "If something happens, just go to the grocery store. Someone will be there." Hannah was reading the box she was using as a plate. "Bunny?"

"I know, Mare," Hannah said, positioning her pizza in front of her mouth for another bite. "Go to the grocery store."

Mary was always like this when they first arrived in a new place. She left for work that night as Hannah was in the bathroom getting ready for bed. "I'll be home before you wake up," she said, loitering in the doorway, watching Hannah brush her teeth.

"I know," Hannah said, her mouth full of foam. She waved. "Good luck!" Then Mary stepped into the hall, shut the door, and the sisters were apart.

On her way to Sea Cliff that night, Mary rolled the windows down and drove the distance as fast as the roads would allow, feeling the wind animate her hair. The windows in the houses she passed glowed yellow in the dark, and the temperature was dropping. Mary turned on the heat, hearing the low growl of the vents as they burst with hot air, feeling it hit her before it rushed out the windows and became part of the night. She loved driving with the windows open and the heat on. It was, to her, an unrivaled indulgence.

When she arrived at Sea Cliff, she parked and looked at herself in the rearview mirror. Then she pulled out her makeup bag. With the interior of the Blazer illuminated only by the lights from the parking lot, Mary drew a dark thick line with an eye pencil along her lashes. It made her look exotic, like some ancient queen. She brushed her hair, stroking it roughly with a pink bristled brush until it was smooth and glossy.

The doorman opened the brass-and-glass door for her when she arrived, nodding cordially. "Good evening." She introduced herself at the front desk and was ushered to the night manager. He gave her a uniform. He gave her a name tag. She was taken on a tour and introduced to various staff working the night shift. The hotel operated with a skeleton crew at night, which was part of why Mary liked it.

"It's slow, your shift," the night manager said, as he loitered by the front desk, his hands in his front pockets. "Just you and Curtis most nights." Curtis was the bellman who stood at the entrance to the lobby, his right arm bent and contorted, his hand resting in his pocket. His left shoulder sunk slightly, and his back curved into an unnatural hump. His uniform hung loosely on his thin, twisted frame. But his eyes, though shadowed, were quick, and they darted around the room with a facility that his body surely couldn't.

"Oh, okay," Mary said. *Oh, okay.* As if she didn't know. As if she hadn't grown up at the Water's Edge. They used to lock the office at night. Put up the closed sign. Anyone arriving later than ten o'clock could fend for themselves or knock until Diane rushed from her bedroom, wrapping her robe tightly. *I'm so sorry. We thought all of our guests had arrived.*

The night manager nodded toward the girl next to Mary. "Sam can tell you," he said, as if Mary doubted him. "She's been on this shift for months."

"Yeah, no," said Mary. "I bet."

When the manager left, Sam and Mary stood in silence.

Sam was supposed to be training Mary, but Mary kept finding her sneaking glances, looking at her in the way that women sometimes did, with a desire and eagerness that wasn't sexual but was desperate all the same. Sam wanted to be her *friend.*

"Where are you from?" Sam asked.

Mary gave her a glance, then turned her gaze back to the vast lobby, with its marble and columns and big beautiful flowers. "Back East."

"How did you end up here?"

"I drove."

"Do you have a boyfriend?"

Mary chuckled quietly. "No."

There was a brief stretch of silence, and Mary picked up a pen from beside the computer's black and green screen.

"I'm moving to second shift tomorrow," the girl offered, hoping to interest, to impress. "I'll get off at ten from now on."

But Mary was silent, her pen winding gracefully over a Sea Cliff notepad. She was drawing Curtis the bellman, drawing him with a cloak and staff. As he sensed her eyes, his chin lifted and he pulled his body ever so slightly straighter, ever so slightly heavenward.

As guests checked in, he slunk up behind them, cart in hand, hauling their bags onto it before they could refuse. Even those ready to voice protest, about to insist that they didn't need any help with their luggage, seemed unable to refuse him—the bent man ready to offer his service.

On his way back from one such delivery, he passed by the front desk. His eyes met Mary's only briefly. "Welcome to the Hotel California," he said, as he hobbled by like some ruined prince.

Mary and Curtis worked in silence those first few nights, each of them assessing the other. And Mary kept waiting for Curtis to sit, for him to sink into one of the plush club chairs that lined the lobby. But Curtis remained upright, though

Mary could see that fatigue burdened his body more than it would most.

On the fourth night, during that dark dead span of time when nothing in the hotel seemed to move, when the bar adjacent to the lobby had gone dark and all the guests that were going to arrive had come, Mary's eyes settled on Curtis. He noticed at once, she could tell, but he kept his stalwart gaze straight ahead for as long as he could. Finally, he looked at her. They stared at each other in silence until Mary asked, "How long have you been here?"

Curtis's brows lifted in mischief or amusement or some combination of the two. "Eight years."

"Why are you still on the night shift?" No one stayed on nights for longer than they had to, always moving to days when someone left and their schedule became available.

A small smile started at the corners of Curtis's lips, and he nodded toward Mary. "Why are *you* on the night shift?"

Mary's head dropped to one side as she looked at Curtis. And without thinking about why, she knew she could trust him. "Because no one's really watching us," she said. It was a sentiment she knew Curtis would understand. He didn't like to be watched either, though for different reasons. She picked up a pen and began to draw. "I'm drawing you," she finally said, her eyes focused on the paper. "Do you want to see?"

Hannah was still asleep when Mary arrived home that morning. She crept through the empty apartment, which was just beginning to brighten in the early-dawn light, and crawled into the sleeping bag next to Hannah. Without waking, Hannah rolled against her, closing the space between them. And there, with her body again part of Hannah's, Mary fell asleep. Her uniform was still on and her name tag still pinned to her jacket, but the rest she found was deep and dreamless. The sort from which you never wanted to wake.

Mary didn't know how many hours had passed when she

finally woke up, only that the late-afternoon sun was pouring through the bare windows. She winced away from the light, rolling so that it warmed her back. With her arms above her head, she arched against it. From the tiny kitchen, not fifteen feet away, she heard Hannah singing along to the tinny music coming from the little clock radio. It was that Madonna song.

Still sunk into her sleeping bag, Mary smiled to herself and listened. From her spot on the floor, she called, "You sound like *Mom.*" She sat up and looked through the doorway at her sister, whose head was bobbing with the music as she pulled a jug of milk from the refrigerator. "She used to go nuts whenever Carole King came on."

Hannah, for her part, continued on. *Like a virgin. Ooo-ooo-oo-oooo, like a virgin.*

Mary pulled her jacket off and tossed it. Then she again noticed the position of the sun. "What time is it?"

Hannah's singing stopped only long enough for her to answer. "I think it's like four." She poured the milk into a bowl of cereal.

Mary eyed her purse, which sat slumped by the doorway to the bedroom. "Want to see what I got from work?"

"Okay," Hannah replied, padding across the floor. She stopped at the doorway to the bedroom, tilting the bowl back into her mouth, swallowing down both Toasty-Os and milk.

Mary nodded toward her purse. "Hand me my bag," she said.

Hannah picked it up, noting its weight, and tossed it over. It landed with an awkward thump. Mary reached inside. After pawing through it for a moment, she pulled out a spoon.

"Here," she said, extending it to Hannah.

Hannah immediately sunk it into her cereal. "Awesome."

"I've got four whole sets." Then Mary dumped the contents on the floor by her sleeping bag and out spilled shampoo bottles, sugar packets, and tiny jam jars. Out came miniature soaps, cashews from the mini bar, and even a guest-room phone.

Hannah immediately reached for a jam jar and read the label. "These are really fancy," she said, intimidated, if one could be, by preserved fruit.

"I know. They've got good stuff at Sea Cliff. We're moving on up, Bunny."

Hannah set the jam jar back down. "You're not going to get in trouble for taking it, are you?" she asked. She wouldn't want to invite trouble. She wouldn't want to leave.

"No," replied Mary. "It's totally fine. They would never even know." But what Mary knew, what Mary had always known, is that when you stay still, leg in a trap, trouble can find you.

Twenty-seven

1989

T HE GIRLS FLEW, THEIR HAIR WAVING behind them, their faces turned to the sun. "You'll probably have to ride to school some days," Mary called to Hannah, who rode behind her. The Chase girls were on their bikes. Their colorful, shiny, fantastic bikes, with spokes that glistened and wheels that hummed. On hers, Mary felt the joy of the kinetic, the profound relief of movement as she watched the sidewalk disappear beneath her.

"Isn't there a bus?"

"Yeah, but the bus sucks," replied Mary. She slowed to let Hannah pass her. "It's all kids picking at their whiteheads and sucking on their egg-salad sandwiches."

Mary remembered the boy who'd taught Hannah how to ride a bike. He worked as a mechanic, and he played in a band. He took Hannah to the parking lot of a chemical factory and put her on his sister's old ten-speed, running behind her and holding on to the seat until she was doing it on her own. Later that night, he double-pierced Mary's ear with a sewing needle, then slipped his grandmother's ruby stud into the hole. Mary felt a trickle of blood run from her lobe down to her neck. Without hesitation, he licked it clean, sliding his tongue up from her collarbone, then wrapping his mouth gently around her tender and swollen earlobe. Three days later, the Chase girls were gone. They didn't leave a note. And for years, the taste of Mary's blood would come to the boy unbidden, and he'd feel his mouth go wet; he'd feel an ache in his groin. And he'd remember the taste of Mary Chase.

The girls rounded a corner, and athletic fields came into view behind a massive brick structure contained inside a chain-link fence. Hannah gripped the hand brakes and her bike slowed. "Is that it?" she asked, her face alert and cautious. It was bigger than she had imagined.

Mary squinted as she assessed it. "That's it," she said.

Hannah stopped and let a foot drop to the ground for balance, and Mary did the same. "Do you think these tests are gonna be hard?"

"Probably not," replied Mary. Then she pressed her foot against the pedal and felt her bike respond by quickly gliding down over the concrete of the sidewalk. "They just want to make sure you know what you're supposed to know."

Mary let the bike gain speed as the hill sloped down toward the school, then she made a smooth turn into the parking lot. Mary stopped in front of a metal bike stand. Beside her, Hannah's bike screeched to a halt, and she wobbled off. She was nervous, Mary could tell.

Mary swung her leg over, dismounted, and looked at Hannah. "You should pretend like something's wrong with you," she said. "When someone introduces themselves, you should just hug them. You should act like some total freak who just hugs everyone."

Hannah chuckled — it was a nervous, jittery thing. "Do you think there are going to be other people?" Hannah asked, her eyes hopeful. "Taking this test?"

"Probably not, Bunny. School started a couple of weeks ago here."

Hannah walked close to Mary as they entered the school, which was like any number of schools. Its cinder-block halls were painted a slick yellow and were lined with a series of handmade posters and trophy cases. The students were in class so the building seemed empty save for the windowed office with a view of the entrance. Mary pushed through the door. An older woman was seated at a desk behind a raised counter. She looked up as the Chase girls entered. "May I help you?" she asked.

Mary walked up to the counter and leaned against it. "This is Hannah Chase," said Mary, nodding toward her sister behind her. "She's here for a placement test."

A phone receiver was lifted, and soon Hannah was greeted by a small friendly-looking woman with an ever-present smile who was all arm rubs and encouragement. "You're just going to take some quickie tests for us, okay?"

Hannah looked at Mary, then looked at the woman and nodded.

"Good luck, Bunny," called Mary, as the woman led Hannah to the testing room. Hannah looked back at her, and Mary mimed a hug. Hannah turned, the smile just visible on her face.

Mary waited as Hannah took her tests, her head resting against the wall behind her, her arms crossed in front of her chest. She felt her eyes drift shut. She had slept for only a couple of hours after her shift before they had to leave for the school.

"It's going to be a little while," the woman at the desk said. Her hair was wiry gray and gathered up on the crown of her head in a bun.

"That's fine," replied Mary, still staring at the ceiling. "I'll wait."

A few more minutes passed. "Are you the mom?" the secretary asked.

Mary looked at her. "Excuse me?"

"There's paperwork," she said. The secretary extended a brown clipboard and gave it a bounce. "Needs to be filled out. May as well get it done now." Mary stood, keeping her eyes on the woman as she took the forms. "Since you're waiting." The office phone began to ring, and the woman lifted the receiver. "William Brown Middle School. How can I help you?"

Mary sat back down and looked at the papers, at the black letters on the white pages. The school needed Hannah's name, the date and place of her birth, the address of the last educational institution she had attended. They needed to know if she had any medical conditions or disabilities. They needed to know the name of her parents or legal guardians. Their places of employment. *Mary Chase,* she wrote. *Sea Cliff.* She brought the clipboard back to the old woman.

"Thank you, honey," she said, taking it from her and setting it on her desk without giving it a glance.

Mary wasn't quite sure how long she sat there. Long enough for the hallway outside to fill up and then empty, then fill up and empty again. Long enough for the woman at the desk to pull out a brown paper bag and eat a tuna-fish sandwich. Finally, Hannah was escorted out of the testing by the woman with the ceaseless smile.

"She did *great,*" the woman said, and Mary understood that she would say this no matter what. "We'll be in touch with the results and placement." Hands were shaken, and the efficient, pleasant woman went back from whence she came.

"How'd it go?" whispered Mary, placing her hand on Hannah's back as she guided her toward the door.

"Good," said Hannah, wincing away from Mary's touch and scanning the hallways for peers.

From behind them, Mary heard the secretary's voice. "Hey, *ummm . . .* girls?"

Mary's and Hannah's heads turned in unison.

The secretary was finally looking at the paperwork. "You forgot the dad's name on here," she said, as she flipped through the pages. Then she looked up at Mary and Hannah over her glasses. "You want to add him?"

Mary felt her head go light, perhaps with fatigue. "No," she replied, ushering Hannah out ahead of her. "We don't."

Mary and Hannah rode home in silence, the sun softened by high clouds that glided slowly past it. "Let's go the long way," said Mary. "By the water." And so the Chase girls passed along the coast, watching the surfers bob like seals as row after row of perfect arcs came rolling in from the horizon.

"It's pretty," said Mary, as she looked at the water, its light shooting in all directions. "Don't you think?"

But Hannah was silent. She remained so as they pulled up to the apartment, as they lugged their bikes up the stairs, and as Mary slid the key in the door.

Mary dropped her purse inside the door. She watched Hannah as she walked to the kitchen area. "I'm gonna go back to sleep, okay?"

Hannah opened the refrigerator, investigating its contents. "Okay," she said.

"Wake me up at like eight."

Mary soon fell into an impenetrable sleep. She didn't know how long she'd been unconscious when her eyes blinked open. The light in the room had changed, had gone black, the only illumination coming from the parking-lot lights of the grocery store. But Mary knew Hannah was there even before she saw her.

"It's 8:15" came Hannah's voice, inches away.

Mary opened her eyes and saw her sister's face. She was lying on top of her own sleeping bag, her hands tucked against the side of her cheek, her body angled toward Mary.

Mary inhaled sharply, acclimating to consciousness. She drew her head back slightly and glanced around the room.

"Mare?" started Hannah, bringing Mary's eyes back to her. "Who was my dad?"

Mary took another breath, the engine of her mind starting to churn. *He was a prince, a warrior. He broke away from his family, which was powerful but cruel. He fell in love with Mom, but he was sworn to another. He had to leave to protect her. He promised to come back for her one day.* These were the things Mary had said in the past, these were the tales that Mary had once told. And now she would tell another.

"He was a friend of Mom's," said Mary. Her voice sounded raw, ragged with sleep. "His name was Barry."

Hannah's face was serious, and she adjusted her hands. "What was he like?"

"He was nice. Handsome. He took Mom to nice places."

"Is he alive?"

"I think so."

"Does he live where we used to? In Sandy Bank?"

"Last I knew."

"Was he your dad, too?" Hannah's questions were clinical, determined.

"No. He wasn't."

"Who was your dad?"

"I don't know for sure," replied Mary. "Nobody does."

"Do you think you'll ever find him?"

"Maybe, Bunny," said Mary. It was soon going to be winter. Winter was such a lovely time of year to visit Sea Cliff. For many longtime guests, it was their favorite time.

"I hope you do," said Hannah.

Mary rested her arm over Hannah. And Hannah did the

same. The Chase girls lay there like that, their arms over each other, their bodies still and curved as if they had been cast in stone, as if they were the recently unearthed fossils of some forgotten cataclysmic disaster. Until Mary had to stand up. Until she had to go to work.

Twenty-eight
1976

D IANE AND MARY SAT ACROSS from each other at the small table in the kitchen of the Water's Edge underneath a Tiffany-style chandelier that cast a weak amber light around the wood-paneled room. Diane's hair hung limp on her head, and the skin around her nose and eyes was red. Every so often, she would drop her head against the table and sob. Mary sat and watched her mother roll with pain until that wave of it subsided and she could once again lift her head.

They had been sitting there for more than an hour before Diane could speak. "I should have been more careful," she said. Her shoulders began to shudder, and she brought her fist to her mouth. "I should never have left you alone so much."

"You didn't," Mary said, her words empty and emotionless. "I left you."

"You wouldn't have been able to sneak out if I had been paying more attention." Her fist slammed hard against the table. "Goddamn it! I should have known better! I *of all people* should have known better!"

Mary knew what she meant. She knew about her father. She heard it in whispers, in subtext. She knew it by what was not said, by what was avoided. And she knew it explicitly after her grandfather, with warm wet eyes, his mind unlocked by medication and disease, told Mary the story of the man who said his name was Vincent Drake. "I want to give it away," said Mary.

"No!" said Diane. She sniffed hard and wiped underneath her eyes. "You are not going to '*give it away*.'" Then she looked at her daughter. "Imagine if I had given you away?" she asked, the thought seeming inconceivable to Diane in a way Mary couldn't quite understand. Then she shook her head, as if shaking off the idea. "No. This baby is blood. You don't give away blood." Diane was silent for a moment, her face grim, her eyes faraway as she stared down what was to come. "We'll raise the baby here. It's going to be mine," she said. "We'll say it's mine." She let her palm slap the table and looked once again at Mary.

"But Mrs. Pool—"

"Alice would never tell a soul. You're like a daughter to her. So am I."

"But people are going to see," said Mary. She pointed to her belly. "I'm going to get bigger."

Diane clasped her hand over her mouth and took a breath as if there were something sustaining in her palm. "We'll cross that bridge when we come to it."

Diane took a sleeping pill that night. She hid them in her underwear drawer and only took them on very rare occasions. Mary knew she would need one. She cracked open the door to her mother's room and found her asleep on her bed, her robe still on, her arms curled around herself, her brow furrowed even in sleep. She would have the sort of dreamless, dead slumber that hardly seemed like rest.

So Mary left that night, walked down to the marina. She took the long way so that she could go along the beach. She feared nothing about the night. Girls she knew at school wouldn't walk on the beach after dark. When she used to hang out with the older kids and they'd gather down at the Perkins Break to drink beer and smoke joints, the girls would always arrive together in groups of three or more, convinced that murderers and rapists lurked around every corner, jumping at the snap of a twig and screaming as they gripped each other. But then Mary would appear, the youngest of all, slinking out of the dark, her bare feet padding fearlessly over the sand.

Joining her on the beach that night were the small darting bodies of ghost crabs, which moved around her like water around a stone. She climbed up over a jetty, lodging her fingers into the crevice of a smooth algae-covered rock and pulling herself up. When she was younger, a wave had smashed her into one of these stones, giving her a gash on her head that needed stitches. They had to shave part of her head to put them in. Diane had cried, but Mary hadn't. She just watched the doctor's face as he leaned in close to her. The in and out of his breath was steadying, and she felt its warmth on her temple.

She slid down the other side of the rocks, slipping so that the seat of her shorts became wet. When she bent, when she climbed, when she moved, she was aware of the hardness in her belly that was growing and growing, that was burrowing into her.

The marina was empty, as it always was this time of night, and bobbing boats, so obedient and ready, instantly calmed Mary. She remembered where the boy's had been. He was coming back. He swore he was.

One of the boats in the marina was called *Esmeralda*. It was owned by a local building contractor who had a mistress with the same name. His wife had no idea, but everyone else did. She'd only give a puzzled smile when she'd call for her husband at his office and be told that he was "cheating on her with Esmeralda." Still, it was a beautiful boat. Mary boarded it.

She lay on the bow and looked up at the stars, her hands beneath the back of her head, her sweatshirt lifted to expose her belly, and she let her hand rest there, not out of affection but out of curiosity, to understand just how big this thing had gotten since her last assessment. She could get an abortion, she knew, but not without Diane's consent. Angelina Murgo got pregnant and wanted an abortion. Her parents had to sign paperwork and go with her. Everyone said that her father never looked her in the eye again.

And the fact remained that the prospect of having the baby didn't frighten Mary. Girls her age were supposed to be scared about having children, but it was the opinion of others that induced the fear. *What would people think?* That threat held no sway with Mary. She almost smiled when she thought of them wondering, staring at her belly and turning to each other with whispers. She would have the baby. She would give it away. It would be simple. But she didn't want it to stay. She never intended for it to stay.

As her eyes began to drift shut on a boat that was not her own and that she had no business being on, she tried to will her body back up, knowing that she couldn't fall asleep there. But as the boat rocked gently in the water, she submitted to unconsciousness. She submitted to need. And Mary was awakened hours later in the still-dark morning by the voices of the early charters as they readied themselves to set out to sea.

Twenty-nine

1989

H ANNAH TESTED VERY WELL IN READING but was below grade level in math. "I don't understand," said
Mary, shaking her head into the pay phone in the
employee locker room at Sea Cliff. "Hannah's great at math."

"The skills she has are strong," conceded the guidance
counselor, "but there are subjects and concepts that she's missing entirely and that her classmates know."

"Like what?"

"At Hannah's age, students have already been introduced to
geometry."

"I'll work with her," said Mary. "Hannah's smart. She'll
get it."

"We don't doubt her intelligence."

In the end, it was agreed that Hannah would start the sev-
enth grade with the rest of the kids her age, but she'd begin
with sixth-grade math and receive extra support until she was
caught up. "This kind of thing can happen," said the guidance
counselor, "when you're working outside the standard curricu-
lum."

• • •

ON THE MORNING OF HANNAH'S first day of school, Mary left Sea Cliff before dawn. She drove slowly, cherishing her time in between places, in the seat shaped to her body, in the vehicle that roared and raced at her bidding like a mythological creature as bound to her as she was to it. She parked and took the stairs to the apartment one at a time, the hood to her sweatshirt pulled up over her head, the too-long sleeves covering her wrists.

When she sunk the key into the door and opened it, she saw Hannah standing in front of the stove, the cooktop illuminated by the range hood's yellow light, and a small pot was placed over the bright red coils of the burner. Her hair was all loose loops of tangles, and she was wearing her underwear and a faded navy blue turtleneck.

"Hi," said Hannah, not looking up.

Mary let her bag drop inside the door; it made its telltale thump. "You're up early."

Hannah watched the pot, watched the tiny bubbles form and then meander toward the surface. "I'm making tea."

Mary crossed her arms in front of her chest and shuffled toward her sister. "Are you nervous?"

"No," said Hannah, not trying to sound convincing.

"What are you gonna wear today?"

"I was thinking my jeans," she said. "And maybe that shirt with the flowers."

Mary gave her an appraising glance. "Want me to do your hair?"

She turned to Mary. "Okay," she said, her eyes wide and hopeful.

In the bathroom, Hannah sat on the avocado green toilet, watching in the mirror as Mary teased her bangs. Mary could sense some confession on the other side of Hannah's lips, words that were building their courage in the darkness. When she finally spoke, it came plainly. "Shawn never wrote me back," said Hannah.

Mary picked up the can of Aqua Net, shielding Hannah's face with her hand as she sprayed. Hannah used the opportunity to close her eyes. "Does he even have your address?"

Hannah nodded. "I sent him a letter as soon as we knew it."

"Well, he might not have gotten it yet," said Mary. "We only just moved in."

"I asked in the grocery store. They said it probably only takes three days for a letter to get from here to Kansas."

As Mary set the can of hair spray on the gold-and-white-flecked vanity top, her eyes darted discreetly to Hannah's face. "Did you guys say you'd write each other?" Mary knew Hannah liked him, but she hadn't realized how much.

Hannah nodded. "He said he'd write me like every day. He just needed my address." The emotion in her voice breached the levies, but only just.

Mary set the can of hair spray back on the vanity and looked at Hannah. "Give it a couple more days, Bunny," she said. "If you don't get a letter, forget about him."

Hannah opened her eyes, and they hung on to Mary like she could save her. "He said he liked me."

"There'll be other boys, Bunny," said Mary, her words soft.

"I don't want another boy."

Well, then, thought Mary, before she could stop herself. *Maybe you are just like your mother after all.*

ON THE WAY TO WILLIAM BROWN MIDDLE SCHOOL, Hannah rolled down her window and let her elbow rest in a position intended to be casual.

"So when we get there, just go to the main office," started Mary. "They'll take you to your classroom. They're expecting you."

Hannah nodded. "I know," she said.

Mary felt the rhythm of the road beneath her. "What are you gonna tell people?" she said. "When they ask where you're from?"

Hannah was silent for a moment. "I was just going to say that we're from Sandy Bank. But we've lived all over."

"That's good," said Mary, as they came to a stoplight. "You should just tell them that I work in tourism, so we used to move around a lot."

The closer the girls came to the school, the more intent Hannah seemed to become on making it look as though she didn't care. When the Blazer came to a stop, she opened the door quickly and hopped out, all in one fluid but shaky motion, like a newly born colt. Hannah wanted to seem like she belonged, and Mary allowed her the dignity of the act, remaining in the car. "I'll see you later, okay?" she said, as Hannah nervously adjusted her backpack. It was too big, a camping pack; but they didn't have the money to get her anything new yet.

"Okay," said Hannah. Then she looked at her sister, her fingers hooked onto the straps of her bag. "Bye," she said. Then Hannah turned and she walked into the school.

Mary watched Hannah's feet as they propelled her toward the door. She was wearing her Keds. Mary had washed them for her in the sink the evening before. Like their hair, they smelled of the shampoo from Sea Cliff. There were kids beside her now, all walking inside. A girl ahead of her pushed through the glass door and held it behind her for Hannah. "Bye, Bunny," she said, when Hannah disappeared into the yellow halls and was engulfed in the crowd of bodies, all moving in the same direction. Upstream. Onward. "I love you, baby."

OVER THE NEXT WEEKS, the Chase girls found their pace, settled in, as they often did in a new place. The first weeks were all discovery and newness. The first weeks were all promise. When Mary would get home from work, she'd find Hannah still asleep, and she'd crawl into the sleeping bag next to her, and for a few precious minutes, the girls would lie like they did on so many countless nights—their breath, their bodies, each facing the other.

Hannah would leave for school while Mary slept, quietly making her breakfast and getting dressed, packing her lunch and leading her bike down the stairs.

Mary would be up by the time Hannah arrived home. They would have from then until Mary left for work to sit on the floor and eat American cheese while Hannah did her homework and Mary drew. She'd draw what she saw, what she had seen, people and places and the eyes of a cat she once found in the swamp. And when she was alone, she'd sit in front of the mirror and draw herself naked. Like a scientist trying to find elucidation in the repetition of study, she was curious as to the power of the beauty that others so coveted.

"Do you know what everyone at school calls Mr. Loogar?" asked Hannah, a textbook open between her legs.

"Who's Mr. Loogar?" Mary was drawing Hannah as she did her homework.

"My social studies teacher."

"What do they call him?"

"Lefty Loogar," said Hannah, trying not to reveal just how hilarious her peer-starved mind found this. "He only has one ball."

Mary made a face as she turned the pencil and erased a line. "What do you mean *ball*?"

Hannah blushed and pointed between her legs.

"What's where the other one should be?"

"I don't know," said Hannah, the life in her eyes quick and brilliant like the silver flash of darting fish. "It's probably just empty."

"Hold still," instructed Mary. Hannah bit her lip, her face settling in as she realized she was being drawn.

The pencil moved quickly in Mary's hand as her eyes moved from Hannah to paper, paper to Hannah.

"You should sell your drawings," said Hannah, trying to keep her chin lifted, her face at the same angle.

Mary chuckled as she worked. "Oh, yeah?"

"Yeah, they're really good."

"Thanks, Bunny," she said, and then she fell silent as she worked, putting Hannah not in their tiny apartment, but in front of a range of mountains that lifted through the sky with an ocean to her left and a desert to her right, and the boundlessness of infinity all around her.

AT WORK THAT NIGHT, Mary stood at the desk as she listened to the low constant buzz of conversation coming from the hotel's bar. There was a boy who worked at the Sea Cliff golf course staring at her, as he often did, from his stool. It was the point in the evening when the bartender would lean against the mahogany that separated him from his guests and top off their drinks with a titch more on the house and begin wiping down the wood. Mary would watch them stumble out, the weight of their lives temporarily lifted as they took uneven steps, swaying to music that wasn't there, inhabiting the safe corner of their minds they could find only with drink.

Mary always felt kindly to the guests; the people who came to Sea Cliff did so to sit by the sea and mourn. That's what grand old hotels by the sea were for: mourning. Mourning the loss of prestige or prominence. Mourning the loss of love. Mourning the children who no longer spoke to you or the person you used to be or should have been. Mourning the loss of freedom or beauty. Mourning a time when all could have been set right again. Mourning the sedimentary layers of mistakes that constituted a life. For that, hotels were sacred ground.

The men would smile when they saw her, and they were always men. They would tip hats that they only thought were on their heads and stare at her as if she were someone else, someone they knew, someone they once cared for more than anyone in the world.

"Can I help you to your room?" she'd asked. She wasn't supposed to leave the desk, but it was the night shift. And besides, she was assisting a guest.

"Well, that would be lovely," they'd say. And she'd slip her arm through theirs, feeling them right themselves, stand straighter with her on their arm. They'd mumble to her in the elevator, asking with whiskey-soaked breath her name and how long she'd been working at the hotel. She'd keep her smile professional and polite, holding the elevator door as they exited, as they thanked her for her time. Sometimes they'd slip her a bill — a ten, a twenty. And she'd keep the elevator door open long enough to see them enter their unlit rooms.

And she'd feel kindly toward them later when she left the desk again. When Curtis's stare followed her down the hall. When hers were the only footsteps in the hotel. When she took the elevator up to the floor she'd escorted them to. When she got off and walked down the hall to the room they had entered. She'd feel kindly to them when she sunk the key into the lock and opened the door, hearing their snoring coming as steadily as the surf. When she walked past them as they lay on the bed in their underwear, their pale bellies exposed, their arms at their sides. When she found their wallet in their pants pocket, when she pulled out several crisp bills, feeling their texture between her fingers.

They would wake the next morning after a sound and drunken sleep, not knowing what happened to the money.

Thinking that they overtipped. Thinking that they bought a round for the bar. And they would remember the girl with the black, black hair, the girl who helped them, who slipped her lovely arm through theirs, making them feel like the men they once were, if only for an elevator ride. And for that, they would have paid anything.

Thirty
1989

MARY CAME HOME FROM SEA CLIFF with more money than she should have. She bought Hannah a backpack. She bought a used couch from Goodwill and a mattress from an ad in the newspaper. It had belonged to an old woman who lived in a beautiful Victorian, an old woman who slept in the twin-size bed next to the twin-size bed in which her husband had died, in the twin-size bed in which she would die. The queen-size bed was never used. Her kids put an ad in the newspaper for most of her things. There was a piano and a dining-room set. Mary got the bed.

The girls didn't know if they'd be able to fit it up the stairs into the apartment, but Mary found a boy in the Laundromat, a boy she recognized from the hotel. The one who watched her from the bar and worked at the golf course. He usually arrived at the greens when Mary was leaving, and he'd slow at the sight of her, looking for a reason to stop, for something to say as she brushed past. She smiled at him and he carried up the bed.

The first night they had it, they slept in their sleeping bags on the bare mattress. The next day, they took the Blazer to a discount home store in a big town fifteen miles away to buy bed linens. Mary let Hannah pick them out. She walked up and down the aisles, pondering the neat rows of plastic-wrapped sheets, as if confronted with the most pleasant but important of deliberations.

"Do you like these ones?" Hannah asked, holding up a set of seafoam green sheets with tiny white seashells.

"Yeah," nodded Mary. "Those are pretty. It'll be like sleeping in the ocean."

They purchased the matching comforter and went home and put the sheets on the bed, right from the package, then spread the comforter on top. Hannah looked at it, at the crisp lines in the sheets where they had been folded, and she smiled. "I like it here," she said. It had been so long since she lived in a home. And if Hannah's devotion had an apex, if Mary's omnipotence did, it was on that day, looking down on the sheets that were the sea, in the town that was beside it.

IN THOSE EARLY WEEKS, it became clear that Hannah enjoyed school. She was a competent though not a standout student, faring well in English but continuing to struggle in math.

"I don't understand, Bunny," Mary would say, reviewing her corrected homework, which was slashed with red lines and corrections. You totally got this kind of stuff when I was teaching you."

"Mrs. Jentiff goes really fast."

"Tell her to slow down."

"I can't, Mare."

And sometimes Mary would be in bed, underwater, but there would be other voices—not hers, not Hannah's—and she'd force her eyes open and swim to consciousness and they would be gone. All that there'd be was the sound of the radio, tinny and garbled.

"Bunny, you need to turn it down," she'd say, her voice dry and bare. "I'm trying to sleep."

"Sorry," Hannah would reply. Lying on her belly, she'd groan slightly as she reached for the knob that controlled the volume.

It wasn't long before Hannah asked to have a friend over. "Her name is Nicky," said Hannah. "She said you might know her mom. She works at Sea Cliff, too."

Mary was still in bed, and she pulled the covers up to her chin. It was getting colder, and they hadn't turned on the heat in the apartment. "What does she do there?"

"Nicky says she works in *events*."

"I don't know her."

Hannah waited expectantly. "So can she come over?"

Mary's lips were a perfect bow as she looked at Hannah. "I guess so," she said. "Just tell me when."

Nicky came on a Thursday. She was pretty in a common way, an unchallenging way, with brown hair and a fine nose. She tossed her hair over one shoulder and extended her hand toward Mary. "Nice to meet you," she said. And Mary noticed the admiring way Hannah looked at the girl.

Mary made herself smile and took the girl's hand. She found little reason to be charming outside of work. "Nice to meet you, too," Mary said, looking from Nicky to Hannah back to Nicky. "What do you guys have planned?"

Hannah grabbed Nicky's hand. "We're just going to hang out," she said. "Come on." She pulled her into the bedroom and shut the door.

Mary sat on the couch, let her head fall back, and she listened. Nicky's and Hannah's voices rose like a piano scale, the words indiscernible but lilting. And Mary let her gaze rest on the white of the ceiling, and she let her breath come and go, her arm draped across her stomach. It drained her, staying in a place, as if roots drew life from her rather than gave it. Then she closed her eyes. They opened only when she heard Hannah and Nicky emerge from the room.

"We're going to make some popcorn," said Hannah, as she led Nicky across the room with a saunter Mary had never seen her use before; she was trying to impress her friend. Hannah opened the cabinet next to the refrigerator and pulled out the metal pan of Jiffy Pop—it was Hannah's favorite treat. "Do you want any?"

Nicky was staring at Mary, twirling her hair and letting her ankles buckle to the side as she rolled over on the sides of her feet. Mary had met girls like Nicky, girls for whom being looked at wasn't a means to an end but the end itself. "No, thanks," replied Mary. The cabinet closed with a clink.

As Hannah heated the popcorn on the stove, she and Nicky made small talk, the self-consciously blasé sort that young girls make when they have an audience. It was all sighs and *so anyways*. When the foil wrap of the pan was distended, Hannah held its handle and led Nicky back to the couch. She and her friend sat in front of Mary on the floor, their legs spread, the pan between them, and Hannah peeled back the foil, the steam hurrying out.

Nicky picked up a single kernel and put it in her mouth. Hannah took a small handful.

"So like," started Nicky, looking briefly at Mary. "You guys live here all by yourselves?"

Mary was stretched out on the couch, her body occupying its entire length. Since she worked nights, this was morning for her. She let Hannah answer.

"Yeah," Hannah said, looking at her handful of popcorn. "Our mom died a while ago."

"Oh, my god," said Nicky, her brow furrowed in sympathy. "That's so sad."

"It's okay," said Hannah. "I mean"—she blushed, not

knowing how to explain herself — "we're used to it. I was four. And Mary was like eighteen."

Mary closed her eyes again and sunk deeper into the couch.

There was a moment of silence. "So, are you going to go to the dance?" she heard Hannah ask.

"I *think* so." Nicky leaned on her side, her hand in her hair, her body arranged just so. "I want someone good to ask me, ya know?"

"I think I'm just gonna go," Hannah said, through a mouthful of popcorn.

NICKY SOON BECAME A FIXTURE at the Chase girls' apartment. Her mother often didn't get home until late evening so Nicky would ride her bike with Hannah after school, and Mary would wake up to their voices, their furtive whispers, their manic laughter. She often heard Nicky coaxing Hannah into calling a boy for her or writing her essay for her or letting her borrow the new shirt Mary had just bought.

"Can you guys keep it down?" Mary would call from the bedroom. And then she'd hear them shush each other through quieted laughter.

"Nicky thinks you don't like her," Hannah said to Mary one evening. Nicky had just left. Mary was sitting on the floor folding the laundry she had hauled up from the Laundromat. Hannah plopped down across from her. Mary didn't look up.

"Am I supposed to?"

Hannah gave an exasperated huff. "Yes!" she said. "She's my *best* friend!"

Mary tossed a pair of Hannah's underwear into her pile. "Sure she is," she replied.

"What is wrong with you?" demanded Hannah. "Why can't you be happy that I *finally* have a friend? That I finally go to a school like a normal kid?"

"Stop being so dramatic, Bunny. I want you to have friends,

and if you want to go to school, then go. But Nicky's just not as good a friend to you as you are to her."

"What are you *talking* about?"

Mary looked at Hannah squarely. "You basically do her homework for her every night while she lies on the floor, eats our food, and watches you."

"I'm *helping* her. That's what friends do."

"That's bullshit, Bunny. And you know it. Friends don't make you give them your Taylor Dane tape."

"How do you know?" spat Hannah. "You don't have any *friends!*" Hannah was wounded and trying to wound back.

"I don't want any," replied Mary.

Hannah shook her head. "You are so messed up." Then she stood and wheeled away from Mary and stomped into the bedroom.

"Bunny," Mary called, as the door slammed. She waited for a moment, her chin lifted. "Bunny, you need to *chill* out."

"No, *you* need to chill out!" Hannah called back to her, her voice muffled.

"You're acting like a total brat!" called Mary, as she mated a pair of socks and threw them in Hannah's pile.

Mary finished folding the laundry, stacking her clothes next to Hannah's, feeling the weight, as she had so often lately, of raising a teenage girl. "Hey, Bunny!" she called after a few minutes. "I think I'm going to get some Chinese!" She had the night off of work. She'd thought they would do something fun.

Hannah was silent.

"What do you want?"

There was still no answer. Mary picked up the phone and called Hunan Garden. *I'd like to place an order for takeout.*

She took the long way to pick it up, driving along the coast with the black silhouettes of the hills on her left and the star-littered sky that faded into sea on her right. She drove with the window down, letting her hand weave through the cool air like a hawk gliding through thermals, then she guided the wheel into a wide turn toward the road that wove its way back to the center of the town the Chase girls now called home.

The restaurant had her order ready when she walked in. And she was in and out of the tidy dark little space with barely a word spoken. They knew Mary there. She paid them, they thanked her, she left. And she drove home wondering if Hannah was still mad at her.

She picked up their mail from the small metal box beside the door that led to the staircase up to their apartment, sticking it under the arm that also held their dinner. Inside, Mary found that Hannah was still in the bedroom. She set the white bag with red characters on the counter between the sink and the stove, and tossed the mail over to the couch. "Food's here!" she called, as she opened the container. She piled her plate with shrimp lo mein and kung pao chicken. "If you want any!"

Mary took a seat in front of the couch, leaning back against it as she wedged her plate between her chest and her bent knees, feeling its warmth rise toward her face. Her nose was red with cold from the drive. She took a bite and reached for the pile of mail. The letter was stuck inside the *Penny Saver;* she hadn't seen it at first.

Her hands were still as she opened it, as she pulled out its contents. They were still as she unfolded it and read its lines once. Then again.

Ms. Chase,

You're a difficult person to contact, but that seems to be your intent. I have spent the last six years grateful that you haven't once again, quite literally, shown up on our doorstep. But that doesn't mean that there isn't business between us that needs to be settled, namely the claim you made in the letter you left with Stefan.

If you had intended to inflict damage to my son, I can assure you that you succeeded. Martina and I have always tried to protect our children, maybe to a fault. But we both were certainly ignorant to what we had allowed into our lives with you. All I will say is that Stefan is now living abroad. Thankfully, I can't imagine a way you can possibly reach him. I am also eternally grateful that it was Teddy who answered the phone on that day you called to make plans for a meeting on that island in the Tammahuskee. You mistook him for Stefan. Had you not, things might have ended very differently.

I will not go into the revelations of your character made, not coincidentally, I now know, on the day of your departure from Northton. The reason I am writing is regarding your claim that Stefan is Hannah's father.

We have done enough investigation to know that you are, in fact, Hannah's mother. And while the timing of Stefan's stay in Sandy Bank might be nothing but coincidence, you certainly have used it to your advantage. In other words, your claim is not inconceivable. And your continued contact in the form of photographs of Hannah is, to say the least, very upsetting to Martina.

I will not pretend to fully understand your motivations or intent, Ms. Chase. I can only imagine, based on the information conveyed by your cousin, that what you would really like is money. So I'm prepared to offer you ten thousand dollars per year until Hannah is eighteen years old, in exchange for your distance, silence, and assurance that all the money will be used to care for your daughter.

You need not reply. Your silence will be answer enough. But if you try to contact us again, the checks will stop.

Patrick Kelly

It was several minutes before Hannah finally came out of the bedroom. And perhaps it was the smell of smoke that drew her out. When she opened the door, Mary was leaning over the sink with a lighter in her hand as flames claimed the last fragment of the check, and Mary dropped it, feeling the heat on her fingers.

"What are you doing?" Hannah asked.

"I don't know," said Mary, her eyes unmoved. She flipped up the handle to the faucet and watched as the water washed the ashes down the drain. "I just felt like seeing fire."

Thirty-one
1977

Diane didn't know that Mary was in labor. She had headed into town to go to the grocery store, the bank, and to find a pay phone so she could make a private call to Alice Pool.

Diane took her time coming back, driving over the bridge that separated the island from the mainland, and she watched the water that had turned gray to match the sky. There was a storm out at sea, its long arms were twirling somewhere over the Gulf. It would miss them, the weathermen said, but the waves would rush in, swollen and dark, with their tales of the great churning beyond.

It was only in the grocery store, when Diane saw the gaudy red boxes of chocolate and bouquets of roses, that she realized it was Valentine's Day. And now, as she looked out at the water, her hands on the steering wheel, she gave a tired chuckle.

"I'd bet you'd be rolling over in your grave, Dad." She was speaking out loud, though she hardly realized it. "If you knew I was here in Bardavista." Her father had considered it a cursed place ever since Vincent Drake had named it. She smiled. "It's nice, though. I think you'd like it. It's got a beautiful beach."

Her head started a slow nod. "The sand's like sugar." Diane had begun talking to her father since she and Mary had come here, feeling more connected to him than she had since he died. She understood him more now that she was facing what he had, a daughter pregnant far too soon.

She pulled into the driveway of the cottage she and Mary were renting and popped the trunk of the station wagon. She didn't buy much food, just enough to get them by. Crackers and bananas and shrimp, which were cheaper than chicken here. She would boil a mess of them, and she and Mary would eat them cold while sitting in front of the television, watching the picture spasm in and out between bursts of static.

"Hi, Mare!" Diane called, when she walked inside. The metal screen door banged shut with a clatter. She set the groceries on the counter. "I'm home! I got some of that cheese you like!" She began unpacking the bags. "Mare!" she called again.

Diane found Mary in the bedroom lying on the mattress facing the wall. At first she thought she was sleeping, but then she pulled back on Mary's shoulder and saw that her eyes were open and focused, that her forehead was damp with sweat. "Oh, Jesus!" said Diane, her hands shaking. "Mary!"

Mary's eyes darted briefly to her mother, then she once again faced the wall.

"Come on," said Diane. "We're going to the hospital."

The nurses didn't look Diane or Mary in the eye as they rushed around the room.

"Would she like an epidural?" one of them asked Diane, her words soft, her drawl heavy with apology. She was sorry for Diane and Mary. All the nurses were. Mary was so very young.

"No" came Mary's voice, sure and emotionless as she lay on her side in the white-sheeted bed. And all Diane could feel was her own heart like galloping hooves inside her chest.

Mary didn't make a noise through childbirth. She didn't

scream or shout or beg for help with the pain. Diane only heard her breath rushing in and out and coming so, so fast. She'd tighten her fists and dig her nails into her palms so fiercely that she drew blood, but she was silent, her jaw hard, her eyes focused on something no one could know.

Diane wondered about the boy. Mary would tell her nothing but that he was a prince. That he had ridden into Sandy Bank on a white stallion. That he was going to come back for her. Diane wondered if her daughter had lost her mind. Or if she had created another beautiful, terrible lie. She wondered if Mary believed it. If she always would.

She was already seven centimeters when they arrived at the hospital, and so the baby was born within the hour. It was a gray February afternoon, and Diane let out a gasping weep when she heard the first cry. "It's a girl," said the doctor, without emotion or joy.

Diane squeezed her daughter's hand, feeling her face turn wet with tears. "Mary, honey, did you hear that?" she choked. It hadn't been so many years since she had lain where Mary was. It hadn't been so many years since she felt the shame of slipping her feet into the cold metal stirrups as a girl.

The doctor handed the baby to a waiting nurse, then reached for a pair of surgical scissors and clipped the umbilical cord. Diane lifted her chin to see her granddaughter. "A baby girl!"

Mary's body had gone limp as she submitted to exhaustion. She watched the baby with a guarded expression, her black hair soaked with sweat, a strand of it like a gash across her cheek.

"She's beautiful," whispered Diane. Bringing her hand to her mouth, she shook her head. "Thank you, Jesus. She's just perfect."

The baby was cleaned and weighed. *Six pounds, eleven ounces.* And Diane didn't let go of her daughter's hand. When the nurse brought the swaddled infant over to them, she looked from Diane to Mary. "Would you like to hold her?" she asked.

Mary simply looked at her, her beautiful face like stone. Diane slowly let go of her daughter's hand. "I'll take her," she whispered, slipping her arms underneath the small bundle and pulling it into her chest. She brought her nose close to her granddaughter's. "Hello, sweetheart." Then she held her so Mary could see. "Mare," she said. "Look at her."

Mary's face registered nothing. And Diane brought the baby back to her chest. She hoped that Mary would be able to be a good sister to the child, as they had planned. She hoped that she'd be able to love her, in her way.

All afternoon, Diane held the baby, stroking her head while keeping a close eye on Mary, who still hadn't spoken since the baby was born.

"You want to hold her?" Diane asked.

Mary shook her head.

"But look how sweet she is, Mare."

Mary let her head roll toward the window.

But Diane noticed Mary's reaction to the baby's cries, the way she'd lurch toward the child almost involuntarily. It broke her heart to see her fourteen-year-old stone-faced and silent, the front of her hospital gown drenched in breast milk that came unbidden, trying to fight her instinct and resist a child she was meant to love.

The baby slept in the nursery that night. Diane slept beside Mary. When she opened her eyes in the black night, she found Mary's opened, too. "They feed her when she's in there, right?" It was the first thing Mary had said since the baby was born.

Diane nodded. "Yeah," she said, trying to hide her relief, her shock, trying not to even move. "They'll give her a bottle."

They brought the baby back in the morning, and Diane

watched as Mary inspected her when they wheeled the bassinet back in, the way her eyes took an inventory. *One head. Two legs. Two arms. Ten fingers. Ten toes.* Then she swaddled her back up and turned away.

The first full day of the child's life passed quietly, the sun making a graceful arc in the sky until the sky had been leached of light and it was night. Mary stood at the hospital room's single window, her forehead resting against the cool glass, her eyebrows tensed as she peered into the night as Diane held the infant in her arms.

Diane looked at the back of her daughter's head and the body that seemed so tensed, so ready to spring. She shifted, feeling the fatigue in her body reach down to her bones.

"Mary, honey," Diane said, her voice cracked with lack of use; it had been a day with few words. "Can you hold the baby for a minute?"

Mary didn't move. Diane shifted slightly in her seat, suddenly feeling the enormity of raising another child on her own. She was going to need Mary, she knew. She was going to need her girl.

"Mary," she said, her tone sapped of patience, her words lingering and long. "I need you to hold your sister."

Mary's eyes found her mother's in the window's black glass, all that was unspoken passing in a look.

"Why?" asked Mary.

Diane held her daughter's gaze. "Because I have to go to the bathroom, Mary."

Mary turned slowly and looked at the baby, her arms at her sides. Diane struggled up, cradling the infant in one arm while pushing herself up with the other. "Mare . . . ," she said, keeping her awkward hold. "Can you?" She felt herself slip slightly, fall back against the chair, and the baby let out a mewling cry.

And to Diane it looked like reflex, like some primal need to protect the being with whom she shared blood. Because Mary darted forward, sliding her arms beneath the baby and pulling her into her chest. Diane watched them for a moment, watched as Mary started to sway, calming the child.

"I'll be right back," she said, but Mary was still looking at the baby, some internal battle silently being waged.

In the bathroom, Diane turned on the water and sat on the toilet, letting it run and run, letting it drown out everything else. She wasn't sure how long she stayed in there. It could have been five minutes. It could have been twenty. And when she opened the door, Mary was sitting in the blue pleather chair, the baby still in her arms. Diane watched them for a moment.

"So," Diane said. And Mary started slightly, as if she hadn't heard her leave the bathroom. "What are we going to name her?"

"Name her whatever you want," Mary replied, though she couldn't quite look away from the baby's small face.

"She's going to need you, Mary," said Diane. It was something Diane knew without understanding how. "Do you know that?"

Diane walked over and sat on the edge of the hospital bed facing her daughter. Diane waited, knowing that Mary was a girl whose loyalty was fierce and rare and absolute. Knowing that Mary was deciding, right at this moment, whether or not to love this child, whether or not to give herself to her entirely. The baby squirmed in Mary's arms and the expression on Mary's face slackened, and at that moment, Diane knew it was done. Raising her chin, Mary looked at her mother, and simply said, "Let's call her Hannah." And with those words, it was as if Mary had slashed the palm of her hand and offered her blood as oath.

Thirty-two
1989

A FTER MARY BURNED PATRICK'S CHECK, after she turned on the water, leaning over the sink and watching the ashes swirl then disappear in the stainless steel of the basin, she looked back toward Hannah. "You want to go to the beach?" she asked, her elbows still resting on either side of the sink, her voice deep and dry.

"Now?" asked Hannah.

Mary nodded.

"But what about the food?"

"We'll eat it in the car."

Hannah glanced out the front window, which was slicked black with night. "But it's cold out," she said.

Mary smiled. In Sandy Bank, she used to sleep on the beach in the winter, bringing a sleeping bag and slinking through the night while Diane lay oblivious in her bed. But that was before Hannah was born. She turned back to the sink and looked at the round mouth of the drain. "Are you getting soft on me, Bunny?" she asked.

Hannah was silent for a moment. "Fine."

On the way to the beach, the girls passed the white containers of takeout between them — Hannah taking huge slurping bites, Mary simply letting the warmth from the food seep into her legs.

"Why aren't you eating?" asked Hannah, her mouth full as she gave her sister a sidelong glance.

"I don't know," said Mary. "I guess I'm not hungry."

They parked in one of the spots along the road that ran along the coast. By morning, they'd be full of cars with surfboards strapped to their roofs and wet suits in the trunks. But now, the girls had their choosing.

They walked down the steep wooden stairs that led to the beach, each of them holding a sleeping bag, Mary also carrying a backpack.

Mary paused, looking out onto the limitless Pacific, which breathed invisibly in front of her in the dark. "It's strange," she mused. "Having the ocean to the west."

"Why?" asked Hannah, who had stopped a few steps farther down to look back at her sister.

Mary just shook her head. "Everything is all flipped around. It's like we're at the end."

Hannah made an annoyed huff and shivered, her sweatshirt hood pulled over her head. "Everything's exactly where it always was," she said, as she started down the stairs again. "You could just as easily say that *this* side's the beginning. The earth's round, remember?"

Mary followed Hannah. At the bottom of the steps, Hannah turned toward her sister. "Where do you want to sit?"

Mary looked down the beach, which dipped into a graceful curve before jutting out into another point. Cottages with pale yellow windows sat with their backs to the black hills behind them. "Let's walk down a little."

They found a spot by an old bleached cypress trunk. Hannah set her bag down, shimmied inside, and pulled it up to her chin. "It's freezing," she said, as she shook off the chill.

"It's not that bad," said Mary, who was stone-still and looking down the beach.

Hannah stiffened. "What are you looking at?" she asked.

Mary lifted her chin toward a pair of yellow eyes making their way down the sand. "It's a raccoon."

Hannah sunk deeper into her sleeping bag. "Is it coming toward us?"

Mary chuckled. "Yeah, but," she said, still watching it. "It's just checking things out. Looking for dead stuff." Mary let her backpack slide off and unstrapped her sleeping bag, then laid it next to Hannah.

"Nicky's dad was bit by a raccoon that had rabies," said Hannah, as Mary slid in next to her. "He had to get shots in his stomach every day for a month."

"Mrs. Pool once went ape shit on a bat that got into her house." Mary looked at Hannah and saw her small smile from beneath her sleeping bag. "She beat the crap out of it with a couch cushion, then ran all the way to the 7-11 in her nightgown."

A spring of laughter, real and true, came from Hannah's lips. She knew Mrs. Pool mostly from stories. Her recollection of Sandy Bank and the Water's Edge was spotty and dim.

Mary closed her eyes and lay down flat in her bag, feeling the familiarity of sand under back. It was like being home. She took a deep breath. "Anyway," she said.

She felt Hannah watching her. "Are we gonna sleep here?" Hannah asked.

"No," replied Mary. "Let's just rest." And she pulled her hand from her sleeping bag and blindly found Hannah, laying her arm protectively over her. "I think we both need to rest."

And that night, as the girls lay beside each other, Mary thought about the continent behind them. About all that had happened. All that had ended. About the sun that had sunk into another sky, as if sinking into the ocean itself.

Mary waited until she heard Hannah's breath slow, until she felt her body lie limp in the sand. Then she carefully got up and walked toward the water. The wind had picked up now, and it blew her hair around her head as if it were something alive, something animated. Above her hung a full, fat moon, watchful and silent. She took off her sweater and let it drop to the sand. She had on a tank top underneath and no bra. She felt the hair on her skin rise.

She slipped off her sweatpants, coaxing each leg down with the opposite foot. She stepped out, leaving those, too, on the sand. She took another few steps toward the water. The frigid waves lapped up to her feet, swirling around her ankles before sliding back into the sea. She stood there for a moment, in her tank top and underwear, until her feet became pleasantly numb. She could dive in, she knew. She could swim and swim until there was no more land. Until her limbs slowed with the cold. Until they no longer responded. She could swim until her lips became vein blue and Stefan and Northton and all that was lost no longer existed.

She closed her eyes, pulled off her tank top, and tossed it behind her. Then she stepped deeper into the water. She felt it meet her knees, then her thighs. She walked farther still, her body immune to shudders, her skin contracting from the cold. She felt the water pass her stomach. She wouldn't go too much farther she told herself. She just wanted to taste the salt on her lips. She felt the water pass her breasts. She was part of the tide now. She felt it moving her back and forth, her hair like bleeding ink around her back, her body weak against the temperature. It wasn't up to her now, the retreating tide took her out bit by bit until the water passed her collarbone, passed her neck, and then she let herself sink. Through her closed eyes, she saw Hannah when she was little, when they were still at Sandy Bank. When they used to face each other, holding hands, and plunge down into the ocean, into a world of their own. Through her closed eyes, she could see the fluid, refractive surface of the water; she could see the sun filtering through. She could see Hannah looking like light; she could hear her calling her name. *Mary!* It was muffled by water and memory and time. But she heard it again. *Mary!* It came again and again. Each time louder, more real. Until the words themselves pulled Mary to the surface.

"Mary!" Her body reacted, shaking violently from the cold. And Mary turned back to the shore. Hannah was wading in after her, frantic and furious, the sea in sprays around her. Hannah was up to her knees.

With sluggish arms, Mary began paddling back to shore. Hannah was up to her hips when they reached each other. She clutched at Mary, wrapping her arms around her waist and hurling her angrily toward the shore.

"What are you doing?" she screamed.

Mary's teeth chattered so fiercely, her words were barely intelligible when she said, "I just wanted to go for a swim."

"What the fuck is wrong with you?" asked Hannah, pushing Mary from behind toward the shore. Mary stumbled against the strain, her arms crossed over her bare chest. "You could have *died!*"

And Mary laughed, though she couldn't have said why.

"Shut *up*, Mary!" said Hannah, as the girls waded out of the water. When they reached the sand, Hannah bent down and, with her hands on her knees, let out a silent convulsive sob.

Shaking so hard, she could hardly grasp it, Mary bent down and picked up her sweater.

From behind her, Mary felt another forceful shove, and she fell against the sand, feeling it on her lips, tasting it. "Don't be mad, Bunny," she said, as she brought herself to her hands and knees.

· · ·

The Chase girls drove home that night with the windows closed and the heat on high, neither of them saying a word, Mary with bare feet and wet hair bleeding onto her back, Hannah with her sleeping bag covering her legs. When Mary put the Blazer into park in front of their apartment, Hannah abruptly pushed open her door and got out of the car. With her shoulders softened and her back slumped, Mary felt another involuntary shudder move through her body. Then she followed her sister out of the truck.

Hannah stomped up the stairs in front of Mary. Mary followed slowly, grasping the handrail.

"Here," called Mary, tossing the keys up to Hannah. They landed at Hannah's feet. She bent over, picked them up, and opened the door, letting it swing behind her after she stomped in.

When Mary walked into the apartment, the water was already running. Hannah had turned the shower on, and the bathroom door was closed. Mary knocked on it. It was thin and hollow, with wood veneer that had grown mottled and yellowed at the bottom from humidity and age.

"I'm in here!" said Hannah.

"I need to come in, too." Mary was still bent with cold.

"*No!*"

"Bunny . . ."

"I'm taking a shower!"

Mary stuck her fingernail into the groove in the center of the doorknob and turned, releasing the lock.

With a slap of the vinyl shower curtain, Hannah's face appeared. "I'm in here!"

"I need to take a hot shower," Mary said. Her teeth chattered in corroboration. "I'm *freezing.*"

"That's because *you* decided to go for a fucking *swim!*"

Without a word, Mary peeled off her clothes, letting them

drop on the floor atop Hannah's. She pushed open the back side of the curtain and stepped in behind her.

"Hey!" said Hannah, covering herself with wet limbs.

Mary was doubled over with the cold. "Like I haven't seen you naked before," she said.

At the sight of Mary wincing against the heat of the water, Hannah softened. "Here," she said, her voice still gruff. She stepped aside so that Mary could stand directly under the showerhead. "You can be here."

But Mary didn't move. She simply looked at Hannah. "Bunny" was all she said. Then she straightened her cold-wracked body and wrapped her arms around Hannah's neck.

"Get off of me!" commanded Hannah, as she pulled Mary's slick arms away. But Mary's arms immediately found her again. "Seriously! Get *off!*" Again Hannah tried to break free, but again Mary's arms reached for her, pulling her close. "What the *hell?*" she demanded, as she tried to duck out of Mary's grasp.

It went this way until Mary felt Hannah's body finally give in. Until Mary felt Hannah's head lean into her shoulder. Until Mary heard a high, sustained cry escape Hannah's lips. "I'm so sorry, Bunny," she whispered, resting her hand on the back of her head.

They stood there like that until the bathroom filled with steam, until the memory of the cold evaporated. Until Hannah was silent. Until all that could be washed away was.

Thirty-three

1989

WINTER CAME AND SETTLED OVER the town by the ocean. The gray whales began their journey from the Arctic to the warm waters off Baja. Come April, they would pass again with their calves, their great streams of blow breaking the horizon. But the Chase girls wouldn't be there to see it.

Mary began driving more. Sometimes after work, instead of heading right home, she would head south, her eyes red and glassy as they blinked against the rising sun. When she'd get back to the apartment, Hannah would be gone. There would be a note on the counter next to the stove. *Going to Nicky's house after school and staying for dinner.* And so Mary would slip into their bed and cover the windows and fall asleep.

Mary's waking hours were spent in the dark. Standing at Sea Cliff's front desk through the night, she'd fill notepads with her drawings, letting the ink find its way into every empty space, letting it crawl between the letters of the hotel's name. One evening, she was drawing herself and Hannah. She was drawing them dashing through the woods, wolves in pursuit, gashes from thorns marking their arms, their cheeks. Blood dripping down to the ground and sprouting roses. She drew groping, gap-mouthed skeletons below, reaching for the girls through the dirt. She drew black, black skies.

She heard a voice from the other side of the counter. "Are you an artist?"

Mary looked up. It was the boy from the golf course. The one who had carried their mattress up the stairs. His voice was slow with alcohol, though Mary hadn't seen him at the bar. Her head drifted to the side. "No," she said, as she stared at him. He had pale blue eyes and thick lashes. Mary wondered what it would be like to have a boy she couldn't leave, a boy she couldn't drive away from without explanation or warning.

"You could be," he said earnestly, nodding as he looked at her picture.

Mary took a deep breath and leaned toward him. "What's your name again?" she asked, her elbow resting against the marble.

"Jake," he said.

"Jake," Mary repeated, letting the sound fill her mouth.

Jake leaned closer. "Do you wanna have a drink sometime?"

Mary shook her head. "I don't drink," she said. She hadn't since the Kellys'. She watched his face fall. Then she leaned closer. "But meet me in the Oak Room at the end of my shift."

"Miss Mary Mack," said Curtis, as he rolled the luggage cart past the front desk. His movements were halting and labored, but his quiet voice was silky smooth. "All dressed in black."

Mary looked up at him. She liked Curtis. "What is it, Curtis?"

He paused and gave Mary a teasing lift of his chin. "I heard you and Greens Fees are enjoying each other's company."

"Where'd you here that?" she asked.

"Where you think?" he said, looking at her with a small smile. "He practically had it written in the *sky.*" He started off again, one foot seemingly heavier than the other. "You just might want to put some construction paper in front of the cameras from now own. Otherwise, the boys in security might decide to get into home movies."

Jake, for his part, proved to be as reckless as Mary. They'd meet in the small conference room that faced the ocean, and Mary would turn to the window. From behind, he'd wrap his arms around her and press his body against hers, kissing her neck, running his fingers over her breasts. Then he'd drop to the floor and lift her skirt. Mary would keep her eyes focused on the sea, on the rhythm of the waves, until her eyes closed involuntarily, until her head rolled back and a quiet gasp escaped her lips.

When Mary was finished, he would stand. "Can I see you later?" he'd ask, his mouth to her ear.

"No" was usually all that Mary would say.

SOON WREATHS ADORNED THE DOORS of Sea Cliff and more visitors came—families who had spent their holidays there for years.

"Are you seeing someone else?" Jake would press, trying to find Mary's eyes.

Mary would look at him. "I'm not even seeing you," she'd reply, before finding something, anything, more interesting than the boy in front of her.

At school, Hannah was doing well. She joined the chorus and came home one day with a pink xeroxed invitation to a holiday concert.

"What's the holiday?" Mary asked, almost to herself.

Hannah looked at her. "Christmas, Mare," said Hannah, as she snatched the invitation from Mary's hands. "It's in like two weeks."

Mary looked back at the paper, feeling disoriented by stillness, by the feeling of time rushing past her as if she were a bystander on a train platform.

That night, Hannah made spaghetti for dinner. "This is good, Bunny," said Mary, as she took a bite.

"Thanks," said Hannah, not meeting her eyes.

"Where'd you learn to make it?"

"Nicky's mom taught me."

Mary swallowed and nodded, feeling the food stick in her throat.

"She's really cool," Hannah added.

"Will she be at the holiday concert?"

"Probably," said Hannah. "She comes to all that kind of school stuff."

"What school stuff?"

"Nothing, Mare."

Mary looked at her. "Not *nothing*," she said. "What school stuff?"

"Just like Back-to-School Night and all that."

"You never told me about Back-to-School Night."

"You were probably *sleeping*."

Mary let her fork drop on her plate. "Cut the shit, Bunny. I sleep while you're at school. I see you every night that you're not at Nicky's. If you wanted me to go to Back-to-School Night, I would have been there."

Hannah looked at her fiercely. When she spoke, her words matched her expression. "Yeah, and you just would have *walked* around and all the dads would have looked at you and people would have thought that you were my *mom!*" And with a slam of the door, she was in the bedroom. And Mary looked down at two half-eaten plates of spaghetti, feeling the unfamiliar sensation of tears as they ran down her cheeks.

When the Christmas concert came, Mary went. She wore jeans and a sweater but noticed that the other mothers were all in dresses. They linked their arms proprietarily through their husband's when they saw Mary.

"You must be Nicky's mom," she said to the woman she had seen chatting with Hannah and Nicky before the girls took to the stage. From the refreshment table, Mary could see Hannah watching.

Mrs. Hashell straightened pertly, extending her hand and giving Mary's a firm shake. "Cynthia," she said, with a fixed smile. "So nice to meet you."

"You, too," said Mary.

"Hannah says you work at Sea Cliff."

"Yeah," responded Mary. "At the front desk."

"I do events. Weddings and whatnot."

Mary looked at her, a response unable to bubble up through the miasma of her mind.

"Well, your sister is adorable," said Cynthia. "Such a great kid."

Mary nodded. "Thank you."

Mary saw her look over her shoulder. "If you'll excuse me," she said. From behind her, Mary heard a loud *hiiiiiiiiiii!* She turned to see Nicky's mom and another woman embrace. From across the room, her eyes met Hannah's.

Mary called Jake that night. She had him meet her in the parking lot before her shift started. "I think I love you, Mary," he said, his lips on her stomach, the words warm and wet in the cold air of the Blazer.

Mary turned her head and exhaled, letting her annoyance escape. "Don't say that."

"But I do."

Mary sat up, pushing him off of her. "Fuckin' A, Jake," she said, grabbing her sweatshirt. She pulled it over her bare chest. "You have to stop." She slid on her jeans, grabbed her backpack, then got out of the truck and slammed the door behind her.

"Mare!" Jake called from the Blazer, as Mary walked through the parking lot toward the hotel. *"Mary!"* But she kept going.

Mary changed in the employee locker room, ignoring the glances of the other women who were ending their days. The hotel was nearly booked, so the bar would be full that night, and she would find men, she knew. Men who would let her link her arm in theirs and escort them to their rooms. They would tell her about when they first came to Sea Cliff. They would tell her about their sons, about what good men they were. They'd tell her about their grandchildren, who'd be meeting them there in a few days. She needed money for Christmas, so she'd speak with several that night. At the front desk, she leaned on the marble and glanced down toward the dark bar, which glimmered and clinked and buzzed with polite conversation.

The second man she escorted to his floor had white hair that was slicked back against his head and the sort of long thin limbs that looked awkward even in repose. He wore charcoal gray wool slacks and a striped button-down shirt. He used to be in bonds, or so he said. He nearly fell asleep in the elevator, so when Mary went back to his room, she did so without reservation.

But when she opened his door and the light of the hallway breached the dark, she saw him sitting in his club chair, his fingers laced, his hands resting in his lap.

"Will you sit with me?" he asked, as if he had been expecting her.

She hesitated for only moment, then walked slowly to his chair, but his eyes hung on the near distance. When she reached him, he looked up. "Sometimes it gets very lonely," he said.

Outside the window, a sliver of moon hovered in the dark. "What does?" Mary asked.

He looked over his shoulder toward the black ocean. "When I was younger, I was in the navy."

Mary sat in the chair beside his so quietly he might not have noticed. "Were you on a ship?" she asked.

"Oh, yes," he said. "A great big ship."

"Did you like it?"

"I did," he said, as if the fact surprised him. "I was stationed in Okinawa after the war. I had a girl there."

"Okinawa?" Mary asked. "Did you know anyone named Stan Pool?"

His eyes searched the space in front of him, as if trying to find the thread of a memory. Then they alighted, and he spoke. "Poolie!" he said. "I knew Poolie! Sandy Bank boy! Knew how to fish! Used to catch us all dinner!" He leaned forward, ecstatic at the connection. "How do you know Poolie?"

"I grew up next door to him."

He smiled for a moment, then chuckled at something far away, giving his hands a single quiet clap. "How did things end up for him?"

Mary smiled. "He married Alice," she said. "They had a big family. Eight kids. He runs a commercial fishing business with his boys."

The man shook his head and grinned the way you do when a story ends up just as it should. "Good for him," he said. Then he let out a chuckle, his eyes like the ripples in the ocean. "Good for Poolie." He put his hand on the armrest of his chair, and his body stilled. Mary rested her hand over his, feeling the rough skin of his knuckles.

Mary sat that way for a few minutes. Then she quietly stood and stepped out of the room, opening the door, then coaxing it shut again. The man's smile didn't change. His expression wasn't altered. He would still look much the same the next day when housekeeping found him. He had died of a massive stroke in the night, a blood vessel bursting quietly and catastrophically in his brain.

Thirty-four
1989

J AKE LOVED MARY THE WAY many men had loved Mary: madly. They'd go to the dark end of the Sea Cliff parking lot, hidden from the bright, graceful swaths of light that crisscrossed the building's exterior. He'd be waiting for her, leaning against his car, his arms crossed over his chest. She'd put the Blazer in park and stare out through the windshield, beyond which was a narrow walkway, a railing, and then a great plunging cliff where the earth seemed to be cleaved into ocean. He'd open the Blazer's door and get in the passenger's seat.

She would feel his hand on her thigh, feel his breath near her ear. "Let's go somewhere," Jake would whisper. He'd grown up poor but took pains to hide it; for him, fucking girls in parking lots held no nostalgic charm.

"No" was all Mary would say, her gaze still straight ahead. She'd unbutton her jeans, arching her back and lifting her hips to slide them off. She'd turn and kneel on the seat, and for the first time that night, she'd look at him. Then she'd lift her leg, move her body on top of his, and he'd reach for the lever that lowered the seat back.

If Mary had a weakness, it was pleasure. And as soon as he pulled off her shirt, as soon as she felt his hands on her bare back, as soon as she felt the warmth of him in the cold truck, Mary would bring her hand to his cheek, and for a few minutes, she would love him back.

And when it was over, when he relaxed against the seat, his breath quick and his body loose, Mary would slide off again. She'd pull her jeans up and put her sweatshirt back on, lifting the hood up to cover her head. Then she'd open the Blazer's door, push it shut behind her, and walk toward Sea Cliff, her hands in her pockets, without a word of farewell.

Jake would watch her while she worked. He'd sit in his car in front of the hotel and stare at the front desk through Sea Cliff's broad sparkling windows as if Mary were something exotic and wondrous. As if she were on exhibit. Sometimes he'd sit there all night.

"I hope Greens Fees isn't going all *Fatal Attraction* on you," Curtis would say. Mary would glance at the spot where she knew he was, though the windows threw back only the lobby's reflection. "You don't have a rabbit at home, do you?"

And Mary felt her face twist, disliking the reference, disliking its irony.

While the morning was still new and black, Mary would leave Sea Cliff. And Jake would follow her home. She'd drive fast with the windows down, and she'd see him in the rearview mirror. This was what it was like, she supposed, to be tracked.

"Who's that guy outside?" Hannah asked one morning, her mouth full of toothpaste. She was brushing her teeth for school and pulling back the metal blinds of the front window, the bathroom less than a dozen steps away. Jake was sitting in the parking lot below watching their building.

Mary walked over and peered out. "You've got to be fucking kidding me," she muttered, as his eyes met hers. Then she stomped out of their apartment without another word.

Jake got out of the car as soon as he saw her. "Hey, baby," he said.

"What are you doing here?" she asked, her arms crossed over her chest.

He put his hands on her hips. She pushed them away. He brought them right back. "I just wanted to make sure you got home okay." He nodded up toward Hannah, who was still looking out the window. "Is that your sister?"

"You can't come here, Jake."

"I just want to see where you live," he said, trying to bring himself closer, trying to brush the hair away from her face. "Where you sleep."

"Don't do it again," said Mary, then she turned and walked back up the stairs, her sneakers squeaking on the treads.

"Who was that?" asked Hannah, still standing by the window.

Mary shook her head, then let her eyes wander around the two small rooms that were their home. She looked at the worn industrial carpet of the living room. At the stained linoleum of the kitchen and the thin metal transition that separated one from the other. She let her shoulders slacken. This place was just for her and Hannah. "Just some guy," she said.

Hannah looked back out the window. She was still holding her toothbrush, her lips rimmed with toothpaste. "He's leaving."

Mary crossed the room, picked up a blanket from the floor, and settled down on the couch, pulling the blanket up over her as she lay on her side. "Good," she said, sliding her hands between her knees.

"He was cute," Hannah said, as his car turned onto the main road away from the apartment.

"I'm sorry," Jake would say, later that night. He and Mary would be in the Oak Room. His hands would be over her breasts, his chest to her back. "I shouldn't have come today."

"You're not my boyfriend, Jake," Mary would say, her eyes closing as he pressed into her.

Then Mary would feel her black skirt slowly slide up past her thighs. "I know," he'd answer. "I know I'm not."

For Christmas, he gave her a pearl necklace. On New Year's, he gave her the matching earrings. Mary continued meet him before work. And when he would buy Mary something, she'd take it. She didn't believe in gracious refusals; she didn't care what it cost him or how he got it. He gave her pleasure and he gave her things and so he could be with her.

Then one day he picked Hannah up from school.

It was early in the morning, and Mary had just gotten home from work. The lights in the apartment were on, and Hannah was awake. "Hey," Mary called, as she dropped her bag on the floor. "You're up early."

"Hi!" Hannah called back. She was in the bathroom doing her hair with the curling iron Mary bought her for Christmas. "Can you drive me today?"

Mary closed her eyes. "Can't you just take your bike?"

"I left it at school," Hannah replied.

Mary paused, her question coming slowly to her sleep-starved mind. "Then how'd you get home?"

Hannah leaned her head out of the bathroom. "Your boyfriend," she said. "Jake."

Mary arrived before him at Sea Cliff that night, waiting in their usual spot at the far end of the parking lot. Mary was already out of the Blazer when he arrived. When he opened his door, she looked right at him. "Hey, baby," he said, his face cautious.

Mary felt the anger that had been building in her pull back in advance of a surge. She reeled back, then lunged forward, putting her hands on his chest and pushing him hard against his car. *"What the fuck, Jake?"*

"What's *wrong?*" he asked, his face concerned as he pulled

Mary into him, as he contained her arms. He was strong, and Mary realized that he could keep her right there for as long as he wanted.

"You went to Hannah's *school?* You drove her *home?*"

"I just wanted to get to know your sister," he said, slackening his arms to find her eyes. "You always keep me away. You never let me in."

Mary twisted away and pushed him hard again. But he didn't even stumble. Then Mary brought her face close to his, her hair falling over her shoulders like a crow's wings. *"Don't go near her,"* she hissed. She drew back to stare at him for a moment longer, her eyes yellow brown, something other than human, then she marched past him toward the hotel.

He watched her silently. Then he followed after her. *"Mary!"* he said, his gate sideways as he tried to make her look at him. *"Mary, come on!"*

She pushed in through the brass revolving door, and he slipped in beside her. Curtis immediately tried to straighten as they burst into the lobby, his eyes moving from Mary to Jake.

Mary stopped and turned. "You need to *leave,* Jake," she said, her voice quiet. She was aware of the empty lobby, of the soft, pleasant din of the bar beyond it.

"Just come *talk* to me."

Mary felt Curtis step up beside her, felt him make himself as solid and formidable as he could. "Come on, man," he said. "This isn't the time or the place."

Jake stared hard at Curtis until a burst of breath escaped and he shook his head, letting his gaze plummet. "Fine," he said. Then he looked at Mary, his eyes expectant. "I'll see you later?"

Mary's body remained stiff.

"Come on," said Curtis. He started to guide him toward the door, but Jake shrugged him off.

"I *got it,* Curtis," he said.

Curtis stood next to Mary as they watched Jake make his way toward the parking lot, his hands in his pockets, his broad, muscled shoulders slumped. "I wish they'd spray that fucking golf course for douche bags instead of grubs," Curtis said.

WHEN MARY GOT HOME FROM WORK that morning, she woke Hannah up. "Bunny," she said, shaking her shoulder; Hannah rolled toward her, blinking. Her skin was phosphorescent white in the dim room. She looked around, orienting herself to the wakeful world.

"I don't want you getting in the car with anyone you don't know ever again."

"What are you talking about?" asked Hannah, her voice still thick with sleep. Mary was home earlier than usual; she had raced there after her shift.

"You got in the car with a guy the other day."

Hannah blinked, running back in her mind to retrieve the memory. Then she looked back at Mary. "Your boyfriend."

"He's not my boyfriend. He's just some guy."

"He said he was your boyfriend."

"I know."

Hannah sat up and blinked, staring down at the comforter. She finally looked back at Mary. "Why are guys like that with you?"

Mary didn't have to ask what she meant. Her body felt tired, like her bones could no longer hold it up. "I don't know," she said.

"You don't even care if they like you, but they do."

Mary was silent.

Hannah squinted, as if looking at something very far away. "I remember one guy you liked back."

"Who?"

"I was little. It was when we lived in that town with all the big houses."

"Northton." The name slithered out before Mary could catch it.

"Yeah!" said Hannah, pleased to hear the long-unspoken word. "Northton. There was that guy there."

"Stefan." In Mary's mind, she pictured a heart bound with briars. She would draw it later. She would draw it over and over.

Hannah looked at Mary. "You liked him."

Mary took a breath and ran her hands over the comforter. "I did like him," she said, her voice rising as if the fact were of little import.

"That town was the last town we really *lived* in. Before this one."

"It was."

And Hannah and Mary looked at each other, some deep truth silently exchanged. Some hidden plea. Some quiet warning. "Do you promise we won't have to leave here?" Hannah asked.

Mary nodded, her throat thick and swollen.

"Cross your heart and hope to die?" Hannah asked.

Mary nodded again.

Thirty-five
1990

O F ALL THE THINGS THAT HAPPENED during that first and last winter at Sea Cliff, Hannah getting her period was not the least among them.

Mary had been sleeping but felt the bed quake as Hannah jumped on top of it.

"Mary!" said Hannah, shaking her sister's shoulder. Mary had just gotten home from work an hour before.

Mary groaned, her face in a pillow.

"I got my period." Hannah's voice was a rush of breath.

Mary turned her head toward Hannah. "You did?" she croaked, her lids still shut.

"Uh-huh," replied Hannah. "It's disgusting. It looks like hot chocolate."

Mary chuckled softly and opened her eyes.

Hannah plopped down next to her and lay on her side, her hands between her knees. "I can't believe I got it."

"I told you you would," replied Mary, angling her body so that it mirrored Hannah's. "Did you find pads?"

"Uh-huh." Hannah pulled the covers over herself. "The ones you use."

As Mary stared at Hannah's face, she thought as she had many times before how very much like Stefan she was. It was the way she seemed to be made of light, beams of it fusing to form something human. It was the way her blond curly hair went straight at the ends; it was the composure of her face when she was listening. It was the way she could forgive and forgive. Until she couldn't. "You know you're like all grown up now."

Hannah smiled, settling into the idea, letting it carry her. "Maybe when I finish high school, we could go to college together," she said. "You and me."

Mary made herself smile. "Yeah," she said. "Maybe we'll do that."

Mary didn't sleep well that day. It was bright. Too bright. She thrashed, her limbs tangling in the sheets, drowning in them. She'd put the pillow over her head until she got too hot, her hair sticking to her neck. Though she had neither spoken to him nor touched him since he picked up Hannah, Jake was still watching her at work, still waiting for her in the parking lot. He still followed her home in the morning. *Please, baby,* he'd say, as he followed her to the door. *Please.*

And on that sleepless day, Mary wanted so badly to feel him. Feel someone. She threw off her blankets and went to the bathroom. She took a shower, turning her face toward the water and letting it fill her mouth, then dropping her head and letting it hit the back of her scalp. She stood there, watching the water run off the ends of her hair. Then she got out, got dressed, and wrote Hannah a note.

Bunny, going for a drive, then going to work. See you in the morning.

Mary drove inland, to where the land flattened and crops grew in huge patchwork fields, spindly seedlings just beginning to rise from the red-brown dirt. She stopped at a restaurant where quiet men with black hair and tanned skin tried not to look at her as they ate their meals.

When the waitress came, she smiled at Mary. Mary pointed to something on the menu, which was in a language she didn't understand. "This one," she said. "Please." The waitress nodded, and Mary sat back and watched the men. They spoke quietly and kept their eyes low, the sound of their words melodic and lovely. And Mary remembered the apartment she and Hannah had lived in when they first arrived in Northton. She remembered listening to her neighbor's voice through the wall, the way it rose and fell like a songbird's flight.

After several minutes, Mary's meal came. The waitress set it in front of her and took a step back, as if to ensure it was to her liking. Mary looked down at a packet that appeared wrapped in an olive green leaf. With her knife and fork, she pried it open. The woman nodded in encouragement.

She ate, feeling the pleasure of anonymity, of hearing voices she did not know or understand. She ate feeling the pleasure of being in a place to which she had never been and would never return. The men seemed to relax. One of them glanced at Mary. She smiled. He looked away.

Mary's gaze turned to the landscape outside the window. Across the road was a field filled with barren trees as far and deep and wide as she could see.

"Hey, what do they grow over there?" she asked the woman when she came to take her plate.

The woman paused, as if letting the words form first in her mind. When she spoke, her voice was deliberate. "Wal-nuts," she said, the word a lovely rolling thing.

Mary nodded and turned back to the window. She thought about the men around her, their arms reaching up through the branches, their bodies always in motion, the landscape always changing, depending on the crop.

Mary paid her check, leaving a generous tip. "*Gracias*," she said to the woman, pausing at the door.

"You're welcome," the woman replied.

Mary drove back toward the coast with a Mexican station playing on the radio. She would go there, she told herself. It wasn't far. She'd go to Mexico and bring Bunny. They'd go there and let their skin go brown. They'd go there, eat food wrapped in leaves, and listen to a language that was like birds.

Jake was waiting for her in the parking lot when she arrived at Sea Cliff. Mary put the Blazer in park, but she didn't get out. She just looked ahead. She loved this spot in front of the ocean. The passenger's-side door opened. She heard his voice. "Where were you today, Mary?" he asked, a proprietary panic beneath his words.

Mary said nothing.

"You weren't at home sleeping."

Mary closed her eyes and brought her finger to her lips. "*Shhhhh,*" she said. Then she slipped off her jeans, feeling her eyes grow damp. Then she threw her leg over and was on top of him.

"Oh, baby," he said, desperate and ecstatic. "I'm so sorry. I love you so much."

"*Shhhhh,*" she said again.

It was the first time they had sex since he picked up Hannah at her school.

At the front desk that night, Mary felt her eyes start to slip shut after checking a young couple into the hotel. She hadn't slept all day.

"Wake up, Miss Mary Mack," she heard Curtis say, as he hauled the couple's luggage onto the cart. "You can get away with a lot of shit at this job, but sleeping isn't one of them."

Mary leaned on the desk in front of her and watched him, watched him force his body into performing the same task he had performed on countless nights before. "Is it hard for you?" she asked. "Physically, I mean."

He shook his head but kept his eyes on his cart. "Nah," he said, brushing his bangs to the side. "I mean, not as hard as it must look."

"Were you born this way?"

"No," he said, his voice full of mischief. "It was a freak rodeo accident." He looked at her, as if anticipating laughter. When her face didn't change, his gaze dropped back to the bags. "Yeah, I mean," he started. "My shit's always been fucked up. I'll spare you the syndrome. It has lots of syllables."

And as he grasped the brass bar of the cart, Mary stared at the twisted bend of his wrist. It reminded Mary of something fragile and new. A seedling. A hatchling. A bunny. And she felt a sadness come over her so suddenly, it was as if it had been injected right into the vein.

Mary didn't escort anyone back to their rooms from the bar that night. She barely even saw them pass. It was in those ambiguous hours between morning and night, when no one ever arrived, that Mary sensed him. It was an animal's instinct, a primal recognition. She stared at the glass door just before he materialized. Surrounded by black, all she could see was the white of his shirt, the white of his eyes, and then the white of his smile. He pushed open the door and stepped into the light. And finally, finally, the man for whom she had come arrived. He walked toward her like a crocodile gliding through the water. And for a moment, Mary wasn't sure he was real.

When he reached the desk, he put his suitcase down, then loosened the collar of his dress shirt as he looked at Mary. "Hello," he said, his voice glass smooth and of no single place. "I'm afraid I don't have a reservation."

Thirty-six
1990

MARY'S FACE REMAINED STILL, but she felt her heart falter as she took a single audible breath. "Welcome back, Mr. Mondasian," she said, her voice raw as she spoke. She recognized him, of course. From more than his picture. He was familiar to Mary in a way she couldn't explain.

Robert Mondasian smiled. He was accustomed to being recognized on occasion. "And your name is?"

"Mary Chase."

"You're new."

"I started a few months ago."

"You're not from California."

"I'm from back East."

"Ah," he smiled. "As am I."

"You prefer an ocean-side suite with a view, correct?" she asked, forcing herself to speak. The paper back in Northton had only mentioned his affinity for the hotel, but Mary checked Sea Cliff's records. He always stayed in a west-facing room. He always arrived in winter. And he never had a reservation.

Robert smiled, his eyes narrowing in interest and curiosity as he slid his credit card across the desk. "That's right," he said. "And how is it that you know me?" He was used to batting about pretty young things who knew something of his reputation. "I shudder to think I've made it into the training manual."

Mary's head tilted as she looked at the face that was so much like her own. "You knew my mother," she said.

Robert straightened slightly and gave Mary a placating smile — he preferred not to know mothers. "How wonderful. Do give her my regards," he instructed blandly. They stared at each other until Mary looked away. She placed Robert's credit card into the imprinter and pulled the handle across.

Hannah was still an infant when Mary walked into the office at the Water's Edge to find Diane sitting on the couch, her pale hand covering her mouth. She was staring at a magazine splayed open on the coffee table in front of her. Hannah let out a squawk and — as if smelling salts were passed under her nose — Diane seemed to inhale her way into consciousness. She closed the magazine abruptly and looked at her daughter, some switch in her mind thrown. *Has Hannah had a nap?* she asked. But Mary's instincts were sharp enough to sense the seismic.

Mary found her again later that night, sitting at the round kitchen table under the yellow light of the cheap Tiffany-style chandelier, the same magazine open to the same page. Mary sat down and looked on. Diane didn't move. She wasn't reading. She was simply staring at the image of a very handsome man standing in front of an enormous photograph of a head wound. Mary reached for the magazine and slid it toward her; Diane continued to gaze at the spot where it had been. The article was on young British artists, but Mary, too, looked only at the man. *Robert Mondasian with* Collishaw's Bullet Hole, the caption read. And she knew who he was without being told.

"You said his name was Vincent."

"That's what he told me," said Diane. Then she brought her

hand to her forehead and closed her eyes. "I can't even say for sure it's him. It was a long time ago, Mare."

But in his face, Mary saw all her beauty and flaws. She saw the parts of her that hurt Diane, the parts of her that lied. She saw her black, black hair. She saw her yellow brown eyes.

Mary pulled the key to room 508 from the drawer and turned to Robert. "Her name was Diane," she said. "You stayed at our motel. In Sandy Bank."

"It must have been quite some time ago."

"Twenty-seven years."

"Well," he said, with a false smile. "Perhaps I'll give it some thought in my room."

Mary extended the key just far enough to make him reach for it. "Maybe you remember my father, then," she said. Her mouth felt dry. "His name was Vincent Drake."

And in his eyes, she saw him tumbling and tumbling across continents and time, through people and places and lies and truths, until he found the reason for its familiarity, the little yellow motel with the oyster-shell parking lot. Until he saw the pretty blond girl shooing off the gulls as she hauled garbage bags into the Dumpster under a bright blue sky. Then he looked at Mary, an invisible line between them like the thin starlit threads that connect the constellations. His eyes darkened, and in that instant, Mary understood his full capacity for cruelty. "Yes," he said, the word slithering out, long and thin and cold. "Handsome chap. Looked an awful lot like me."

A burst of air escaped Mary's lips, and she released the key. Robert Mondasian smiled. "Do give him my regards," he said. Then he turned and was gone.

Mary stood motionless for several minutes after Robert walked down the marble corridor, his footsteps echoing through the empty lobby. She didn't hear Jake come through the doorway behind her. "Who was he, Mary?" he asked, his breath on her hair, his hands wrapped around her wrists. "You knew each other. I could tell."

Mary was silent.

"Is he who's keeping you in that apartment?" he asked, his grip tightening. "Is he who you went to see today?"

His words vaporized before they found her ear.

"Is he your boyfriend?"

"He's my father," she said, without looking at Jake, her voice weak.

She felt him press into her. "Please don't lie to me, baby. Please don't lie."

And in some reserve, some pocket tucked deep inside her, Mary found the will to loosen her body, to lean her head back against Jake. "I promise. He came from England today. He lives over there. With his wife."

Jake loosened his hold on her wrists. "Why didn't you tell me?"

"I was going to." Then she turned and pressed her hips into his and brought her hand to the back of his head. "But you haven't been yourself lately."

He lowered his head, let it hang. "I'm so sorry."

"You should go home," she said. "Get some sleep. You've been spending too much time taking care of me."

His eyes snapped to hers. "I *want* to take care of you."

"I know," she said, twisting her finger through his hair. "I know. But go home and rest. For me."

Jake brought the back of his hand to her cheek. "I love you so much."

Mary smiled. "I love you, too."

As soon as Mary saw Jake's car turn out of Sea Cliff's long straight driveway, Mary turned and pushed through the door to the desk, back into the staff quarters and the locker room. With urgent but discreet speed, she ran the combination on her locker, pulled out her bag, and slammed the door shut again, hearing metal hit metal. She burst from the locker room and stopped short of bumping into Curtis. Mary looked into his eyes for only a moment. She said nothing, but he knew. He stood and watched her as she disappeared. There were four hours left on her shift. She would not return.

She took the back way to the parking lot, the hidden way, avoiding windows and the corridors frequented by guests. She pushed open a back door to the hotel and was hit instantly by a wild wind that took her hair up and threw it about. Below, she heard the ocean, churning and spraying and bearing witness to all.

Mary slunk through the night. If you weren't looking for her, you'd never see her. She moved like liquid black. She got into the Blazer and started it up, then drove quietly and smoothly away. She kept her windows up and the radio off as she drove. She watched the branches of trees move in the dark like arms thrown up in warning.

When she arrived at the apartment above the Laundromat, her eyes moved around the parking lot, looking for Jake's car. But it wasn't there. She parked in an unlit corner behind the Dumpster at the back of the building, pulled up the hood of her sweatshirt, and tucked her chin. As she rounded the side, she saw two employees from the grocery store smoking a joint by the loading dock, their voices faint but full of happy bravado. *Yo, yo, yo, check this out.*

Mary slipped her key into the door of the building and slinked inside. She took the steps quickly but quietly, opening the door to the apartment and shutting it behind her just as fast. In the dark, Mary took a moment to look around. Hannah had hung some of Mary's art around the room, and there was a candle that smelled like vanilla. It was a peaceful place, the apartment. Mary would miss it.

Mary paused in the doorway of the bedroom, watching Hannah sleep. It used to be that she could pick her up and carry her to the car, letting Hannah's head rest in her lap while she drove. It used to be that Hannah wouldn't even know they had left until they were three hundred miles away. But things were more complicated now.

Sliding into bed next to her, Mary waited until her breath matched Hannah's. Until her inhale was with hers. Until her exhale was the same, too. Then she stroked Hannah's face. "Bunny," she whispered.

Hannah stirred, a barely conscious reflexive groan coming from the back of her throat.

Mary spoke again. "Bunny," she said. "You need to wake up."

Hannah opened her eyes. They focused on Mary for a moment, then swam around the room, resting on the alarm clock's glowing red digits. "You're home," she said, her brows drawn together, her face plump with sleep.

"Bunny," she said, bringing Hannah's gaze back to hers. "We have to go."

"What?" asked Hannah, as if she hadn't understood. Whether it was the fog of sleep or the statement itself that confused her, Mary did not know.

"We have to go," she said. Jake would be back soon, if he wasn't on his way already. "It's time."

Hannah looked back to the clock, staring at it as if there were some answer there. "You said we wouldn't have to go anymore," she said finally.

"I know, Bunny."

"You said we were going to stay here."

"We're going to find another place to stay," said Mary. "This town isn't right anymore." And the landscape that had been forming in her mind became sharper. She could see the baked earth with cacti twisting up out of it. She could see the flat red hills in the distance, the desert covered with scrub. She could see the small low towns and the women who'd rest their hands on their lower backs, squinting into the sun as she drove by. "We're gonna go to Mexico. You'll like it. There'll be hotels I can work at."

Hannah shook her head. And for the second time in a single night, Mary felt like someone could see right into her chest past the wet lashes of muscle, past the cage of her ribs, to her flawed, fragile, and ferocious heart.

When Hannah spoke, her voice was high and cracked and hopeless. "You're a liar," she said, her face growing red. She stared at Mary, waiting for her to refute it. "We were always going to leave. You said we wouldn't, but you knew we were."

Mary reached for Hannah's hand, but she pulled it away. Mary felt her eyes turn hot and wet. "I didn't want to, baby."

Hannah's face was angry now. And her tears darkened the pillow beside her face. "Don't call me that," she said, shaking her head. "I'm not your baby."

Mary looked at Hannah. "Yes, you are," she said. Then she reached for her like a mother would. She reached for her like she always had.

But Hannah's hands landed hard on Mary's chest. *"You're a liar!"* she screamed. And she pushed Mary away.

Thirty-seven
1990

MARY DIDN'T KNOW WHERE she was going or when she was going to go back, but she needed to drive. Her mind was void of thought as she sped over the road, traveling faster than she had in a very long time, feeling the thrill of the velocity find its way through her body, into her fingertips, into her legs. She felt the Blazer strain with the burden of it, but it was soothing, that rush of motion.

She hadn't spoken another word to Hannah before she left. She had grabbed her bag and flew from their apartment, her hair waving behind her as she took the stairs. She pushed the door open and let it slam back against the wall, metal to brick, and then close again. She wasn't trying to hide now. She didn't care if she was seen. She started the car and screeched out of the parking lot, passing the kids at the grocery store who were still out back smoking weed. They would laugh as they watched her speed away. *Shit! You in a rush?*

At first, Mary didn't think at all. Didn't think of Hannah or Stefan or Jake. She just drove. Every so often she'd rub her eyes with her closed fist to tamp out the fatigue, but she drove until her mind emptied, as if with a tide. She drove until it filled up again with something quiet and dark. Until it filled again with the swamp. It was of the still water reflecting the earth above it that she thought. It was of the place where sky was land and land was sky. She saw it through eyes that were not her own. And in that way, she wasn't thinking at all. She saw the movement of every snake in the water, the darting path of every animal. She saw the swamp from beneath the brush and from a perch in the branches of a tree. She saw the strange and lovely flowers open up to draw in flies, then close again, their delicate teeth like crisscrossing briars. She saw heat and coolness and the lovely white gray moss dripping from the trees it shrouded.

She felt herself running, placing each footstep, darting between the cypresses, feeling the brush against her coat. She felt the ancient instinct for motion, for sensing it, the instinct that had kept her alive for hundreds of thousands of years. That had fed her. It was primal, her rush toward the small brown body. It was food. She watched its hind legs pedal in unison to race away from her, watched its small white tail point to the invisible sky. Her need for it was her beginning and end. In her chest, her heart pumped savagely. When she had nearly reached it, she opened her mouth. "Bunny," she whispered.

And suddenly, she was back. She saw the curve of the road in front of her and the cliff to her left, and she cut the wheel. But the lights from the car behind her shone so brightly in her rearview that they filled her eyes, that they blinded her. She tried to follow the road, to turn in the other direction, but the road was no longer there. She never let go of the wheel even when the car left the earth, when the wheels spun not on asphalt but air. But suddenly, she could see everything all around her. She could see beyond time. And that feeling of motion when the car was in freefall, when it was in its glorious descent to the hungry sea that was the end — well, that was bliss.

Thirty-eight

BUNNY

*W*HAT, *WERE YOU GOING TO DIE OF OLD AGE, MARE?*
Were you going to wither in a world that was in-
comprehensible? Was your skin going to loosen and
your hair drain of color and your body shed its beauty? Was
your mind going to go? Were you going to grip the hands of
visitors whose faces you did not know? Were you going to die in
a bed?

I don't remember much from right around the accident. I
know they questioned that guy who thought he was your boy-
friend. He was behind you that night. They thought he might
have run you off the road. But in the end, they decided that you
lost control of the car.

I don't remember the police coming to the door. I don't remem-
ber staying at Nicky Hashell's house. I don't remember the social
workers. I don't remember giving them the names I did. Where
the shreds of my memory start to fuse is when Alice got there.
She was one of the people I told them about. Alice and Martina.
Alice dressed up to come and get me at Nicky's. She had lipstick
on. Her hair was set, and she had on a white blouse with red dots.
She pulled me into her chest, and somehow she felt like home. She

took me to a Burger King for dinner, and then we spent the night in a hotel down the highway.

I remember the plane ride back East. It was the second time I'd ever been on a plane. I remember staring at the shiny foil packets of peanuts, not eating them, but just rolling them around in my hands and looking out the window, seeing the tiny houses and the tiny cars. Seeing the world in miniature. Nothing looked real.

Before we got to Sandy Bank, Alice had warned me that the Water's Edge was gone, but I didn't really remember it anyway. They had torn it down just a couple of months before to build some single-families. Alice had gone in years before and saved all of our stuff. You have to be astounded at that, don't you? Alice, who had no idea where we were or if she would ever see us again, filled boxes full of our things and kept them in her attic. That's Alice, right? I keep hearing Mom's voice. Salt of earth. She's the salt of the earth. *That's mostly how I remember Mom —through snatches of her voice, glimpses of her face. But I remember you like I just saw you this morning.*

I was only back in Sandy Bank for a couple of days before Stefan came. Alice opened the screen door one night and there he was, with a duffel bag in his hand, moths circling his head under the light. Alice nodded—she and Martina had been talking, so Alice expected him. But for me, well, I can't tell you the relief I felt at seeing him. I rushed to him, and he brought me into his chest and put his hand on the back of my head. Then he folded onto me. I never heard him cry again, but I did that night. I had never heard a man break like that before. And it was so comforting to know that someone else missed you. Missed you like I did. Mrs. Pool let him sleep on the floor next to me. I suppose that was when I first understood that he was something more than your old boyfriend. That's when I understood that Mrs. Pool knew it, too.

Stefan was the one who told me everything, but not for a long time. He stayed at Sandy Bank for the rest of that winter, then I went to Northton for the summer. We were on the boat and he was holding my hand and he asked me if I knew what the stars were. I looked up at them, and I said I thought that they were light. And he laughed, but it sounded sad. And he said that that was only part of it, that they were more than that. Then he told me that he loved you. And he always would. And that I was a part of both of you. That was all he said at first. Now he introduces me as his daughter without hesitation. But Patrick only told him the truth of it all when you died. Martina says that it took years for Stefan to forgive him for that.

I used to spend the school years in Sandy Bank, but Stefan would come down all the time. And he'd bring me up to Northton for summers and holidays, and I'd stay with Martina and Patrick. Stefan and I would walk together, and he'd tell me about when he first saw me. When you and I first appeared on his doorstep. He said I was wearing earmuffs and tights with holes in the knee. And then he'd stop, and I'd know he was remembering you. It was hard for him when you left, Mary. Harder than you realized, probably. I still remember that night — the night we left Northton. So does Stefan. He said that you left him a letter and that he read it over and over again, smoothing it flat, until the paper softened, until the words blurred. He said that after we left he didn't know what was true or real anymore. He said that as far as he knew we just disappeared.

He has a girlfriend now, and I like her very much. Her name is Anna. They came to stay with Daniel and me for a week, and we were up late, talking and drinking martinis. He'd rest his hand on her shoulder and she'd smile at him. It's good to see him in love, Mary. Martina once said she wasn't sure he could be again.

On the last night of their visit, Anna went to bed early and Daniel followed. Then it was just Stefan and I on the deck. He patted the spot next to him, and I sat down. "Hi, Dad," I said. I *only ever called him that when we were alone. It has always felt like something just for us. He smiled, and his eyes went far away. And he reminded me of the time he was in Sandy Bank and the sea bass were running. Stan had caught a mess of them. Alice broiled them and the four of us sat on the porch eating off the same platter, our fingers smelling like lemon. Stefan asked where I got my nickname, and Alice let her head tilt to the side, and she told us a story.*

She said it was right after I was born. You were standing on a jetty, just watching the water. A storm was coming, and the ocean was all gray chop. Mom had sent Alice down to come get you, to make you come inside, because the weather was turning so quickly. She said she could see you clearly and was shouting your name, but the wind was so loud and you were still so far that you weren't responding. You were just staring into the water, statue still. When she got closer, she could see that you were soaked through. That your hair was stuck in curves against your shoulder blades. And that you were hunched forward, holding something in your arms. She called your name louder, but you still didn't move. Alice had to climb all the way up onto the rocks before she could see that you were holding a little rabbit in your arms. You said you had seen it in the water and that it had almost drowned, that you dove in after it. No one knew how a rabbit ended up in the water, but there it was, helpless and vulnerable and in a place it shouldn't be. And you saved it.

After that, you called me Bunny.

Acknowledgments

I am grateful to have been edited by the wonderful Helen Atsma, whose intelligence, thoughtfulness, and vision have been such a pleasure. And Stephanie Rostan is the best kind of agent. Her advice has made me a better writer.

Thanks to my dear parents, Maureen and Peter Enderlin; my brothers, Jonathan Enderlin and Matthew Enderlin; my sisters, Jennifer Enderlin Blougouras and Erin Enderlin Bloys, who are always my first readers.

Thanks to all the friends and family who have shown up for me over the years—especially Sheila White Moore, Jim White, Marlow "Buster" White, Audrey and Tom Healy, Phyllis Donohue, and all the other Enderlins, Healys, and Whites. Also, a special thanks to Kristen Deshaies, who throws both her head and heart into everything she does—including manuscript reading.

This book was written in snatches of time, and it was my husband, Dennis Healy, who helped me find them. True to form, he was as giving and steadfast in his support as he is with everything else.

And finally, thank you to my sons, Noah, Max, and Ollie Healy. They've taught me everything about love.

About the Author

Sarah Healy is the author of *Can I Get an Amen?* and *House of Wonder*. She lives in Vermont with her husband and three sons.